FIRST PITCH SWINGING

LINDA FAUSNET

My books contain steamy sex, bad words, and human beings of all sorts, include gay people. If you're not a fan of those things, you may want to stop reading now. If you're cool with that stuff, come take my hand and join me on this journey...

This book is a work of fiction. References to real people, events, establishments, organizations, or locales are intended only to provide a sense of authenticity and are used fictitiously. All other characters, and all incidents and dialogue, are drawn from the author's imagination and are not to be construed as real.

Published by Wannabe Pride 2021

Editing by Linda Hill

Cover Design by Chuck DeKett

FIRST EDITION.

Library of Congress Control Number: 9781944043612

ISBN: 978-1-944043-61-2

❀ Created with Vellum

CHAPTER 1

yric

IF I DON'T GET a shot of coffee into my system in the next thirty seconds, I might very well pass out.

The line at Richmond Roast was barely moving, and it was all I could do to remain upright. While nobody standing in the line in front of me looked particularly lively this Monday morning, I was willing to bet I looked the worst. I'd barely had any rest this weekend between studying and volunteering at the hospital, yet somehow I was gonna have to rally to make it through a full day of classes.

Someone gently cleared his throat behind me, and I realized I was holding up the line while nearly falling asleep on my feet. I shuffled forward, grateful there was only one person in front of me now. I shook my head vigorously in an effort to remain conscious.

"Good morning," I said to the barista with a smile. She smiled back, which lifted my spirits a bit, making me glad I'd made the effort to be nice, despite my exhaustion. "A large coffee, a shot of espresso, with one cream and one sugar."

Fortunately, the kind folks at Richmond Roast were quite efficient, and my drink was prepared in no time. They gave you your order right away instead of making you step to the side to wait for it, which was one of the reasons the line took so long.

"Thanks," I said. I pulled the plastic tab on the lid so hard, I nearly ripped it off. Swigging my coffee, I turned around way too fast and slammed right into the poor man standing directly behind me.

"Fuck!" he yelled as hot coffee splashed across his chest. His *huge* chest. My God, this guy was big. I had to look up ... and *up* to see his face.

Horrified at what I'd done to this guy and his crisp white shirt, I stammered, "Oh my God, I'm sorry. I'm so sorry!"

The man laughed. Lucky for me, because judging by the size of his biceps, he could probably kill me with one arm.

"It's okay. Sorry for my colorful language." He glanced around at the other patrons then turned back to me.

"I'm so sorry," I repeated, unable to think of anything better to say.

"Accidents happen," he said with a grin. He reached behind me to grab some napkins that the barista was trying to hand him, but I was standing in the way.

"Sorry, sorry." I stepped to the side, sloshing more of my coffee in the process. "Please, at least let me pay for your coffee."

"That's really not necess—"

"Please, it's the least I can do."

The big guy smiled again with kindness in his dark brown eyes. "Okay," he said with a nod. "I feel bad, but I was gonna get some muffins, too."

"Go ahead. Anything you want. Please."

2

He chuckled softly and gave his order to the lady behind the counter. Though he was very sweet to her, she acted nervous for some reason. The guy was gigantic but he seemed gentle at the same time. He didn't seem like he was somebody to fear. After all, he'd taken it in stride when I'd tried to burn his torso.

After I finished paying for his order I stumbled over to a table in the corner. Crowded as it was, I was lucky to find a place to sit. I normally just grabbed my caffeine-in-a-cup and split, but I figured it wasn't a great idea to wander around while I was this tired. Better to let the coffee work its magic for a few minutes before attempting to tackle my day. Instead of waking me up, though, a renewed sense of exhaustion swept over me as I sipped my coffee and thought about the day ahead. My classes were tough this semester. Today alone I had to tackle physics and biochemistry.

"Mind if I join you?" The deep voice startled me, making me jump and splash my coffee on myself this time. Good God, I had to pull it together already. I blinked as I looked up at the guy with the huge muscles and the coffee stain on what I now saw was probably an expensive shirt.

"There, uh, don't seem to be any other tables left," he said when I took a beat too long to answer.

"Oh yes. Sure, of course. Please, have a seat." I gestured at the empty chair across from me.

Is he hitting on me or did he really need a place to sit?

The man was strikingly handsome, with dark hair, strong jawline, and rippling muscles. He could be an underwear model or something.

Yeah. Definitely just looking for a place to sit. Guys like him do not hit on girls like me. Not that I was looking to date anybody anyway. Not with my current schedule.

"I'm Lyric, by the way. Lyric Rivers."

"That's a beautiful name," he said with a smile. It *sounded*

3

like he was trying to pick me up, but that wasn't possible. Was it?

I shrugged. "I guess. Both my parents are musicians, so ..."

"Ah, I see. My name's Brady." He hesitated for a second, then added, "Brady Keaton."

"Nice to meet you, Brady. Sorry for the dramatic introduction," I said, glancing at his chest. "I hope that shirt isn't ruined. Feel like I should offer to pay for it, but I doubt I could afford it."

"It's okay, really. No big deal."

"Thanks for being so nice about this."

Brady shrugged to show he wasn't upset, then bit into one of the muffins I'd bought him. Rather than watch the guy eat, I glanced around the coffee shop.

And realized that almost everyone in the place was staring at us.

My muscles tightened with unease. What was their problem? Hadn't they ever seen anybody make a fool of themselves by crashing into a stranger and dumping hot coffee on him? When it happened, I'd been too stunned to think about how I had looked. After that, I'd been too tired to care. Now, though, I was starting to feel embarrassed.

"Jeez, everybody is staring at me," I said quietly. "Guess they've never seen an idiot as clumsy as I am."

"They're not staring at you, Lyric," Brady said kindly. I found I liked the way he said my name.

"Yeah, they are. Look."

But Brady didn't look. He kept his eyes on mine. "They're not staring at you. They're staring at me."

"They are?"

"Yeah. Truth is, I'm kinda famous."

"You are?" I asked incredulously. I realized too late that

sounding shocked might have been insulting, since I clearly didn't know who he was.

Brady nodded.

"Oh. I'm sorry to say I don't recognize you."

He chuckled. "Yeah, I kinda figured. It's okay. I take it you don't follow baseball."

"Oh. Baseball," I said dismissively. It took my foggy brain a moment to realize I'd said those words out loud.

"Yeah. *Baseball*," he said, sounding genuinely annoyed. And who could blame him?

"I'm so sorry." Apparently, that was all I knew how to say today. My exhaustion was no excuse for how poorly I was treating this perfectly nice gentleman whom I'd managed to attack physically and now verbally. "I didn't mean for that to sound as rude as it did. I just meant that you're right; I don't follow baseball. Or any sports. You could be the most famous athlete on the planet and I wouldn't recognize you. That's how clueless I am."

"You're not clueless," he said, eying me carefully. "But you're obviously very tired."

"Yes, I am," I said. "And I really appreciate your patience with me."

He shrugged again.

"I mean it. Thanks for not being a jerk."

Laughing, Brady said, "Well, I do my best. So what, did you just come off working the night shift or something?"

"No, unfortunately my day is just beginning. Just had a busy weekend. Had a ton of studying to do. I go to the University of Richmond. Pre-health major."

"Pre-health. What does that mean, exactly?"

"It's basically pre-med."

Brady's eyes opened wide with interest. "Pre-med? Like, you're gonna be a doctor?"

5

"Eventually. Someday. At least that's the plan. Got a looong way to go."

"So I guess you gotta get through college and then med school."

"Exactly." I shook my head. "I don't mind telling you, college alone is kicking my ass, so I can't begin to imagine what med school will be like. Right now, on top of my classes I'm volunteering at St. Theresa Hospital to get some experience, and I'm studying for the MCAT."

"And the MCAT would be ..."

"The Medical College Admissions Test. I'm not taking it 'til June, but it's a lot of work."

"Is that like studying for the bar for law?"

"I guess you could say it's kinda comparable."

"Damn," Brady said. "Sounds like a *helluva* lot of work. I'm impressed."

"Thanks."

"Dr. Rivers. That has a nice ring to it."

A ripple of excitement went through me. It *did* have a nice ring to it, especially when spoken in Brady's deep, sensual voice. Hearing "Dr. Rivers" out loud helped to center me somehow. It reminded me of why I was pushing myself so hard. I was going to be a doctor, and I could really make a difference in people's lives someday.

"Of course, tough as it is, getting *into* medical school is just the beginning. I don't know how the hell I'll be able to pay for it."

"Scholarships? Financial aid?"

"Yeah, that'll take care of part of it," I said, rubbing my temples wearily. "I'll have to take out loans to pay for the rest. I'm already in debt for college, even though I took a few years off after high school to work and save money. I really hate the idea of taking more time off after college to save up, but I'm not sure I could handle having a job while I'm in medical school."

"Damn," Brady said. He breathed in the scent of his coffee before taking a healthy sip. "Makes me tired just hearing about it."

His expression of concern and respect gave me a warm, pleasant feeling all over. I was so used to burning myself out with work and studying that sometimes I forgot how strong my work ethic was, until I spoke to somebody else about it. My "business as usual" was pretty grueling by most people's standards, and I rarely gave myself a break.

"Here I am rambling on and on about myself, and I haven't asked a thing about you. So, baseball. Do you play for the local Richmond team? Or are you in town with the opposing team?"

"I play for the Richmond Dominoes," he said, his dark eyes lighting up as he spoke. He looked like a child who'd been asked to talk about his favorite toy. I had to admit, it was rather charming. "But don't get too attached."

I narrowed my eyes, trying to figure out what he meant by that.

I think you're cute. Doesn't mean I want to marry you. Get over yourself.

Brady laughed at my expression. "I just mean I don't plan on staying here in Richmond. After this season I'll become a free agent, so I can play for whatever team I want so long as they'll have me. So I'm gonna play for Baltimore."

"And you're certain they're going to have you?" I asked.

"Pretty sure," Brady said with a grin. "I've had a batting average of more than .300 for the last two years, and I won the Silver Slugger last year."

"Impressive."

"You don't know what any of that means, do you?"

"Nope. But I'm assuming the Silver Slugger is an award

and your batting average must be good, or you wouldn't have mentioned it."

"Correct," he said with a laugh. He had a way of talking about his accomplishments without sounding like he was bragging, which was kind of nice. With his good looks, talent, and most likely tons of money, he surely could have gotten away with being a huge jerk. The *Do you know who I am?* kind of asshole who yells at baristas, not to mention women who pour hot coffee on him. But apparently, that wasn't his way.

"It's not just that, though." He popped a piece of muffin into his mouth. I watched his Adam's apple bob up and down as he swallowed. Even his throat looked sexy. "I'm willing to take less money to play for Baltimore."

"Really? And why is that?"

Brady's voice grew softer. "Because I grew up there. Ever since I was a little boy, I dreamed about being a Baltimore Bay Bird. My hero growing up was Ray Renner Jr., shortstop for the Birds. I wanted to be just like him. God, I would give anything to play for Baltimore."

I'd never understood the sappy phrase about getting lost in someone's eyes, but I swear that was what happened to me as I listened to Brady Keaton talk about his childhood dream. It was like I could feel how much he wanted it, and I admired him tremendously for working so hard to make his dream come true. If I'd passed this hulking athlete on the street, I surely would have dismissed him as just some dumb jock. I winced inwardly as I remembered my earlier *Oh. Baseball* remark.

Unable to tear my gaze away from him, I said in a voice that was nearly a whisper, "Well, I really hope that happens for you. I hope you get to play for Baltimore."

"Thanks," he said. "I 'ppreciate that. I mean, don't get me wrong. I've really loved playing for Richmond these past three years. They're an expansion team, and it was an honor to play for them from the very beginning. I'll always be a part of baseball trivia, no matter what happens in the rest of my career. I get to say I was on the very first roster for the Richmond Dominoes. How cool is that?"

I laughed softly, still reveling in Brady's adorable enthusiasm. Scanning the room again, I saw that people were still watching us.

"Does this happen everywhere you go?"

"Ah, kinda," Brady said modestly.

"Does it bother you?"

"Not really," he said with a gleam in his eye.

No. It definitely did not seem to bother him.

"Ugh, I would lose my mind," I muttered.

"Really?"

"Oh yeah. I'm not the type who enjoys a lot of attention. I just kinda keep to myself."

"Huh," Brady said thoughtfully. He seemed intrigued by the idea of somebody not wanting to draw attention to themselves. And unless I was completely mistaken, he seemed intrigued by *me*. When he sat down I was afraid he might hit on me, but now? I was afraid he *wouldn't*.

Don't they always say you meet someone when you're not looking? And I definitely was not looking. Funny how when I first saw him, intellectually I could see that he was conventionally handsome, but I hadn't been particularly attracted to him. Now, after chatting with him for a few minutes and seeing how cool he was, I was *definitely* physically attracted to him. It was like watching a movie starring a handsome actor. At first, you don't feel anything, but after watching the man be all sexy and charming and whatnot for two hours, by the end you've got a crush on the guy.

Cold reality crashed down on me as I realized that landing Brady Keaton as a boyfriend was every bit as impossible as landing a movie star. Whether I'd heard of him before or not, he *was* a celebrity. And he was gorgeous and athletic with tons of charisma. What the hell would he want with a science and medical nerd like me? Besides, he clearly loved attention and was probably a big-time partier. The type who loved to be around people, especially women, and he could probably bed any woman he wished. As charming as he was, he didn't strike me as the type to want a serious girlfriend. Even if he did, I highly doubted he would be interested in me.

Great. Now I felt sad in addition to being exhausted. As much as I enjoyed talking with Brady, there was no sense in dragging out the inevitable. Besides, I had a really long day ahead of me.

"Well, I guess I better get going. It was really nice meeting you, Brady. I hope you have a great baseball season, and I expect to see you wearing Baltimore colors next year."

Brady seemed taken aback when I stood up to leave. He was probably used to women falling all over themselves for him. Granted, it was tempting given the fluttery feelings he had stirred in my stomach and, well, *lower*. But I had no interest in being a notch on his belt or a bump on his cleat or what have you.

"Um, okay," Brady said, standing up. "It was great meeting you too, Lyric."

Damn. I hated what hearing my name on his lips did to me. More stomach flutters.

"Good luck with school and everything else you got going. Take care of yourself, okay? You can't help patients too well if you burn yourself out."

"Thanks," I said, melting all over at his sweet words. "I really needed to hear that."

With a somewhat forced smile, I drained the rest of my coffee cup and tossed it in the trash before making my way out the door of Richmond Roast. I zipped up my jacket as the chilly early-April air whipped around me. The coffee shop was only a short distance from Dominion Park, and I caught sight of the baseball stadium as I walked toward the University of Richmond. I'd never paid any attention to the place before, but this time, seeing where the Richmond Dominoes played felt like a punch in the gut.

Wow. That's new.

CHAPTER 2

rady

AFTER SIGNING a few autographs for fans on my way out of Richmond Roast, I walked back to my apartment a few blocks away. The first thing I did when I got home was step out onto the patio. Located on the twelfth floor, my place offered a great view of the city, and my eyes immediately went toward Dominion Park. That was one of the best parts about my luxury apartment. That I could see the ballpark from here. I still owned a big house back in Baltimore, but this place was perfect for me while I played for Richmond. Three bedrooms, big kitchen, and spacious living room; it was just what I needed to be comfortable during the season.

Gazing out into the city from high above it, I was surprised to find myself thinking of Lyric. I met women all the time and they never had much of an effect on me. Not once we left the bedroom anyway. Lyric hadn't seemed to notice my physique much, and she hadn't cared that I was famous. For some reason, I found that kinda hot. Her dream of being a doctor was rather sexy too, but *damn* she looked exhausted. Lyric had the most beautiful ice-blue eyes I'd ever seen, even if they did have dark circles under them. With her dark hair, pale face, and petite body, she looked more like a delicate ballerina than a doctor. Still, she must be a tough little thing to handle everything she had going on. Weird how I wanted to fuck her senseless but then tuck her into bed after to make sure she got some rest.

For a few minutes there, I'd felt like we sorta had a connection going. Then she'd just gotten up and left, clearly having no problem with the idea of never seeing me again.

Why did I even care? She obviously hadn't been interested in me, and that was all there was to it. I've never exactly been the relationship type, no matter how much my mother wished I would settle down and get married and give her some grandkids. I always thought it was so bizarre how people called getting married "settling down" like that alone made you more mature.

Whether or not I was the relationship type didn't really matter. Problem was, I liked this girl more than I cared to admit, and her rejection stung. A lot. Best to just forget her, I guess. For all I knew, she had a steady boyfriend. Some smart guy. A scientist or a future doctor like her. Not a high school graduate like me. Even if she did go out with me, she'd probably get bored with me pretty damn quick. My life was baseball. It wasn't just what I did for a living, it was who I was as a person. Remembering the disdain in Lyric's voice when she'd said *Oh. Baseball*—maybe she wasn't right for me after all.

Trying to put the petite med school princess out of my mind, I turned my attention back to the ballpark in the distance. A soft breeze wafted across my face, and I was pleased to feel the air turning slightly warmer as the day went on. *Springtime.* Baseball season. After nearly six years of being in the majors and several years playing in the minor leagues, that jittery, excited flutter in my stomach never got old. God, I loved baseball. Richmond had been good to me these last few years. I would miss it, but Baltimore was where I truly belonged.

Game time wasn't until 7:05pm with batting practice starting a few hours earlier, and I was antsy. We were only a few days into the season, and I was eager to get going. I'd gotten used to waking up earlier in the off-season, and now I had too much time on my hands. Once the late nights at the ballpark and the travel schedule kicked in, I'd start sleeping in later.

I sat on my patio and played on my phone for a while, then I went back inside to watch TV. Becoming a game-show addict came with the territory of having a job where you're home for most of the day. Putting my feet up on the coffee table, I settled in to watch some of my favorites, including *The Price is Right* and *Family Feud.* There was also a cable game-show channel where I could catch some old-school shows that aired years ago. Old or new, I often found myself on the edge of my seat, cheering on the contestants. It was a relaxing, non-physical way to unwind and recover from the previous day's baseball game.

After lunch, I was bored again. Wandering aimlessly around my apartment, I was debating going to the ballpark to work out when my cell phone rang. The caller ID said it was my agent, Doug Ryerson. Maybe he had a new advertising deal. He'd managed to get me some great ad contracts over the years. I was no actor for sure, but the commercial shoots were fun, and they gave me something to do in my down time.

"Hey, man. What's up?" I said as I flopped down on the couch.

"I'm 'fraid I got some bad news for you," he said.

"Really?" I wondered what it could possibly be.

"Dude, I'm really sorry, but ... Baltimore passed."

It took several seconds for my brain to register his words.

"Wait, what?"

"I know. Sucks, man. It really does."

"What the fuck? I'm not even a free agent yet. You can't even make a deal until after the World Series ends in the fall."

"Right, but I reached out to the owner now to get the ball rolling. I wanted him to know you were interested and, you know, try to get you as good a deal as possible."

I shot up off the couch and started pacing. "I don't give a shit about getting a great deal. You know that. I just want to play for the Baltimore Bay Birds."

"I know, buddy. Believe me. My plan was to start negotiating now and see what we can get and go from there. But they passed."

"Tell them I'll sign for less. Doug, I know this goes against every bone in your agent deal-seeking body, but you need to tell them I will agree to whatever they want."

"I did, Brady," he said wearily. "And believe me, it was physically painful for me to say the words out loud. They just ... Dude, I hate sayin' this to you, but they just don't want you."

"How can they not want me?" I roared into the phone. "With my track record and my agreeing to whatever terms they want? What the *fuck*, dude?"

"The owner said you're too big of a risk."

"A risk? A *risk*? What does that even mean?"

"Devilbuss says he doesn't want a guy on the payroll who gets drunk and trashes hotel rooms."

Shit. So maybe I partied too hard sometimes. So what? I always paid the damages and apologized. It was all in good fun, and most of the time the hotel owners enjoyed the notoriety. We always parted on good terms, and I never got kicked out of anywhere.

"Are you serious? That's his problem?"

"You know how he is. Gary Devilbuss prides himself on being a family man. He expects his players to be squeaky clean, and there's a reason Baltimore fans have the best reputation in baseball. They work hard at keeping Old Bay Stadium kid-friendly, and they don't want rowdy, drunk fans in the stands."

My fans did tend to get a bit out of hand sometimes, but was that really my fault?

"There's gotta be something we can do, man."

"Sorry, dude. He was pretty damn clear he wasn't interested. Look, you got plenty of time to think things over. Maybe see how the season goes with Richmond and then you can decide if you want to stay in Virginia or try for another ball club."

"I don't want another ball club," I said, knowing I sounded like a petulant child. "I want Baltimore!"

Doug sighed. "I know. Look, I gotta go for now. Just ... try to keep your cool here, okay?"

He sounded worried, and rightfully so, about how I would handle this blow.

"No promises," I said grimly and ended the call.

Baltimore passed.

I couldn't believe it. I was one of the hottest players in the entire major league, I was willing to take less money, and the Baltimore Bay Birds had been on an unprecedented losing streak for the last five years. It hadn't occurred to me for one second that they could turn me down.

Physical pain exploded in my chest. I felt like I'd been punched right in the heart. I'd grown up watching the Baltimore Bay Birds play, and Old Bay Stadium had been my second home growing up. The whole time I played ball in high school and all those years in the minors, I'd been working toward playing for Baltimore. Even when I finally made it to the show, playing my first major league game for the Boston Red Rebels, I still thought about being with the Bay Birds. The first time I played at Old Bay Stadium, albeit for the opposing team, I actually *cried*. Thank God none of my teammates saw me; I got there super early so I could have a moment to myself on the field. After being drafted by Boston and then playing for Richmond, finally after this season I'd have put in my six years the majors required to become a free agent, so I would be free to try to go where I wanted.

And the Baltimore Bay Birds fucking *passed*.

My lifelong dream and everything I'd worked for, gone in the blink of an eye.

Rage suddenly replaced my heartache. I stared at my apartment wall, sorely tempted to punch my fist through it. I sure as hell felt like trashing a room now, since I had nothing to lose. Not wanting to destroy my own place, I grabbed my gym bag and charged out the door. Better to take my aggression out on an actual punching bag.

Shoulders hunched and tense, I stormed down the street toward Dominion Park. Good thing there weren't too many people out on the street because for once I was in no mood to be recognized. I passed by Richmond Roast, which didn't exactly help my mood. It reminded me of Lyric's rejection.

Nobody wants me right now.

My spirits lifted slightly when I arrived at the ballpark. If nothing else, I would get to play baseball today. Once I got to the weight room inside the park, I jammed in my earbuds and tried to tune out the world with the loudest rock music I could stand. When one of my teammates came into the room, the look I gave him was enough to make him turn right around and walk out. I knew I was being a dick, but I couldn't help it. I needed to be left alone.

Working out and blaring music was cathartic. Immediately afterward I felt slightly better. But it wasn't long before the exercise adrenaline wore off and all the emotional pain came flooding back.

I wasn't going to play for Baltimore.

Much as I tried to push those thoughts away and concentrate on the game that night, it was impossible. I went 0 for 4 after falling back on my nasty habit of swinging at the first pitch. My nature is to be impulsive; it had taken years to learn to be more patient at the plate.

Impulsive.

Yeah, that was me. That's how I'd wound up drinking too much, destroying hotel rooms, and smashing my own dreams because of it.

As much as I loved playing for the Richmond Dominoes, the truth was that with every game I played, in the back of my mind I imagined someday it would be for the Baltimore Bay Birds. Tonight was the first game I played knowing that wasn't going to happen.

I sat on the bench in the locker room after the game in a daze. I didn't even see my friend and teammate Tyler Maxwell walk in, and I had no idea how long he had been staring at me.

"So you gonna tell me what the hell is the matter with you, or what?"

"Ah! What?"

"I said what the hell is wrong with you?"

"Baltimore passed." How I hated saying those words out loud.

Tyler slowly sank down on the bench next to me. "Shit."

He knew damn well how much I wanted to play for the Bay Birds. Well, everyone knew. It was no secret. But he was one of my best buddies on the team, and he understood more than most guys.

"How could they pass on you? Weren't you willing to play for pretty much anything they offered?"

"Yep. Devilbuss thinks I'm too much of a risk. Too wild."

A look of understanding crossed Tyler's face. He knew exactly what they meant. Hell, Tyler was usually partying right next to me when I got into trouble.

"Damn." After a moment of silence for the death of my dream, he added, "Let's go get drunk."

I scoffed. "That's how I got into trouble in the first place."

"But what's it matter now?"

"Good point."

Though I knew it was irresponsible of me, there was nothing I wanted more right now than to drink my sorrows away.

"Let's go," I said.

We went to a place we frequented when we were in town. Though I usually gobbled down the food they had for us at the park post-game, tonight I hadn't eaten anything. All the better to get where I wanted to be—blind drunk—as soon as possible. It only took a few shots to dull my pain, at least temporarily. I tried not to think about the fact that it was mostly alcohol and my immaturity that got me into this mess.

I drank when I was happy after a win. I drank when I was bummed out over a tough loss. I drank when I was bored or just in the mood to party. Not that I was an alcoholic, but I did have a tendency to overdo it. Right now it was hard to care, though.

"'Nother one," I said to the bartender, my words sounding slurred in my own ears.

"Cheers, buddy," Tyler said with a wink as he toasted me with his own shot.

A pretty blonde lady walked over to me, her eyes wide with recognition. I was, by far, the most famous baseball player on the team. In fact, I might even be the most famous player in all of major league baseball right now. I'd learned long ago that just because a woman recognized me, it didn't necessarily mean she followed baseball. She might have seen me in TV commercials or on magazine covers. Still, that recognition frequently got me laid. But I was not in the mood tonight. I offered her a weak smile then turned away. She got the hint, and she sat next to Tyler at the bar. With his blond hair and green eyes, even I knew Tyler was a hot guy. No doubt he had no problem getting laid on his own, but sitting next to me usually made it a lot easier.

While Tyler chatted up his new lady friend, I kept on drinking. I picked up my phone, which was never a good thing when I was drunk. Just as well I didn't get Lyric's number because I probably would have called her and spilled my guts about what had happened with the Bay Birds. Not sure why, really. She barely knew me, and she didn't even like baseball. But for some reason, I felt like she would understand why I was so crushed.

No, that was completely insane. I talked to her for what, ten minutes? And I expected her to care about my life?

So I drunk dialed somebody else.

"Angel? Angel, my boy," I said, talking loud so I could be heard over all the bar noise.

"Brady? You okay?"

I felt bad. He sounded tired, and I realized I had no idea what time it was. Angel was my best friend from Maryland. We played together in the minors, and now he played for the Baltimore Bay Birds. He had a lovely wife named Jana, who I'd probably woken up with my late-night phone call. Shit.

"Sorry for calling so late," I mumbled. "I'm sorry for everything."

"What are you sorry about? Dude, you okay?"

"Fucked it all up. Gary Busydevil ... Devilberry ... Devilbutt ... the owner of Baltimore guy. He don't want me 'cuz I'm a screwup. He won't let me play for the Birds."

"Oh, man," Angel said, and the sorrow in his voice tore me up inside. We were supposed to play together in Baltimore. That was the plan. Now it wasn't gonna happen.

"Yeah. I'm sorry. Go back to bed. Just hadda tell you."

"You all right? You got somebody to get you home safe?"

I glanced at Tyler, who was no more responsible than I was. Still, I could probably make it home okay. It wasn't that far.

"Yeah, I'll be fine." I somehow managed to press the button to end the call.

I didn't feel fine. Once again, anger started taking the place of my sadness. The more I thought about what had happened, the more pissed off I got. Who the hell did that Gary Devil guy think he was? He thought he could do better than me? His team hadn't seen the playoffs in years. I was the best chance he had, and nobody—and I mean *nobody*—would ever play with more heart than I would when it came to playing for Baltimore. I belonged in that town. I was supposed to be there.

Yet, I wasn't.

I picked up my shot glass and threw it hard against the wooden bar. The goddamned thing bounced instead of breaking. Good Christ, I couldn't do anything right today. I picked up an empty wine glass from the bar and threw that down. The glass shattered with a satisfying crash.

"Okay, okay, buddy, I think it's time to go," Tyler said with an apologetic glance at the girl who'd been cozying up to him. He grabbed me by the shoulders. I shrugged him off too hard and he fell to the floor. I winced. I hadn't meant to embarrass him in front of that girl. I just had an uncontrollable urge to smash everything in this place until it was as broken as I was.

"Sorry, man. Sorry."

Tyler glared at me as he got up.

"Time to go," he said firmly. "Unless you wanna get cut from the Richmond team too."

It was a cruel thing to say, but it was the wake-up call I needed. I could very well fuck up my entire career if I got too out of hand.

"Yeah," I said, stumbling toward the exit. "Yeah."

* * *

I SLEPT in the next morning and woke up with a dry mouth and a slight headache. After years of drinking, my body was used to alcohol punishment. It took me a few seconds to remember why I'd been drinking. Did we win last night? Did I have fun?

It didn't take me long to realize that the answer was no to both questions. My chest ached all over again. I'd been rejected by Baltimore.

Groaning, I heaved myself out of bed. Memories of last night came trickling back; I owed Tyler big for keeping me out of trouble. I jumped in the shower, using that time to try to get my head on straight. Get some perspective. I couldn't afford to sit around feeling sorry for myself, no matter how angry and hurt I was. I was still a major league baseball player, something most guys would give their left nut to be. My heart might be with Baltimore, but right now my loyalty needed to be with the Richmond Dominoes. I'd let them down last night by getting into my own head, and that wasn't right. Those guys deserved better.

I got dressed, wandered into my kitchen, and stared at my coffeemaker. I desperately needed coffee, but I debated whether or not I felt like taking a stroll down to Richmond Roast.

Nah. What were the odds that Lyric would be there again? Other than her, I didn't feel like talking to anyone. I was trying, but it wasn't easy to pull myself out of my funk. I had to face facts. Losing Baltimore was gonna hurt for a really long time.

After breakfast, I took my coffee out onto the patio since the day was warming up nicely. I scrolled through my phone, reading over the news and sports and all that good stuff. Then I moved on to my social media accounts to see if anything interesting was going on. As usual, there were some comments from fans as well as some haters.

My heart nearly stopped when I saw a photo I'd been tagged in—a picture of me sitting with Lyric at the coffee shop. It wasn't the photo itself that shook me up. People took pictures of me out in public all the time, so it was really no big deal. I was just surprised at my reaction when I saw her face.

Scrutinizing the photo, it was no wonder I'd gotten the wrong idea. She really did seem interested in what I was saying. The way she was looking at me in the photo, the way she was leaning in, it was like she was fascinated by whatever I was saying. Weird to think just a few minutes later she'd been like *Welp, gotta go!* and out the door she'd gone.

After I finished staring at the photo and into Lyric's clear blue eyes, my focus drifted downward and I realized this wasn't just some random photo snapped by a fan. It was a news article. Well, a tabloid gossip article.

Brady "The Crusher" Keaton Shares Intense Convo With New Girlfriend?

Photos of me with women hanging on me while I partied was nothing new. There were pictures of me with different women in cities all over the country. Strange they would think Lyric was my girlfriend when they'd never said that before about any other woman. Made me feel better that they'd clearly been as fooled as I'd been. That was what I thought at first. Then I read the next two words of the article.

"Yeah, right."

Then the rest of the article was pretty much trashing me and scoffing at the notion that I would ever "settle down." And, of course, it went on to talk about my wild partying and drinking and all that. To add insult to injury, the article mentioned that I'd expressed an interest in playing for Baltimore and that they'd turned me down. At first, I was super pissed at the whole article. Who the fuck were they to judge me? But then I had what people like to call "a moment of clarity."

Settling down was the exact opposite of what they were judging me as — a playboy partier. A wild man. And no one was judging me more than Baltimore. But if I could convince Devilbuss that I had finally "settled down," he might just give me a shot.

Staring at the photo, I knew exactly what I was going to do.

I was gonna ask Lyric Rivers to marry me.

CHAPTER 3

*L*yric

I GLANCED at Dominion Park as I walked back to the house after classes. In the few days since I'd met him, I'd gotten an inkling of just how famous Brady "The Crusher" Keaton really was. Yesterday, while standing in the checkout line at the grocery store, I was shocked to see his face—and gorgeous body—gracing the cover of *GQ* magazine. So the guy wasn't just baseball-famous, he was, like, actual celebrity-famous, since *GQ* wasn't even a sports publication.

I bought a copy and read through the article. Apparently, Brady had been in a bunch of TV commercials for deodorant and men's soap and things like that. No wonder he'd thought it was weird that I hadn't heard of him. His nickname was The Crusher, which wasn't surprising. With his huge build, I was sure he crushed home runs on the daily. Now that I knew how famous he was, I realized he was even farther out of my league than I'd thought. I was sure he had women all over the country lusting after him. It was laughable that I'd thought for even a second that he might be interested in me.

Laughable or not, I couldn't deny the twinge of sadness every time I caught sight of the ballpark or heard mention of the Richmond Dominoes. Brady would be off playing for Baltimore soon enough anyway, I figured. Best to forget him.

Besides, I had a tough biochemistry test tomorrow, and I had a lot of studying to do. I opened the door to the creaky old house where I was staying to find all four of my roommates sitting in the living room. Right away I knew something was up because seeing them together was rare. They had busy social lives and were constantly coming and going at all hours of the day and night. It was a horrible setup for somebody like me who was actually in college to learn, but it was the cheapest living arrangement I'd been able to find.

"What?" I asked while all four women stared at me.

"Are you dating Brady Keaton?" Kerry asked, blue eyes wide. With her long blonde hair and slender frame, she was a Barbie doll come to life.

How the hell could she possibly know I had met Brady Keaton? For one paranoid moment, I was afraid I'd been talking in my sleep or something.

"What are you talking about?"

Kerry handed me her phone, and the next thing I knew I was staring at a photograph of me sitting with Brady at Richmond Roast. It was a tabloid article. I quickly scanned the first paragraph, noting that the headline briefly speculated about us dating but then quickly dismissed the notion. Apparently, Brady Keaton was not the type to settle down. I found that unsurprising to say the least.

"No, we're not dating," I said, forgoing the idea as quickly as the article had. "I met him once and dumped hot coffee on him."

"You did?" Kerry asked. "What did he do? Hit on you? Grab your ass or something?"

"No, no. I didn't do it on purpose. I just wasn't paying attention and accidentally splashed him. Then I bought him some coffee and muffins to make up for it, and we talked for a few minutes. End of story."

"Oh," Kerry said.

"Did you really think a guy like Brady Keaton would go for a girl like me?"

Their silence hurt more than it should have. But it was the truth. What would a gorgeous celebrity baseball player want with boring old me?

"Of course he would," Jill chimed in. With her lovely blue-green eyes and strawberry blonde hair, she was as attractive as Kerry. Her words were charitable yet unconvincing. "Why wouldn't he?"

The other women finally stammered their agreement, but it was a little late.

Forcing a smile, I said, "He seemed like a nice guy. It's funny. I honestly had no idea who he was at first. Whatever. I've got a ton of studying to do, so I'll catch you later."

I hurried up the narrow steps to my tiny bedroom, eager to be alone. I grabbed the sweater I kept draped across the chair since it was always cold in my room and sat down at my desk. After waking up my computer, I quickly searched up the article so I could read it through more carefully. I smiled as I looked at the picture. Pretty sure I could pinpoint the exact moment in the conversation when somebody had snapped the photo. The way I was gazing so intently at him, I knew it was when he'd talked about why he wanted to play for Baltimore. That had been the moment I'd realized there was more to him than being just a dumb jock. Guilt pricked my stomach at having judged him so quickly in the first place.

"Oh, no," I said out loud when I read down to the bottom of the article. Apparently, the owner of the Baltimore team had rejected him. And, as it turned out, I wasn't that far off with my first impression of the guy. He really was the playboy party type, just as I'd pegged him. And now that reputation had cost him his dream.

My heart broke for him. I could so clearly remember the look in his eyes when he'd talked about playing for the Baltimore Bay Birds. He probably felt the same despair I would feel if I found out I hadn't been accepted to medical school.

That poor guy. Though I understood where the Baltimore owner was coming from since it could be a risk taking on a guy with a wild reputation, I still wished they would give him a second chance.

I sighed heavily, knowing there was nothing I could do about it. Forcing myself to study for my test, I shoved my earplugs in my ears, but it didn't really block out the loud talking and giggling coming from downstairs. The music also did nothing to drown out my thoughts of Brady.

* * *

"LYRIC!" a man's voice called to me on campus as I exited the science building.

My brain was pretty foggy after a grueling sixty-minute biochemistry test, but unless I was completely losing my mind, Brady Keaton was jogging toward me.

"Brady?" I asked, actively resisting the urge to rub my eyes with my fists like a cartoon character trying to clear her vision.

"Yeah. It's me." His eyes were wild when he caught up to me in front of the building. "This is the only place I could think of to find you. I've been to Richmond Roast every morning for the last week, but you weren't there."

"No. I wasn't," I said, staring up at him. The man really was gigantic. Wracking my brain to figure out why he had hunted me down, I started to feel afraid. What if he was some crazy stalker? I clutched my books to my chest and took a step back. I was still close enough to the glass doors of the school building that I could run in and scream for help if necessary.

"Oh, I'm sorry," he said as his dark eyes softened with concern. "I didn't mean to scare you. You must think I'm insane running up to you like this."

"Well, the thought had crossed my mind."

"There's something important I need to talk to you about. That is, if you have some time now?"

"Uh, well. I guess," I said, glancing toward the safety of the doors again.

"We can talk in public if you feel safer. Wherever you're comfortable."

My tense shoulders relaxed. Though I knew I still had to keep my guard up just in case, there was something in his eyes, his demeanor, that told me he didn't mean me any harm. Still. A public place. Definitely.

"There's some picnic tables over there where we can sit and talk if you want." I gestured to them a short distance away.

"Perfect," Brady said with a smile. He walked toward them while keeping a careful distance from me, which I appreciated. Ever since I started school here, campus safety had been drilled into my head. I'd done my best to remain vigilant.

Brady took a seat at a picnic table in the sun to ward off the chill of the April breeze, and I sat across from him. Despite the cool wind, there was a hint of summer smell in the air. Since it was too early for lunch, we had the place to ourselves.

"So," he began. "I don't know if you saw that tabloid article with our picture?"

"I saw it," I said grimly.

"Oh." Brady seemed disappointed by my reaction. I guess a lot of women would love to have people think they were dating him. "You really don't like that kind of attention, do you?"

I shook my head.

He nodded, looking worried. It was weird. What did he want to talk to me about? Maybe he was trying to work up the nerve to ask me out? That seemed impossible. Not only was he literally out of my league as a celebrity MLB player, he did not seem the type who needed to gather his courage to hit on a woman.

"You're not married, right?" he said.

"Right. I'm not."

"Are you seeing anyone?"

"No. Not at the moment."

Not yet anyway.

"Okay, good."

That was all he said. Again, it was weird.

"So, it turns out Baltimore doesn't want me after all," he said at last. Certainly not what I expected him to say.

"I know."

"You do?"

"Yeah. It was in the article."

"Oh. Right."

"I'm really sorry, Brady. I felt so bad when I heard about that. I know how much playing for that team meant to you."

"Thanks," he said sadly. "I appreciate that." He stared at me intently. "I was hoping you might be able to help me with the whole Baltimore situation."

"Me? What could I possibly do to help you play for Baltimore?"

"I have a proposal for you," Brady said with a wicked grin. "And it's literally a proposal. I want you to marry me."

My muscles tensed. Brady might actually be out of his mind. I wasn't sure whether to laugh or run away. Sheer curiosity kept me in my seat for the moment.

"*Marry you?* What, are you from another country and need to marry an American citizen or something?"

"No, nothing like that. The Baltimore owner thinks I'm too wild and crazy to take a chance on. I kinda have a reputation for drinking a little too much sometimes and getting into trouble."

"Sounds like marriage material to me," I said dryly. "Sign me up."

"See, that's the problem. Nobody thinks of me as marriage material right now. And everybody thinks that when you get married it means you've 'settled down.' If I get married to some nice stable girl, the Baltimore owner won't think of me as such a risk anymore."

I stared at him for a moment. I'd had several impressions of Brady Keaton since I'd met him. Big scary guy who might kill me for scalding him with hot coffee. Man who turned out to be pretty nice after all. Famous TV commercial spokesperson and magazine cover model. Playboy partier. But I'd never taken him for a lunatic. Until now.

"You have lost your mind," I said, grabbing my books and standing up.

"Please," he said, and there was something so plaintive in his voice that I couldn't walk away. Not just yet. He might be crazy, but he was also desperate. He was hurting. "Please hear me out."

Sighing, I sat back down.

"I will totally make it worth your while."

There was no way in hell I was ever going to agree to this

harebrained, sitcom-esque scheme, but I would at least listen to what he had to say.

"Lyric," he said, and my insides fluttered at the sound of my name. "If the Baltimore owner thinks I've fallen in love with a woman and changed my partying ways, he might really give me a shot."

In that moment, he didn't *seem* crazy. Just passionate about going after what he wanted.

"Why me? You must know lots of other women."

"Well, yeah. I do."

Ouch.

"But they're either underwear models or cleat chasers."

"What is a cleat chaser?"

"Like a groupie for baseball players."

"Gotcha." You learned something new every day.

"Not exactly the type you bring home to mother. Or to the boss for a job you're trying to get. But you? A nice, safe college student? Perfect."

"Perfectly boring is what you mean," I said, feeling defensive.

"You're not boring," he said kindly, because of course he did. He was trying to talk me into doing him a ridiculous, monumental favor. "You're very sweet and smart and really pretty. And we looked like a great couple in that photo. Admit it. That's why they speculated that we might be together. Because we *look* like we belong together."

"I am not going to marry you so you can get a job, Brady. That's insane."

"Lyric, I'll pay for your medical school."

"What?"

"I will pay all your schooling expenses. Med school, books, fees, whatever you need. I'll even pay off whatever you need to finish college."

My heart seized in my chest. I'd always known I'd be in

debt for half my life to pay for everything I needed to be a doctor. It was a given. If I took Brady up on his offer, he could make all that go away. And I wouldn't have to take any time off after college to work and save up for medical school.

All those thoughts raced through my head for a few brief, euphoric seconds before I came back down to planet Earth.

"That's crazy. That's like hundreds of thousands of dollars."

"I make *millions* of dollars every year," Brady said bluntly. "I won't even miss it."

Damn. I knew he was right about that. It was mind-boggling. Despite what was in it for me, the whole idea was still ludicrous.

"You can't honestly expect me to say yes to this," I told him.

"I'll get down on one knee and make it all official. I'll buy you the biggest rock you've ever seen for the ring. I could propose at Dominion Park in front of the whole world!"

"Ugh," I said, involuntarily wrapping my arms around myself for protection. Just thinking about that kind of attention made me want to break out in hives.

"Oh, right," Brady said, wincing. "The whole hating attention thing."

"Yeah," I said. "That kind of crap might be a fantasy for all your underwear models and cleat chasers, but not for me."

Brady nodded and gazed at me with what looked like respect.

"I appreciate your generous offer, Brady, and I sympathize with your plight. I really do. I wish I could help you get in good with Baltimore, but I just can't. Not like this. You might be the bad boy of baseball, but I'm a Goody Two-shoes and proud of it." I was pleased with the defiance in my voice. Those other women might melt into a puddle of goo around this hotshot, but not me. "My dream is to make the world a better place by becoming a doctor, and lying to the whole world is not part of that plan. I'm sorry."

Brady swallowed hard, and I watched that sexy Adam's apple again. For a second, I questioned my sanity at turning down a once-in-a-lifetime opportunity. How often does a rich, handsome man offer you your dreams on a silver platter? But no. I had principles.

"I understand where you're coming from. And God knows I respect you for it. But you're my last hope, Lyric."

Gazing into his pleading eyes, I realized that Brady Keaton wasn't really crazy after all. Just excitable. And passionate about what he wanted.

"I respect you, too, Brady. I love your reasons for wanting to play for Baltimore, and I understand how much you want this. But I'm not gonna be your fake bride to help you do it. There's no way I can lie to my parents and everybody else about something like that. I just can't do it."

"Well, what if we were just engaged? You could just pretend to be my fake fiancée for a little while before we call it off? No public proposals or anything like that. I just quietly get you a ring and we play that angle."

I thought about that for a moment.

Watching me carefully, he tentatively continued. "We would just be engaged temporarily. Until after I sign my contract with Baltimore, and then we break it off sometime after that. I'll say you left me. I'll say you found somebody smarter, which wouldn't be hard, believe me."

Something in the way he said that made me sad. Like he thought he was dumb or something. I certainly had never thought that about him.

"Same deal as I said before. You pretend to be my fiancée, and I pay for all your schooling."

Brady held his breath while he waited for a response. It was painful to look at him, since the answer was still no.

God, it felt like I was turning down a real marriage proposal. But I could not get sucked into this crazy scheme.

"I'm really sorry, Brady."

He looked so crushed I could hardly bear it. That was my initial reaction. Then I got mad.

"Look, I am not the bad guy here. What you're asking of me is insane, so stop acting like I'm a horrible person for saying no."

"You're right. You're totally right, Lyric," he said, seeming genuinely apologetic. Then he reached across the picnic table and took my hand in both of his.

A sudden jolt of attraction sizzled through my body, taking me by surprise. Brady was, after all, a seriously sexy hunk of a man. And it was hard not to be turned on by a guy who spoke with such passion, even if the passion wasn't directed at me.

"This is an awful lot I'm asking of you," he went on. "I understand that this is way out of your comfort zone. You're a respectable woman."

"Which is what makes me so perfect for your scheme."

"Yeah. That's true," he said, holding his gaze steadily on me. "Okay. Final offer. What about you just pretend to be my girlfriend?" He glanced around at the campus and then back at me. "You probably live in a tiny dorm on campus, right?"

"No. I live off campus."

"In a cramped apartment?"

"Nope. In a house."

Brady's expression fell, but then he brightened. "You got roommates?"

"Four of them."

"A-ha! And I bet it's noisy with a bunch of college kids coming and going at all hours." He grinned when he saw my expression. "Pretty hard to study."

"Yeah. True. So?"

"So I propose you become my live-in girlfriend. I have a luxury apartment a few blocks away. It's within walking distance of this place." He gestured to the campus. "Most nights I'll be at the ballpark and then other times I'll be on the road. So you'll have a nice, quiet, comfy place to study all to yourself most of the time. You'll have your own bedroom of course."

I hated how rational this whole thing suddenly sounded. It scared me. Because there was a danger I might just cave in and agree to it. I knew I had to strengthen my resolve.

"Brady, this whole idea is crazy."

"But it's just crazy enough to work," he said with such enthusiasm, I couldn't stop myself from laughing. Damn him and his annoying charm. "You could quietly move in. We don't even have to say anything to the press. Just let them find out on their own when they see you coming and going at my place."

"Does the paparazzi follow you a lot?" I asked, a knot of anxiety forming in my stomach.

"Not a *lot*. I'm not a movie star. But they do follow me *some*."

"How long would you expect this arrangement to have to go on?"

Brady's eyes flashed with excitement like he was taking my questions as a good sign. God help me.

"Well, it's April now. Season's just beginning, so we have some time to let this all play out. I know I can't change my reputation overnight. Bottom line is I become a free agent at the end of the season. Contracts would be negotiated a few days after the World Series, so we're talking October. Do you know where you're going to med school yet?"

Med school. This man is actually willing to pay for my med school. My excitement was getting harder and harder to contain.

"No. I have another year of college to go first. After this one."

"Okay. So this little arrangement won't disrupt your plans. It'll be over before you even attend medical school. You can go any place you want. Money is no object."

I held my breath. I watched as he held his. My excitement quickly turned to panic.

"Brady, I can't ..." I was going to say *I can't do this* but the words wouldn't come. Because maybe, just maybe, I *could* do this. "I need time to think about it. I can't just make a snap decision."

"Of course you can't. You need to think it over." I heard the cautious optimism in his voice.

"Yes."

"Take a few days," Brady said. "Think about it. I'll pay for your college and medical school and give you free room and board for several months. A quiet place to study. All in exchange for you agreeing to hang out with me for a while."

"You make it sound so easy," I said skeptically.

"I will make it as easy on you as possible, Lyric. I swear to it. Listen, I'm going on the road with the Dominoes for the next six days. Give me an answer when I get back?" he asked.

"Okay. That's fair."

Brady fished out his wallet and pulled out his business card. "You got a pen?"

I retrieved a pen from my pencil case and handed it to him.

"This business card just has my agent's info on it, but here's my personal number."

"I wonder how many cleat chasers would kill to have that number."

He laughed and nodded. "A good many."

I tried not to think about that as I took the card from him. Shakily, I stood up to leave.

"Have a safe trip."

"Thanks. Talk to you in six days. If not sooner," he said, eyes wide with enthusiasm.

I nodded numbly. "Six days."

It was gonna be a long week.

CHAPTER 4

rady

GOD, I could really be an idiot sometimes. I was lucky Lyric hadn't run away screaming when I showed up unannounced on her school campus. Showed what a bubble I lived in sometimes. Until she looked at me with fear in her eyes, it never once occurred to me how frightening it would be to have a huge athlete, a relative stranger, come running up to a woman like I had.

Drawing in a deep breath as I walked home from the University of Richmond campus, my eyes naturally drifted toward Dominion Park. As wonderful as it had been playing there for the last few years, I felt renewed hope that next season I'd be playing there as a member of the visiting team. Wearing Bay Birds orange and black.

With Lyric in the picture, my dream of playing for Baltimore still had a fighting chance. After I'd talked to her for a while, she had seemed to stop worrying I might hurt her, so that was good. She'd still looked at me like I was nuts, though, which was fair. It wasn't until I'd said the words *I want you to marry me* out loud that I'd realized how crazy an idea that was.

Even if Lyric did agree to this deal, it was critical that we were convincing as a couple. Sure, I had a reputation as a womanizer and a partier, but I was also known for my sense of loyalty. I'd always been fiercely protective of anybody close to me—my friends, my family, and my team. Though it was no secret I wanted to play for Baltimore, I didn't want the Richmond Dominoes to doubt my devotion to them for a second. As long as I wore a Dominoes uniform, I would remain totally committed to them. But it could cause trouble if they knew the lengths I was willing to go to in order to play for Baltimore next season.

Lyric was a nice girl, and I should have known she would never agree to get married unless it was real. I thought the compromise we'd worked out was pretty good. If she agreed to do it, being my fake girlfriend would work just fine. It was a lot more believable than me just up and getting married out of the blue.

As a solid, hardworking student, Lyric exuded sincerity, and we did seem to have good chemistry together. Yeah. It was totally believable that I could fall in love with a sweet girl like her, change my hard partying, and become the ideal candidate to play ball for a family man like Gary Devilbuss.

All Lyric had to do was say yes.

I'd given her my phone number but didn't get hers. That was deliberate. If I knew how to contact her, I wouldn't be able to stop myself from pestering her over the next few days. She needed time to think it over, so I would give it to her. The hardest part would be trying to put it out of my mind for the next six days while she made her decision.

* * *

I HAD A PRETTY good game that night at Dominion Park. The next day the team headed to Boston for a three-game series.

The first game was a blowout with the Dominoes winning 10-2. I decided to hit the Boston bars hard, thinking of it as a last hurrah before I "settled down" and worked on fixing my reputation.

By the time we hit the second pub I was pretty hammered. It was great, tossing back shots like water. I was really gonna miss this. Becoming a Bay Bird would make it all worthwhile of course, but that didn't mean it would be easy.

"You're Brady Keaton, aren't you?" came a female voice from just behind me at the bar. I turned to see a pretty brunette batting her eyelashes at me. Her equally attractive blonde friend looked me up and down appreciatively but backed off when the first girl gave her the death stare. The blonde shrugged and turned her attention to Tyler.

"Yep, I sure am," I said, annoyed at the slur in my speech. As usual, I'd had too much. I hated how my drunk voice made me sound stupid.

"Are you here with anyone tonight?" the brunette asked. I knew all I had to say was *I am now. Wanna go up to my hotel room?* and the girl would be mine for the night. Any other night, that was exactly what I would have done. But not tonight.

"No, but I'm kinda tired. Gonna have a drink or two for the road and then hit the hay."

"Oh," she said, pouting. She got over it pretty damn quick, though. Joining her friend, she turned her attention to Tyler. Pretty sure I'd just set my buddy up for one hell of a threesome.

You're welcome, Tyler. Ya lucky fuck.

Weird how I'd turned that girl down. After all, this was supposed to be my last night of living it up. Shouldn't that include one last wild fuck before I had to pretend to have a serious girlfriend? I told myself I'd turned her down because I didn't want to risk being seen with another woman; it might mess up my scheme. But deep down, I knew that wasn't the truth.

Crazy as it was, it would have felt like I was cheating on Lyric. I just couldn't do it.

I threw back a couple more shots and paid the bill. At least I hoped I had, I thought on the way up to my room. The last thing I really remember was being in my hotel bed picturing Lyric's pretty blue eyes before I fell asleep. Thinking of her made me smile.

CHAPTER 5

L yric

I AGONIZED over the whole fake-girlfriend scheme, changing my mind dozens of times. Every time I had my mind made up one way or another, I'd go back on it again. It was making me crazy. I'd be studying, my roommates making their usual racket, and I'd think, *That's it. I'm doing it. I'll live at Brady's for a few months. What's the big deal?*

Then I'd think about lying to my parents. I *never* lied to my parents. Since I was a little kid, I'd had the virtues of honesty drilled into my head. They often told me that screwing up was one thing, but lying to cover it up was much worse. Then I'd decide that no, I wouldn't do it. But it was just a tiny white lie, right? So my parents would think I had a boyfriend for a few months. They'd probably be happy for me. As it was, they worried that I worked too hard and didn't make time for a social life. That might be true, but that was the life of a future doctor. I had to work my ass off, or I'd never make it. I got good grades most of the time, but I really had to work for them.

But then my mom and dad would be sad for me when I eventually "broke up" with Brady. They would probably try to comfort me after the relationship ended, and I would feel terrible that they were worrying about nothing. So many sides to consider for this deal, at least for me. Brady seemed to have no doubts about the plan.

As much as I loved my parents, it was times like this I wished they weren't the airy-fairy artsy type. They were musicians. Pretty good ones, actually. A talented duo, with my dad singing and my mom playing guitar and sometimes keyboard. My parents wrote their own songs and even had a few minor hits. But they were the quintessential starving artists, playing gigs whenever they could and working odd jobs in between. My parents had always taken good care of me, their only child. There had always been food on the table and a roof over my head. I was grateful for that, but they were exactly zero help when it came to helping me pay for school.

Though I loved my parents dearly, we had almost nothing in common. They didn't understand my science-oriented brain any more than I understood their arty ways. But they still loved and supported me in everything I did. They were cool like that. My mother had looked so sad when I'd told her I would need to take some time after high school to work, in order to save money for college. She'd told me how sorry she was that she and Dad couldn't help me more, which about broke my heart.

Still, the selfish part of me wished they had at least some money to donate to my schooling. Then maybe I wouldn't be forced to even think about this whole pretending to be a rich guy's girlfriend scheme. Was I selling out if I took advantage of this bizarre opportunity? Was I selling ...

myself? It did have kind of a *Pretty Woman* vibe. Brady had been a perfect gentleman, thank God. He hadn't even hinted about any kind of sexual component to the deal. If he had, I wouldn't have even considered his proposal. I believed his sincerity—that he was only doing this because it was his lifelong dream to be a Baltimore Bay Bird. Though I didn't understand his passion for baseball any more than I understood my parent's passion for music, I did respect it.

Back and forth. Yes, I'll do it. No, I won't. This went on for days. Good thing Brady had asked for an answer in six days, because I didn't think I could go on like this for much longer. I was afraid I wouldn't know my decision until it came out of my mouth once the time was up.

That was what I'd thought until I went to the hospital on the fifth day. I'd been a volunteer there for a few months, and it had been an incredible opportunity to shadow doctors in various disciplines as they treated their patients. I'd gotten some experience with oncology, endocrinology, pediatrics, obstetrics, and recently I'd been working closely with my mentor who was a cardiologist. Dr. Benita Bennett was a brilliant, dark-skinned woman with a deep knowledge of all things medical, and she had a generous heart. As a Black female doctor, I couldn't imagine how tough things must be for her sometimes. Still, she always found time to answer all my questions and allay all my fears. I simply worshiped her.

On the day before Brady was due to return from the road, Dr. Bennett had handed me Mrs. Woodburn's chart. "Lyric, I'd like you to deliver some very important news to our patient." I opened the chart and bit the inside of my cheek, trying to keep my poker face.

"Mrs. Woodburn, I'm afraid we won't be seeing much of you around here anymore," I told the delightful old lady who had charmed everyone in the cardiology department. "But you've improved so much, we have no choice but to send you home."

Almost immediately, Mrs. Woodburn began to cry, and we all knew why. Right before the dear woman had been rushed into emergency surgery, her daughter had given birth. Now, at last, she would be able to go home and meet her new grandson. Dr. Bennett grinned at me and I smiled back, trying not to cry myself. How gracious of her to let me deliver the good news when she'd done all the work to heal the patient.

Standing by Mrs. Woodburn's bedside, I knew what I had to do. The fastest, most efficient way to get on the road to becoming a doctor and helping people like Mrs. Woodburn was to take Brady up on his offer. This time, the decision felt different. This time, I knew I wasn't going to change my mind.

* * *

I WAS RELIEVED to have finally decided, but I knew the hardest part lay ahead. I was actually going to have to go through with this strange charade.

As exhausted as I was after a full day of classes and then working at the hospital, it was hard to sleep with all the racket going on downstairs. Sometimes my roommates went out to party. Tonight, they'd brought the party home to our place. I hated never having any peace and quiet, and I also hated the way they made me feel like a stick-in-the-mud for not partying with them. I knew they thought I was lame and boring, but my future was important to me. It was like *studying* in college was a novel concept. Somehow, I was the crazy one for putting in the work. Considering how ungodly expensive school was, the idea of throwing it all away to just get drunk all the time was enough to make me sick. Easy for those girls not to care when their parents were footing the bill.

Even with Brady paying for it, I was still going to work my ass off, no matter how lame people might think I was.

Brady.

My pretend boyfriend. I smiled when I thought about him. Thank God he was a nice guy, and even nicer to look at. I shuddered to think if some creepy guy had made this offer. Gorgeous and masculine as he was, Brady still seemed like a little kid who just wanted to play ball. It was utterly endearing.

The morning of the sixth day, I figured I should look him up on the Internet to make sure he didn't have a crazy criminal record or something. A quick online search brought up a bunch of boring sports articles, most of them without pretty pictures of Brady to look at. Nothing criminal that I could see. I knew he was a drinker and a partier, so I figured I'd better check to make sure he'd never been accused of domestic abuse or anything like that.

I did find several tabloid articles about his partying, which wasn't surprising. The photos of him with women hanging all over him hurt me more than I'd expected. Stupid, I knew. He wasn't really *mine*. It was just pretend, but still. I was still hurting a bit that he hadn't seemed genuinely interested in me. When he'd shown up on campus I'd been a little scared. But then, for a second I'd thought he'd come to find me because he wanted to date me. But he'd just needed my help.

I found another article about Brady "The Crusher" Keaton. I groaned out loud as I read the article. Turned out his nickname had nothing to do with baseball. Instead, it was a reference to a wild night out when they'd found more than a hundred crushed beer cans in his hotel room, plus several other items in the room that he'd demolished.

47

Oh dear God, what am I getting myself into?

I was trading four sorority-type college girls for one overgrown frat boy.

No. I'd made my decision and I was sticking to it. I had to keep my eyes on the prize. Not only would I be working toward my medical degree, but I would be helping Brady achieve his childhood dream. They were both worthwhile goals. The end justifies the means. It would be fine. Everything would be fine.

I had to keep telling myself that.

CHAPTER 6

rady

EARLY AFTERNOON on the sixth day, I got a text from an unfamiliar number.

Can we talk somewhere? Not in public.

After a few seconds, she added, *It's Lyric btw.*

Adrenaline surged throughout my body. She must have made her decision. Was it a good sign she wanted to meet in person? If the answer was no, wouldn't it have been easier on her to blow me off through text? No use wasting time with speculation. I'd know soon enough.

Sure. You can come to my place if you want.

Lyric wrote back *Works for me,* and I texted her the address. She explained she had a little time before her afternoon class and that she would head right over.

I called the front desk to give them a heads-up that a pretty, blue-eyed lady was coming to see me soon and it was okay for the doorman to let her into the building. The clerk at the front desk chuckled and agreed to let her in. It was not unusual for me to have female visitors. If things worked out, Lyric would be the only woman visiting me for the next several months.

A short while later there was a tentative knock on my door.

She's so pretty, was my first thought when I opened the door and saw her standing there. Her dark hair cascaded down past her shoulders, and I watched as she lifted her eyes from my chest, up to my face. I liked the way she had to look up at me because I was so much taller than her. It was like she was still getting used to my height.

"Hey," I said. "Any trouble finding the place?"

She shook her head. She appeared nervous, tentative, and I wasn't sure what that meant. Was she scared about saying yes, or worried about having to tell me no? All I knew was I had to be careful not to do anything to scare her off.

"Come on in," I said, stepping aside. Lyric scanned my large living room, glanced toward the kitchen, and then back at me.

"Your apartment is beautiful," she said.

"All this could be yours," I said before I could stop myself. Lyric winced and nodded.

"Here, come sit down." I walked over to the couch and sat down on the end, giving her enough space to sit if she wanted. She didn't, choosing a seat on my Barcalounger instead. My plan was to allow her to ease into the conversation, give her time to say what was on her mind.

"So, whaddya think?" I said instead. As usual, my impatience got the best of me. Six days, and I simply couldn't stand the wait anymore.

"Well," she began in a small voice. "I've decided ... I'm going to take you up on your offer."

"That's great!" I yelled, making her jump.

Calm down, you fuck, before she changes her mind.

"Sorry, sorry," I said, lowering my voice.

Lyric laughed, quickly recovering from her scare. She seemed rather amused, like she thought my enthusiasm was cute.

"It's okay. I know how much this whole thing means to you. Playing for Baltimore, I mean."

"Ah, this is so great. I really wasn't sure you were gonna go for it."

"Believe me, neither was I," she said uncertainly. "I just … There's just no way I'd be able to pay for my school without being in debt for the rest of my life. That, and I honestly do like the idea of helping you."

"Cool. Wow, okay. Now I guess we need an actual plan. First thing is to move you in here."

Lyric nodded, glancing around my apartment. "Yeah, I guess so."

"Here, lemme show you around," I said, getting up. I fought the urge to pump my fist in the air and scream and yell, but I knew I had to play it cool. "That's the kitchen obviously." I gestured toward the room just off the living room. Walking down the short hallway, I said, "Over here's my bedroom."

The door was open, and Lyric peered inside. The master bedroom was big for an apartment. My whole place was fairly spacious, though. I had a king-sized bed with red sheets and a black comforter. Manly-looking, or at least I liked to think so. Big-screen TV mounted on the wall, bathroom attached to the room.

I walked over to the bedroom next to it and said, "This one's yours. The guest bedroom."

"Wow, it's beautiful," she said, blue eyes lighting up. She stood tentatively in the doorway.

"Go on in," I encouraged her.

She smiled and entered the room. "This one has its own bathroom, too?"

"Yup. So you'll have plenty of privacy."

I watched as her shoulders visibly relaxed, and I felt my own body react the same. Until then, I hadn't noticed how tense I'd been. As much as I wanted this whole thing to work out, Lyric's nervousness worried me. The last thing I wanted was for her to feel miserably uncomfortable for the next few months.

Lyric ran her hand over the soft, light blue bedspread on the queen bed. Walking over to the window, she said, "This will be a great place to study."

"Yeah, I guess it would."

The room also had a big-screen TV mounted on the wall, so she could spend as much time in here as she wanted. Except for food, hopefully this room had everything she needed.

She stood still for a moment, then she asked, "Is it always this quiet?" She seemed so hopeful.

"Yep, it is. Sometimes I get back from the ballpark or from a road trip late at night, but I'll be sure to keep it down when I get home so I don't wake you or interrupt your studyin' or whatever. But yeah, no noisy neighbors. You don't hear much of the city noise from up here, but you still get the nice view."

After taking another moment to look at her room, she followed me to the patio.

"This place here has the best view," I said, gazing through the glass patio doors from inside.

"You can see the ballpark from here," Lyric said softly.

My insides turned to mush when she said that. It was cool that she noticed.

"Uh-huh," was all I could think of to say. "So, do you have a lease or something that we need to get you out of?"

"No. At least nothing signed and official or anything, but I do share the rent on the house with four other students."

"Got it. Okay, so we'll buy them out for the rest of the school year. I'll take care of it."

"Won't that seem kind of suspicious?" Lyric asked. "How do we explain why some random guy is giving them all this money?"

"We'll just say we've been secretly dating for a long time. Kept it secret because I'm famous or whatever."

Lyric grinned slyly.

"What?"

"I like the idea of my roommates thinking I'm sleeping with you."

Brady laughed. "Would they be jealous?"

"Damn straight they'd be jealous. That, and I know they think I'm boring and lame because I actually study instead of partying."

"I know how that feels."

Lyric burst out laughing. "I highly doubt that."

"No, I'm serious. I admit I can be a little wild nowadays, but I wasn't always that way. Worked my ass off in the minors to get where I am today. Teammates made fun of me because I never went out drinking with them, but I was super focused on what I wanted. Just like you. You're not boring or lame, Lyric."

The sheer gratitude in her eyes took me by surprise. She must have really needed to hear that.

"Thanks," she said.

"And I will totally make out with you in front of your roommates if you want."

Lyric laughed. "That won't be necessary."

Damn.

Not only would it have been fun to make out with Lyric, we needed to make sure our public displays of affection were believable. She was understandably timid around me right now, but we'd have to work on that if we were gonna pass as a couple. Still, the last thing I wanted to do was pressure her into any physical contact right now. Though taking things one step at a time was not exactly my strong suit, I wanted to take care to make sure Lyric was comfortable with all this madness.

"We'll get all your stuff moved in. Bring whatever you want, and any furniture or whatever that we don't have room for, we can put in storage."

"I don't have much. Just my desk and clothes and personal stuff. Nothing else in that house belongs to me."

"Cool. That'll be easy enough."

"If you say so," Lyric said with a worried sigh.

"Everything's gonna work out just fine. You'll see." I had her on board now, and it didn't seem likely she would change her mind. Now my job was to reassure her that she would be okay.

Walking into the kitchen, I said, "Help yourself to anything that's in here. Coffeemaker's a little fancy and complicated, but I'll show you how it works. Feel free to use it anytime. I usually get my groceries delivered, so you can put anything on the list you want, and I'll take care of it."

"I can get my own groceries, Brady," she said defensively.

"Okay. Sure. Whatever you want."

"I'm sorry. I guess I feel a bit like a kept woman."

"That's not what this is, Lyric. And I don't think of you that way. I hope you know that."

Lyric nodded wearily.

"I'll understand if you're more comfortable with buying your own food and all of that, but I hope you'll consider just letting me take care of it. All I'd have to do is add a few more things to my grocery list and get everything delivered here all at once. Otherwise, you'd have to take time out of your busy schedule to go out and shop and shlep all your food back here. I want to make this whole experience as easy on you as possible."

"I appreciate that," she said, rubbing her temples.

"Hey," I said, moving closer to her. Taking a bit of a risk, I put my hands on her shoulders as I looked into her eyes. She flinched a little, and I tried not to take it personally. "We're friends, right? At least I like to think so."

"Yeah," she said with a small smile.

"We're just helping each other out. I want to play for the Baltimore Bay Birds more than anything, but I'm also really rooting for you to get into the medical school of your dreams. We're gonna do this together, okay? It might even be fun!"

Lyric laughed softly. "Maybe it will."

"It'll be okay, Lyric. I promise. Thank you for agreeing to go on this little adventure with me."

"I guess I could use a little adventure in my life," she said.

Dear God, she was beautiful when she smiled.

CHAPTER 7

yric

A FEW SHORT DAYS LATER, Brady arranged to have my things moved from my house to his apartment. It was an odd feeling to leave the house in the morning and then go "home" to his place after school.

I knocked on the door, and he opened it with a grin.

"You got a key card, right?"

"Well, yeah, But I didn't want to just barge in." He had given me the code to get into the building as well as a key to the apartment. Though he'd told me I could come right in after class, I just couldn't. Not the first time, anyway.

"This is your place now too, Lyric," he said after I'd stepped inside. "You come and go as you please, day or night. As long as the tabloids don't catch you making out with another man, you do whatever you want, okay?"

"Okay," I said, glancing around uncertainly.

"I had them put your desk in front of the window in your room, but I can easily move it if you want it someplace else."

"That sounds perfect."

I had a ton of homework to do, and I was eager to get to it. Still, I felt weird about just walking away from Brady.

"Make yourself comfortable, and give a holler if you need anything," he said.

He sat down on the couch in the living room where the television was on.

I let out a sigh, relieved that Brady was good about giving me some space. Though I had no intention of backing out, I still wasn't sure I'd made the right decision by agreeing to be his pretend girlfriend.

I went to my new bedroom and shut the door behind me. It made me smile to see my desk against the window as promised. It was the perfect place to study, and it was still blissfully quiet. Diving right into my work made me feel surprisingly comfortable in my new room.

After several hours of studying, I heard a soft knock at my door. I opened it to find Brady with his gym bag over his shoulder.

"Sorry to bother you. Just wanted to let you know I'm heading out. Normally, I won't bug you every time I leave. For 7:05 games, I usually head over to the park at about five or so for batting practice. You can text me anytime if you need anything, and I'll answer when I can."

"Okay. Good to know. Thanks."

Brady peered over my shoulder into my room and back at me. "Everything good?"

"Oh, yeah. It's perfect. That's the longest I've had quiet to study since I started school. This is amazing."

"Glad to hear it."

Brady stood there for a moment like he wanted to say something else.

"What?"

"I was just thinking, eventually we'll have to be seen together in public, you know?"

"Of course."

"It's just that … well, you really tense up when I get too close. Before when I touched your shoulders, I could tell you were uncomfortable."

"You're right," I said. "I'm sorry about that. It's nothing personal. Really. I'm just getting used to this whole thing."

"I know. I get it. That's perfectly natural." After a pause, he asked, "Lyric, can I give you a hug?"

"What?"

"I figure it's a good place to start. Help you ease into physical contact now, when there's nobody around. And no pressure."

"Sure. Why not?" I said, knowing it was the least I could do. I realized how lucky I was that Brady seemed so aware of my feelings, my comfort level. God knows I'd had plenty of guys grab me and hug me without my consent. This man was paying me to be here, and he still asked my permission before coming near me.

"Okay," he said, opening his arms wide. "I'm comin' in!"

That made me laugh, which relaxed me. He wrapped his arms around me firmly but not too tight, and I found it easy to hug him back. There was something protective and sweet about the way he embraced me. His touch was warm and comforting, and it reminded me of how long it had been since anyone had touched me. Before I knew it, it was over.

He stepped back and smiled. "Not so bad, right?"

"Not at all. It was nice. Thanks for being so cool with me. You're so patient. With all the money you're shelling out for me just to be here, you could easily lord that over me."

"I would never do that," Brady said firmly.

"I know you wouldn't."

Standing there with Brady smiling at me, for the first time I wasn't scared to death that I'd made a big mistake in coming here. I already felt at home, and I knew deep down that his intentions were pure. Brady wasn't going to take advantage of me, nor of the situation. All he wanted was for Baltimore to give him a chance.

"Well, I better head out," he said.

"Good luck. Have a great game."

"Thanks. Happy studying."

After he left, I sat at my desk for a moment reveling in how good Brady's touch had felt. He was big and strong, and I couldn't help thinking how amazing he would be in bed. Biting my lip, I allowed myself the luxury of fantasizing about what it might be like to have sex with him. Me on my back against those silky red sheets he had on his bed. Him inside me, my legs wrapped around his back.

I let out the breath I hadn't even realized I'd been holding. Wow. It was so unlike me to indulge in sexual fantasies about anyone, but somehow Brady had that effect on me. I'd never been one to fantasize about having sex with celebrities or anything, but then again, I'd never thought of Brady as a celebrity. The more I was getting to know him, the more fond of him I was becoming. Yeah. That must be it. I felt safe around him, and he was a good-looking guy. That, and it had been a while since I'd been with a man. It was only natural that his touch had turned me on.

It occurred to me that knowing Brady's reputation with women, if I wanted to sleep with him, all I would have to do was ask.

That was completely out of the question. This was an arrangement of convenience and nothing more. Though I was no prude, I was not the type to have sex with a guy just for fun. I had never gone to bed with a man unless we were in a serious relationship, and I was not about to start now.

Shaking off my naughty thoughts of Brady, I headed into the kitchen to grab some dinner. He had asked me to text him a list of the food I wanted so I would have everything I needed when I moved in. I had to admit, it was a delightful luxury not to have to worry about grocery shopping.

For once, I actually took the time to cook a real dinner. I put a seasoned chicken breast and some broccoli together and roasted them in the oven. I had rarely bothered with any real cooking when I lived with four roommates. Usually, I'd tried to make food as quickly as I could and took it up to my room.

Scanning Brady's spacious apartment, I could not get over how blissfully quiet it was. Though I certainly didn't mind having Brady around, it was lovely to have the place to myself.

After enjoying a leisurely, quiet meal, I headed back to my bedroom. With its dark blue walls, queen-sized bed, and a television mounted on the wall, it was the height of luxury. I wondered how I could have thought of *not* taking Brady up on this offer.

I got in a little more studying, and then I settled in my comfy bed. Flipping through the channels, I found the Richmond Dominoes baseball game. The other team was up to bat now. They were playing New York, and the crowd sounded pretty riled up. I never could understand how people got excited about baseball. I wasn't interested in any sport, but baseball seemed especially boring. At least with hockey and basketball there was a lot of action. Football too, I guess, but it seemed like the action stopped every five seconds with that sport.

Yawning, I watched the Dominoes pitcher strike out a batter. Before they went to commercial, they mentioned the names of the three men who would be up to bat next. Brady was one of them. Tired as I was, I couldn't go to bed now. I had to at least see Brady in action.

The first guy managed to hit the ball but somebody on the other team caught it, so he was out. Brady was up next. I smiled as I watched him. He looked so serious as he concentrated hard on the ball. I might not have fully understood why he loved baseball so much, but I sure enjoyed hearing him talk about it. He was so cute. And he looked downright sexy in his Dominoes uniform. I couldn't deny that it turned me on to watch him in action.

What an idiot I'd been to get so tense around him that he'd to give me ample warning before he hugged me. There were probably thousands of women who would give anything to be in my position. I resolved to try to do better. He'd been nothing but a perfect gentleman with me, and I owed it to him to do my "girlfriend" part better.

Brady swung and connected with the ball, but the announcer said it was a foul ball. I knew the basics of the game, but not much else. Good thing Brady hadn't expected me to know anything about the sport in order to qualify as his fake girlfriend. Next time, he swung and missed. The announcer said he had two strikes.

"How is that two strikes?" I yelled at the TV. "He only missed once." Then I figured out that a foul ball must count as a strike. Ugh.

Maybe I should read over the baseball rules on the Internet tomorrow.

Brady swung and hit another ball foul, and I felt bad that he was out. Except he wasn't. I grabbed my phone and looked up the foul ball rules. Apparently, a foul ball didn't count as your third strike. In theory, you could foul balls all night long and never be out. For a minute, it looked like that was what Brady was going to do. He hit several more balls foul. Then he got a hit.

I sat up and cheered when he made it to first base. Chuckling to myself, I wondered if maybe baseball wasn't so boring after all. But this was different. With Brady, I was emotionally invested in the outcome.

It was kind of scary to realize how true that was. I was quite fond of Brady, but there was nothing wrong with that. Like he'd said, we were friends. He wanted me to get into medical school as much as I wanted him to make it to Baltimore.

I tried to watch the rest of the game, but I just couldn't stay awake. When I called it a night, the Dominoes were up 3-0 in the seventh inning, and I hoped their lead would hold.

Burrowing into my luxurious, soft bed, I drifted into a peaceful sleep knowing I would not be awakened by a bunch of giggling girls.

* * *

THE NEXT MORNING, I checked the baseball score on my phone before I even got out of bed. Richmond did end up beating New York by a score of 5-2.

"Yay," I said out loud, then headed to my awesome private bathroom to take a nice, relaxing shower. No more running out of hot water after four other people had taken showers before me. It was glorious. My first class wasn't until 11am, so I could take my time, too.

Brady was watching some game show on TV when I came out of my bedroom. I wore jeans and a T-shirt, since there was no reason to dress up for school. I did, however, put on a touch of makeup, which I didn't normally do. I wanted to look nice for him, and I knew how black eyeliner made my blue eyes stand out.

"Hey there," Brady said with a smile.

"Okay, I'm trying to be better about this, so bear with me."

"Better with what?"

I sat on the couch next to him, put my arms around him, and squeezed for a few seconds. "Good morning, *dear.*"

After I let go, he chuckled. "Ooh, that was nice. I could get used to that."

I laughed too. Funny how hugging him really wasn't too awkward the second time. It *was* nice.

"Great game last night."

"You saw it?" he asked, sounding surprised.

"Caught some of it. It's tough for me to stay up too late, but what I saw was good. I saw you bat. You looked great out there."

He wrinkled his nose. "Didja see me strike out twice?"

"No, I saw you get a hit."

"Oh. Cool." He sounded relieved that I'd seen what might have been the highlight of his game. "You ever been to a Richmond game?"

"I've never been to any baseball game, ever."

"Are you serious?"

"Not one."

Brady looked physically wounded.

"Sorry. Baseball just always seemed boring and kinda ..."

"What?"

"I don't know. Frivolous, I guess. I just don't get the point of it."

"I assume since you want to be a doctor, you want to save lives, right?" Brady asked, his voice taking on a hard edge I'd never heard before.

"Yeah," I said cautiously.

"What do you think patients do when they finally get out of the hospital?"

I stared at him, not sure what he was getting at and not wanting to say the wrong thing.

"They go out and live their lives. They do fun things. Go

to movies and to sports events, even stupid, boring baseball games."

"I never said baseball was stupid."

"You didn't have to," he snapped. He was right to be mad. I was being condescending about the very thing that meant the most to him in life.

"Believe it or not, a lot of people enjoy baseball games. They have fun going with their friends and families, and it's exciting to root for the home team together. Nothing makes me happier than when I'm walking down the street and I see somebody wearing a Dominoes shirt or a hat. Or when I see two strangers strike up a conversation about the team when they're in line at the grocery store or something. Doctors might keep people alive, but sports players and writers and actors and artists and people like that give people something to live *for*. Something to look forward to in between the shitty times in life, like when you're in the hospital."

"I never thought of it that way," I said, a deep sense of shame overtaking me.

"Obviously," he said with a steely glare. "You really should go to a game sometime."

"Yeah. I should," I said in a small voice.

Brady's expression softened. It seemed like the storm was over as quickly as it had started. "Did you sleep well?"

"So well. Better than I can ever remember sleeping."

"Glad to hear it. I didn't wake you when I got home?"

I shook my head, and he smiled and nodded.

"Does class start soon?" he asked.

"Not 'til eleven."

"Do you want to go get some coffee? We could go to Richmond Roast. Give us a chance to be seen in public again."

"Sure," I answered immediately, still feeling awful about offending him.

"Cool. Let's roll."

Brady got up, and I quickly grabbed my schoolbooks and stuffed them into my backpack. We headed out the door and rode down the elevator in silence.

Once we were out on the street, I finally spoke up.

"I'm really sorry, Brady."

"It's okay," he said with a grin. He wrapped his arm around me and gave me a quick squeeze. I wasn't sure if it was for show in case anyone was watching or if he was just being friendly, but I liked it, whatever the reason. Though I didn't enjoy making him angry, it was kind of hot to see how fired up he'd gotten. The man sure did love baseball.

The morning air was a little chilly, but the sun was out. Walking with Brady felt nice; natural, even. Having a minor argument made us feel like a real couple.

He held the door for me when we got to Richmond Roast, and we stood in line together. Weird to think just a short while ago he'd been standing behind me in line as a complete stranger. If I hadn't dumped coffee all over him, none of this would have happened. My whole future had changed because of that one moment. I'd owe tuition money for half my life instead of being debt-free.

When it was our turn to order, Brady asked, "What do you want, hon?"

Nice touch.

"A large coffee, a shot of espresso, with one cream and one sugar."

"You want something to eat? You didn't have breakfast yet."

"Actually, yeah. Can I get a breakfast sandwich? A bagel with egg, cheese, and bacon," I said to the barista.

Brady ordered a black coffee and some muffins for himself. The place was less crowded than last time, and we easily found a place in the corner to sit. Almost as soon as we sat down, a young man approached our table.

"Um, I'm real sorry to bother you, but … do you mind?" the guy asked, holding out a napkin and a pen.

"Oh, sure. No problem," Brady said. "What's your name?"

"Derrick," he said. "With two Rs."

"Okay, Derrick with two Rs," he said as he scribbled a personalized message. "Here ya go."

"Thanks, man," the guy said, his face lighting up when he took the napkin. "Really appreciate it."

Derrick walked off with a huge grin. It was rather sweet to know I'd witnessed an event that the man would probably remember for the rest of his life.

"That happen a lot?" I asked.

"All. The. Time. For real, Lyric. Get used to it," he warned.

I let out a soft sigh, and Brady frowned with worry. It would take some time to get used to this kind of attention. But I had known from the beginning that this was part of the deal. I silently vowed to make a conscious effort to tone down my anxiety when I was out in public with Brady. The last thing I wanted was for him to worry about me every time we stepped out together. Besides, it was him they wanted to see and not me.

After taking a moment to breathe in the scent of his coffee, Brady took a healthy sip. "So what classes you got today?"

"Physics, which I hate. But I also have organic chemistry, which I don't mind. I took inorganic chemistry last semester."

I took a bite of my sandwich. It was delicious. Good thing Brady had suggested food; I hadn't realized how hungry I was.

"What's the difference between organic and inorganic chemistry?"

"Well, the short answer is organic compounds always contain carbon and most inorganic ones don't. Living organism molecules are organic. Ones like nucleic acids, sugars, proteins, enzymes, even hydrocarbon fuels. Inorganic compounds would be salts, metals, and substances comprised from single elements and other compounds that don't contain carbon bonded to hydrogen."

"Wow," Brady said. He looked decidedly uncomfortable.

"What's the matter?"

He sipped his coffee and then shook his head. "Boy, are you gonna get bored with me real quick."

"Why would you say that?"

"Because I only have a high school education. That's when I got drafted for single-A ball."

"So?"

"So I can barely understand what you're talking about."

"So the hell what?" As far as I was concerned, Brady "The Crusher" Keaton was as far away from boring as you could get. "You think my friends understand any of this science stuff? My parents? They don't know anything about medicine or science, nor would I expect them to."

I laughed, and at first, Brady took it the wrong way. He looked defensive; his muscles tightened up.

"Brady, last night while I was watching the game, I had to Google the foul ball rules because I didn't understand why you hadn't struck out after hitting a bunch of them."

I giggled again, and this time Brady laughed too.

"You're the expert in your field. And I'm in school trying to become an expert in mine. We can learn from each other. As long as we don't judge each other, we'll be just fine."

"You're right," he said with a smile.

"Excuse me," came a voice from just behind me. I jumped, not realizing another customer had walked up to us.

"Sorry," the young woman said to me. "Mr. Crush—I—I

mean, Mr. Keaton ... I'm so sorry to bother you ... um ... ah..."

The young lady blushed, and I watched Brady's expression soften as he looked at her. As much as he enjoyed attention, he didn't like seeing anyone uncomfortable.

"It's okay. Would you like an autograph?"

"Yes, yes that would be so great. But I don't really have anything for you to sign ... I just wanted to tell you that I love baseball and you're my all-time favorite player. I was scared to come up and say that, but I knew I'd hate myself if I didn't!"

The poor thing was literally trembling.

"Hey, I'm sure I've got some notebook paper in here," I said, picking up my backpack. I grabbed a sheet of paper and a pen and handed them to Brady. He asked the girl for her name, and she said it was Wendy. I let out a soft sigh as I watched Brady take the time to scribble out another personal message for a fan. It was so sweet. Wendy was probably in her late teens. I wondered what it would feel like when women closer to my age inevitably clamored for Brady's autograph. It wasn't like we were really together, but witnessing it would still be tough.

Wendy squealed when she took the autograph, and Brady laughed.

After she walked away, Brady turned to me. "Sorry, Lyric. Where were we?"

I shrugged and drank some of my coffee.

"Oh, I know what I wanted to ask you," he began, but then another fan interrupted us. Another guy. I saw the briefest hint of irritation cross Brady's face, but it vanished as soon as it appeared. He went through the same routine again, asking the fan's name and writing a message for him.

"Be honest, doesn't that get old after a while?" I asked

quietly so as not to offend any of his fans who might be within earshot.

"Yeah, it does sometimes. I admit it." He paused for moment, then said, "When I was growing up in Baltimore, my hero was the shortstop."

"Ray Renner Jr.," I said, and Brady looked shocked that I knew the guy's name. "You mentioned him the day we met."

"I did? Wow, thanks for remembering," he said with a smile. "He was so light on his feet. Watching him turn a double play was like magic. Though he wasn't a big home-run type, he got on base all the time, tons of RBIs, that kind of thing. A great producer for the team, you know?"

I nodded and stifled another sigh. Brady was never sexier than when he got on a baseball tangent, especially when it involved his beloved Baltimore.

"I *idolized* him. Then one day I got the chance to meet him." Brady's face turned serious, and I felt my stomach clench. "He grew up in Maryland, so he lived there year-round. I happened to see him walking down the street in downtown Baltimore once."

Brady's face was serious as a heart attack.

If this Ray Renner Jr. did anything to break Brady's heart, I will hunt him down myself and destroy him.

"I was sixteen years old. Hangin' out with a bunch of buddies of mine. They told me not to bug him, but I couldn't pass up the chance. I just couldn't. So I stopped him on the street." Brady paused.

"So what did he do? What did he say?"

"Oh God, I was such a blithering idiot when I talked to him. Told him he was my idol, my hero, and how I wanted to be just like him," he said, wincing as he shared the memory. "Such a stupid kid, I was."

"And? What did he say?" I asked again.

Brady smiled. "He told me how much he appreciated me

telling him that. Then he asked me my name and auto-graphed the baseball card I had of him that I carried in my wallet. Wrote me a personal message: Brady, can't wait to see you in the big leagues. Ray Renner Jr."

There was a twinkle in Brady's eye and an adorable catch in his voice when he spoke. I let out the breath I was holding. *Thank God.*

"I was at such a critical age back then. Junior year of high school, playin' my heart out, dreamin' big. It would have killed me—*killed me*—if it turned out he'd been a jerk. He could have made me feel so stupid for babbling on like that, but he didn't. Could have blown me off, but he didn't. I just … I try to keep that in mind with every fan encounter, you know?"

Staring at him dreamily, I nodded.

"I know people get nervous when they talk to celebrities, and I hate for anybody to feel embarrassed when they talk to me. They know they only get one chance, and sometimes they're so nervous, they stumble over their words and all that. I pretend not to notice 'cuz that's what Renner did with me." Brady laughed. "Well that and I have to confess there is a bit of ego involved, too. I do like being recognized, and frankly, I don't want people to think I'm an asshole. So I do my best to play nice, even if I'm not feeling like it. Toughest part is playin' nice after a bad loss. Gotta somehow suck it up and be good for the fans."

"It's nice that you do that. It's a little annoying to be inter-rupted all the time, but when you see how happy it makes them …" I said, glancing over at Wendy's table where she was giddily talking with her friend.

"Exactly." He bit into a muffin.

"So what did you want to ask me?"

"Huh?" he asked, looking confused.

"You said there was something you were gonna ask me before we got interrupted again."

"Oh, yeah. Right." He wiped his mouth with a napkin. "I wanted to ask if you know what kind of doctor you wanna be. Like, what do you want to specialize in?"

I smiled at the question. "I've been thinking about that a lot lately. You know I volunteer over at St. Theresa Hospital? Well, I work with all kinds of doctors in different disciplines to get a feel for what it's like to work in different areas of medicine. A few months ago I got to watch a C-section. How cool is that?"

"Very cool," Brady agreed. "Do you think you want to be a baby doctor?"

"No, I don't think so. Right now, I'm working with my mentor in her department. She's an incredible doctor. Dr. Bennett. She's a cardiologist, and I just love her. She is the best. I wanna be her when I grow up," I said with a laugh. Brady smiled warmly at me, and I tingled all over.

"So you wanna be a heart doc?"

"No. I do want to be an awesome doctor like Dr. Bennett, who is super smart and unbelievably cool under pressure, but I'm actually leaning toward oncology. Cancer treatments are getting more advanced all the time, and with oncology, you get to help the same patients over a long period of time."

"That sounds great, Lyric. After all, just about everybody knows somebody who had cancer," he said, his voice tinged with sadness.

"Who did you know?" I asked gently.

"My grandad. He was the best. Biggest baseball fan you ever saw."

"He must have been so proud of you," I said.

Brady sighed. "Yeah, he would have been. Died before I made it to the majors, though." Laughing softly, he added,

"Used to always say, 'Baseball, hot dog, apple pie, and Chevrolet!' It was from some commercial I think."

"That is so cute."

Brady chuckled. "He was cute. I like that you'll be helping people like that."

"Me too," I said, my eyes lingering on his. "Well, I know your biggest dream is to be a Bay Bird. Other than that, what's your greatest baseball fantasy?"

"That's easy. To play in the World Series. Every big leaguer's dream, I guess. Even if it wasn't for Baltimore. Damn, I get chills just thinking about it. To play on the national stage like that? To get a shot at a World Series ring?" He shuddered with exaggeration. "Chills."

I laughed and he joined in.

"That would be amazing. The Dominoes are pretty good this year, right? You think they've got a shot?"

"Hopefully. That would be amazing. So, you got any brothers and sisters?" He laughed. "That is such a lame first-date question." Then, in a goofy tone, eyes wide, he asked, "Do you come here often?"

I cracked up at that.

"But for real, I do wanna know. What family do you have, and where are they?"

"I'm an only child. My parents live in Virginia, but they're a few hours away. In Alexandria, close to you."

"What are your parents like?"

I rolled my eyes and he laughed.

"Oh, that's awful of me. The truth is, they are wonderful parents. They really are. I guess we just don't have much in common. They're the 'artsy' type," I said with air quotes. "They're a musical duo. My dad sings, and my mom plays guitar and other instruments."

"Wow, that's cool. I' d love to hear them sometime."

"Wish granted," I said, pulling out my phone. It didn't take long to search them up on YouTube. After making sure the sound wasn't up too loud, I played a clip of a video of my parents for him. My mom and dad played folksy-type music, and I was afraid Brady might think my parents were cheesy. Though I *did* think they were cheesy, I was allowed to think that.

Brady watched the video with genuine interest. "Your dad has an amazing singing voice. And your mom sounds beautiful on the guitar."

"They write their own songs."

"Oh, wow," Brady said. I had planned to stop the video after a few seconds, but he seemed into it, so I let it play to the end. "They're really good."

"Yeah, I guess so," I said with a shrug. "They play gigs whenever they can get them, and then do odd jobs in between. They're always broke, so I don't know why they keep doing it."

"Because they love it," Brady said, eying me curiously. He looked more confused now than when I'd explained the difference between organic and inorganic chemistry. "I guess that's why they named you Lyric. Because they love music, and they love you."

"Yeah. I guess so."

"You have a beautiful name, Lyric. Beautiful name for a beautiful girl."

It should have sounded like a cheap pickup line, but it didn't. Not the way he said it.

"Thanks," I said. "What about you? Family?"

"My parents are divorced but get along pretty well, thank God. I have a stepdad, but my father never remarried. I have a little brother. Eric. He's a great kid, but I worry about him."

"Why?"

"Can't be easy being in my shadow all the time," he said. "He is so fucking smart, and I am so damn proud of him. I

73

tell him that all the time. He's a systems analyst. Makes good money and all that. But it must be tough having me as a brother. If we're in the same room together, people either act like he doesn't exist, or they spend all their time asking about me. He takes it in stride, though."

"I'm sure he's proud of you."

"Yeah," Brady said with a smile. "He is."

After swallowing the last of my coffee, I glanced around the room. It still wasn't too crowded, but most of the people there were staring at us. Again. Funny how I'd lost track of time talking with Brady. In a way, it was rather like a first date in that we'd learned a lot about each other. But it wasn't awkward like most first dates.

"Well, I guess I'd better get to class."

"Need a ride? Can I call you an Uber or something?"

"Oh, no. Thanks, though. I actually enjoy walking when it's nice out. Helps clear my head before and after class."

"So," Brady began hopefully. "Do you maybe want to go to the Richmond game sometime? If you're not busy?"

Going to a baseball game was not high on my list of desirable things to do, but it was impossible to say no to this guy when he looked at me like that. Besides, I was eager to do anything to make up for being so obnoxious about his beloved sport earlier, and hurting his feelings.

"I'd love to. I can't go tonight because I've got to work at the hospital, but tomorrow should be okay."

"Sounds great."

The grin on his face made my decision well worth it already.

CHAPTER 8

rady

It was a good thing Lyric hadn't been able to come to last night's game. Not only did we lose, but we lost 1-0. For real baseball fans, a pitcher's duel like that was exciting, but it could be a nightmare for people who already thought baseball was boring. With any luck, tonight's ball game would be more of a slugfest, with lots of home runs and a higher scoring game. Also, it would be nice if we won.

I was sitting on my couch watching *SportsCenter* on ESPN when Lyric wandered into the living room. Her hair was wet from the shower, which of course had me thinking that she'd been naked just a few minutes ago. My pants tightened a bit when I pictured her showering, eyes closed and slowly washing her hair like in a television commercial.

"Hey," she said with a smile.

"Hey there, Doc," I said.

Her smile broadened. "Doc. I like that."

"Am I the first one to call you that?"

Lyric nodded.

"Cool." I resolved to call her that as often as possible. Maybe I'd get a smile every time.

She flopped down on the couch near me and said, "I should have a nickname for you. I could call you Crush since you're The Crusher."

"And because you have a crush on me."

"Of course, *dear*," she said dryly. But she blushed a little. I was sure of it. "I always thought your nickname was The Crusher because you crushed a lot of home runs."

"It's not."

"I *know*," she said, rolling her eyes. "I read up on your origin story."

"It's not like all those crushed beer cans were mine, ya know."

"I hope not. Even you couldn't drink that many. The article said there were more than a hundred."

I shrugged. "What can I say?"

"I don't know," Lyric said, shaking her head. She sounded more amused than judgmental, though.

"Oh, hey. See that guy right there?" I said, pointing at the TV. "That's Angel Jimenez. He's my best friend back in Maryland. We were on a farm team—you know, the minors —together. We always hoped we'd play for the Bay Birds together." I sighed heavily. "Feel like I let him down. Screwin' around like I did and fucking up my chance with Baltimore."

"You still have a chance, Brady. More than a chance. You're gonna make it," Lyric said firmly. Her confidence gave me hope.

"That's his wife, Jana," I said.

"She's beautiful," Lyric said, watching the screen.

Angel's wife was quite pretty. Petite with dark hair and green eyes. She was also very sweet. I was the best man at their wedding. Though I'd never thought there would be a woman good enough for my best buddy, Jana really was. She always had his back, and I loved her for it.

"She's the best. The *best*," I said enthusiastically.

Their love story was incredible. Jana had been a witness to a terrible accident involving Angel, who was out on a date with another woman at the time. While his date had bailed, Jana went to the hospital to make sure he was all right. She had stuck by his side during his recovery, and they had fallen in love.

"Why are they all dressed up?"

"It's some baseball charity event. Some fancy dinner or what not." I turned to look at Lyric. "You know, we might have to go to some of those."

"That's fine," was her reply, but I saw her wince.

"You don't want to go, do you?"

"You know how I am with being the center of attention."

"You love it. You adore it. You soak it up and never want to let go! Oh, wait. That's me."

She laughed, and her face relaxed. I glanced back at the television screen, unable to stop myself from smiling.

"Jana's pregnant."

"You know, I was gonna ask," Lyric said as she looked at Angel's wife on the television. "She's so petite, with just that cute little basketball baby bump. Hard to tell for sure if she's expecting."

"Yeah," I said. "Angel's gonna be the greatest dad. He already said he wants the kid to call me Uncle Brady."

"Awww," Lyric said with a sweet smile. "You're gonna be such a fun uncle."

"Better an uncle than a dad."

"You don't want kids?" she asked.

"I'm not sure."

"Me neither."

"Really?" I asked, shocked.

"Not all women want to be mothers, you know."

"I know. You're right."

Lyric smiled at me again.

People usually got all judgy with me when I said I didn't want kids. It's not that I don't like kids, because I actually do. *Other* people's kids. Boys and girls who loved baseball were especially cool. The fans I met, the kids I saw laughing and running the bases on the field after minor league games. I would love it if my brother got married and had kids someday so I could be Uncle Brady to them, too.

"It does feel kinda rare to meet a woman who doesn't want kids," I said.

"Fair enough. I figure I'm gonna be career oriented. It's possible I'll change my mind someday, but motherhood is definitely not on my radar right now."

Sitting there so close to her on the couch, I realized I wanted nothing more than to kiss her sweet mouth. I also realized that all I had to do was ask.

"You know, if we do go to baseball events, and even when we go out in public, we kinda need to make it clear that we're together."

Lyric nodded uncertainly, and my stomach clenched. The last thing I wanted was to act like some kind of creep and make her uncomfortable, but what I was saying was the truth. I wanted to kiss her, but I actually *needed* to kiss her too. For business purposes.

"We need to be able to kiss comfortably and easily in public."

"You're right," she said. She didn't seem too upset or uneasy, thank God.

"In fact, the best thing we could hope for is that some gossip rag snaps a photo of us kissing. That would be the quickest way to show the world that Brady Keaton is off the market."

Lyric laughed. Such a pretty sound. "Yeah, I guess it would."

"So, would it be okay to practice just a little?" I asked tentatively.

"Yes, I think that would be fine," she said. "Brady, I can't tell you how much I appreciate you putting me at ease like this. Really. Once we're out on the street, you could have easily grabbed me and kissed me and shoved your tongue down my throat just for the camera's sake."

I grimaced. "I would never do a thing like that."

"I know you wouldn't. But a lot of guys would. So, thanks."

"Well, it's not as though kissing a beautiful woman is some terrible sacrifice," I said with a smile. "You ready?"

She smiled and nodded, but she did look a little nervous. Discussing a kiss beforehand instead of just going for it was an odd thing, to be sure. But in our case, it was the right way to go about it.

I scooted in a little closer to her on the couch. She drew in a nervous breath. Gently caressing her face, I looked into her lovely blue eyes. I swear, my heart skipped a beat.

This was supposed to be pretend, but in the moment, it felt very, very real.

As tenderly as I could, I pressed my lips against hers. Lyric eagerly returned the kiss, and I felt her body relax at my touch. I was not exactly known for my gentle, sweet kisses, and I was surprised at how well I managed it. Most of the time when I kissed a woman, it was a direct prelude to sex.

With other girls, I was always eager to get to the next part. Kissing Lyric, well, I found it hard to stop. Her lips on mine felt so sweet, so natural. Still, I broke off the kiss before I wanted to. I had to make sure she was all right.

Pulling back, I gazed at her. "Was that okay?"

"Better than okay," she said with an adorable blush. "You're a great kisser, Brady."

"Thanks. You're no slouch yourself," I said with a grin.

"If the cameras catch us doing that, it will be easy for people to think we're in love."

"Uh-huh," she said, looking slightly dazed. Then she snapped out of it. "Well, I'd better get something to eat before class."

She got up to head to the kitchen.

"I made some coffee," I called after her.

"Great!"

"Hey, Doc?"

"Yeah?" she said, turning back around to face me.

"Do you still wanna go to the game tonight?"

"Absolutely," she said with a gorgeous smile.

"Cool. I'll leave you a ticket at the will call window at the ticket office. Just use my name. For good measure, tell 'em you're my girl."

Lyric laughed. "I'll do that." Then she headed into the kitchen.

My girl. I rather liked the sound of that.

CHAPTER 9

$\mathcal{L}$yric

I WALKED over to Dominion Park in the early evening. The guy at the ticket counter seemed dubious when I told him that Brady Keaton should have left me a ticket. Then he seemed quite impressed to find I was telling the truth. I wanted to say that I was Brady's girlfriend because I knew he wanted me to, but I just couldn't bring myself to say it. If it came up naturally in conversation, it would have been fine. Had the guy asked me how I knew Brady, I would have said he was my boyfriend. Just saying it for no reason would have felt like bragging or something. I was sure most other women would have shouted from the rooftops that they were dating Brady "The Crusher" Keaton, but it just wasn't my way.

I must have looked lost and confused once I got into the park, because a kindly usher took pity on me and asked if he could help me find my seat.

"Please," I said gratefully. "I've never been here before."

"Well, welcome to Dominion Park," the gray-haired man said with a smile. "Right this way."

With that, he led me down, down, and down the steps, very close to the field. Brady had gotten me an excellent seat. I felt bad as I scanned the upper decks. No doubt there were hard-core baseball fans up there who would have given anything to sit where I was.

They announced the starting lineup for the visiting team and then they announced the Richmond team players. Most of the guys got cheers, but Brady's name got the loudest cheer of all. I was so proud.

It was a little overwhelming; all the noise and excitement, and the idea that soon enough everyone would know we were together. Or at least they would *think* we were together. People would know me. My name. And they might recognize me on the street. It was kind of frightening.

The person on the loudspeaker asked us to rise for the national anthem, and I did as I was told.

The song they played first was definitely not *The Star-Spangled Banner*. It was *O Canada*. I was confused at first, but then I remembered the opposing team was from Toronto. It was heartening to see all the Richmond fans in the crowd standing quietly and respectfully during the song.

A local school choir performed the U.S. national anthem, and they did a lovely job of it. Scanning the crowd, I saw a lot of baseball hats placed over hearts, and the jumbotron alternately showed images of the choir singing and of the flag waving high on its flagpole.

Baseball is known as our national pastime, and it truly felt like it. It was rather touching to see so many people gathered to watch the game. Though it might be silly, it made me proud to be an American.

When the game began, I watched the Richmond players

run out onto the field to tremendous cheers and applause. Naturally, I was fixated on Brady as he took his place at shortstop. He wore the number 8, which I knew was in deference to his hero, Ray Renner Jr.

My heart pounded in my chest as I watched him.

That kiss.

I just could not get that kiss out of my head ... and my heart. No man had ever kissed me like that before. His lips had been gentle at first, but then became more forceful. *Passionate.* He was a terrific kisser, and I was glad I'd told him that.

Letting out a deep sigh, I reflected on how sweet Brady was. He was huge and could be imposing, but in reality, he was gentle and kind. He took such care not to treat me like a kept woman, like I was a prostitute who'd agreed to this deal out of desperation. Brady's heart was clearly in the right place, and his focus was on Baltimore. Though in a sense he was using me to get what he wanted, he was careful not to make me *feel* used. And I adored him for it.

The truth was, I adored *him*. And it was scary. It would be all too easy to get lost in those dark, soulful eyes. That boyish enthusiasm. That passion he had for all things baseball.

None of this was real, and I would do well to remember that. I had to keep my feelings in check. Once this was all over and he'd made it safely to Baltimore, he would likely go back to his drinking and womanizing ways, just on the down low to keep it out of the papers so he could keep his job.

The first half-inning was over pretty quickly. Three up, three down as the sports announcers on TV would say. I was pleased that I was starting to pick up on baseball lingo. In the bottom of the first inning, the second guy up to bat made it to first base. The next guy hit the ball, but one of the Toronto players scooped it up and tossed it to first base, so he was out.

Brady was next. The loudspeaker blared *More Human Than Human* by White Zombie, which they always did when he was up to bat. That must be his signature song. Though the crowd had cheered for him when he was announced as part of the lineup, they really went nuts this time. People were *screaming*. And a lot of those screams were female. In fact, the group of teenage girls seated just behind me screamed so loudly, it hurt my ears.

A nice family sat next to me. Parents, a little boy about six years old or so, and a cute little girl of about two years who was climbing all over the seats. She had an infectious giggle and was having a grand old time, despite being too young to understand baseball. Her mother and I exchanged a mutual annoyed look when the girls behind us got especially loud.

I watched Brady steady himself as he stared down the pitcher. Damn, he was sexy when he was in the zone like that. He didn't swing at the first pitch, which turned out to be a ball.

"Brady! Sign my tits!" screamed one of the girls as the rest of them exploded into obnoxious giggles.

The poor mother next to me winced as she looked at her kids.

"So you like baseball?" I asked her little boy to try to distract him from the decidedly X-rated conversation going on behind us. His mom smiled gratefully at me.

"Yes, it's my favorite," he said excitedly. "Do you like baseball?"

I wasn't about to answer that honestly.

"Well, I'm still learning about baseball. But it can be fun." That was true. It could be fun. According to tens of thousands of fans all around me.

"Are you here by yourself?" his mother asked me curiously.

I knew Brady wanted to start spreading the word that we

were together as much as possible, and here was the natural opening I needed.

"One of the players is my boyfriend," I said, gesturing to the field. "So my date's on the field."

"Really?" the lady asked me with great interest. "One of the Richmond guys or the opposing team?"

"Richmond. Brady Keaton."

"Oh, yeah right," yelled one of the girls behind me. "Like Brady's really your boyfriend."

"You are so full of shit," said another mean girl.

I turned around and said, "Can you please watch your language in front of the kids?"

The girl sneered at me but kept quiet for a few seconds. Then they started giggling and making fun of me for being a "pathetic liar." I briefly considered taking out my phone and pulling up the photo of me and Brady from the Internet, but then figured they weren't worth it. Besides, trying to prove myself to a bunch of immature high school girls *would* be kind of pathetic.

"Brady Keaton is your boyfriend?" the kid asked.

"Yup," I said with a smile. "And I don't know much about baseball, so maybe you can help me."

The boy's eyes lit up. "Okay, yeah."

Brady connected with the ball, and we were sitting so close, we could hear the crack of the bat. My heart thumped wildly as I watched him speed toward first base. I suddenly had tremendous empathy for baseball wives everywhere. This was rather stressful to watch, and it wasn't even a critical game like the playoffs or the World Series. I breathed a sigh of relief as he made it, rather easily, to first.

"See Brady's on base and now Jamie Mathers is all the way on third now," the boy explained.

"Oh right," I said with a laugh. "I almost forgot about him."

The kid laughed.

"My name is Lyric. What's your name?"

"Hayden. It's my birthday."

I gasped. "It is? How old are you today?"

"Seven."

"Well, happy birthday!" I said loudly, trying to cover the F-bombs being dropped from just behind me. I also heard my name several times, and I knew they were still making fun of me.

"Thank you," Hayden said politely. He was so freaking adorable. Better to concentrate on him than those awful girls anyway. Yes. I would take the high road, no matter how hard it might be. "That's why we got really, really good seats. For my birthday."

"Well, that is super fun!"

"Yeah, he's about as big a baseball fan as they come," Hayden's proud dad said as he sipped his beer. The little two-year-old girl eyed me curiously. She smiled when I waved at her. They were such a cute family.

The next guy up to bat hit the ball hard on the third pitch and it sailed all the way out to the bleachers. Little Hayden, along with many of the spectators in the park, jumped out of his seat and yelled with excitement. Just like that, the Richmond Dominoes were up 3-0. The jumbotron exploded with digital fireworks and loud rock music played.

I had to admit, it was fun and exciting. I loved seeing Hayden and his family so happy, and there was something heartwarming about seeing people of all ages and ethnicities wearing Dominoes hats and T-shirts, and all supporting their team together.

This was what Brady had meant when he'd asked me "What do you think patients do when they finally get out of the hospital?" All around me, I saw friends and families getting together to watch the game and having a good time.

Though I still felt like baseball was kind of a frivolous thing, I was starting to understand it more. I was starting to understand *Brady* more. And the more I got to know and understand him, the more I liked him.

When I closed my eyes, I could almost feel his lips on mine. If he kissed that way when it was just pretend, what would it feel like when he kissed a woman he loved?

I shook my head, reminding myself to get a grip. Brady "The Crusher" Keaton was unlikely to fall in love with *any* woman, least of all me. A poignant reminder of that was the loud female screams that erupted every time he was up to bat. Such an unsettling feeling to think Brady could have his pick of any woman in this entire ballpark. I shuddered to think of how many women he'd already been with during the course of his career. He could have a girl in every city for all I knew.

The rest of the game was pretty exciting, with lots of back-and-forth scoring. The final tally was Richmond 11, Toronto 8. Watching a baseball game live was a very different experience to seeing one on TV, and I had to admit it was a lot more interesting than I'd thought it would be.

Except for the persistent mean-girl chatter, much of it revolving around me every time Brady showed up, I had a great time. Hayden jumped up excitedly at the end of the game and started yelling at the players as they walked toward the tunnel that I assumed led them to their locker room. It was so cute that he knew every guy's name and told them, "Good game!" When Brady walked toward the tunnel, Hayden yelled for him, but of course the mean girls started yelling at Brady too. It made me so mad that those awful teenagers were drowning the poor kid out. A couple of the players had smiled in Hayden's direction when he'd called out to them, and I was sure Brady would have done the same if only he could *hear* the poor boy.

Then I got an idea.

"Brady!" I yelled, trying to rise above all the noise of the crowd. "Brady! *Hey, Crush!*" That got his attention. He turned his head and caught my eye.

"Hey, Doc!" he said with a grin.

I rushed over to where he was walking and leaned over the rail.

"Hey, I've been sitting next to this utterly adorable little kid and it's his birthday. I know he would love it if you said hi or something."

"Oh yeah, sure," Brady said, taking a few steps back so he could look up to where we'd all been sitting. He caught sight of Hayden and smiled. Then he turned away for a second. "Hey, ump?"

One of the umpires turned around to see Brady holding up his right hand. The man nodded. He pulled a baseball out of his pocket and tossed it to Brady.

"Thanks, man." Turning toward us, he asked, "Who's the birthday boy over here?"

"Me! Me!" Hayden screamed, making everyone around him laugh at his infectious excitement.

"This is Hayden. He's seven years old today," I said.

"Well, happy birthday, Hayden," Brady said, carefully tossing him the baseball. Hayden caught it easily, and I wondered if perhaps he played little league.

"Wow! Thankyouthankyouthankyou!" he said joyously.

Brady saluted him and smiled.

"Thanks," I said.

"You're welcome. See ya at home, hon," he said to me before disappearing into the tunnel.

Immediately, I turned around to look at the brat pack of girls, who had finally been stunned into silence. After briefly shooting them an "I told you so" look, I turned back to

Hayden and his lovely family. His parents thanked me profusely, and I assured them it was my pleasure.

I arranged for an Uber to pick me up in the parking lot of the stadium, but I had a little time before it arrived. On my way out, I stopped at one of the little souvenir shops and bought a Richmond Dominoes T-shirt. Naturally, I chose one with Brady's name on it and the number 8 on the back. He would probably be happy to see me wearing it, and the thought made me smile.

Though I knew I'd never be able to compete with the countless gorgeous women that Brady no doubt had in his life, I had to admit to myself that I was liking him more and more every day. He was such a good guy and so much fun to be around that it was impossible not to like him. As attracted as I was to him, I had more respect for myself than to become one of those one-night stands he was notorious for, according to gossip rags everywhere.

I decided to simply be grateful that Brady Keaton was my friend.

 rady

I woke up a bit later than usual on Saturday morning. I was starting to get back in the habit of being out late at the game and then sleeping in. Lyric wasn't home when I got up. She didn't have class today, so I wondered where she was and hoped she was okay.

I took a moment to smell my delicious coffee before taking a sip and that little action helped clear my head. Lyric was a grown woman, and I'd told her she was free to come and go as she pleased. It was silly to worry about her. It was broad daylight out, and we lived in a safe area.

Then a scary thought occurred to me. What if she never made it home last night? Had she walked home by herself? God, what an idiot I was for not taking her home myself or at the very least, arranging a ride for her. Though I hated to violate her privacy, I rushed to her room to make sure she'd slept in her bed last night.

Her bed was neatly made, but that didn't mean anything. Lyric was a neat person. She never made a mess. I went into her bathroom and saw her towel hanging on the door. It was damp. Relief flooded through me as I realized she must have showered here not long ago.

Chuckling at my own idiocy, I went back into the kitchen and grabbed my coffee. I really liked Lyric, and I couldn't help worrying about her. But she obviously knew how to take care of herself. She'd gotten along just fine without me until now.

I flipped on the TV and watched ESPN for a few minutes. Since they were only talking about golf, I switched over to the game-show channel. In no time, I was thoroughly invested in an episode of *Match Game* from 1982. By the time it was over, my stomach was growling. Seeing that it was 11am, I knew I had an important question to answer—did I want breakfast or lunch?

I heard a key card slide into the lock, and I looked up to see Lyric coming in. She had her backpack on her shoulder, and she was wearing a white blouse and blue jeans. She smiled at me, those bright blue eyes lighting up when she looked at me. Women smiled at me all the time, but there was something, I don't know ... *genuine* about her smile. I guess it was because we were actually friends as opposed to strangers, like most of the women I used to be with.

"Good morning," I said, cheering her with my coffee mug.

"Good morning to you."

"You're out and about early."

"Library," she said with a shrug. "Nothing exciting."

"Have you had breakfast yet?"

"Yeah. Well, I had coffee and a bagel. Hours ago, and I'm hungry already."

"Wanna go grab some lunch with me somewhere?" I asked.

"Sure," she said. "That would be nice."

"I know a place about fifteen minutes from here. I can drive."

"Okay. Sounds good."

I put my coffee mug in the sink and walked toward her. "Hey, how did you get home last night?"

"An Uber. Why?"

"Felt bad that I didn't even think about giving you a ride home. Sorry about that."

"It's okay. I didn't want to rush you, anyway. I wasn't sure how long you needed to stay."

"Usually not too long," I told her, and she nodded.

On the way to the restaurant, we chatted about the stuff she was studying and how much she admired my car, a dark blue Maserati. Again, lots of women were impressed by my car, but none as adorably as Lyric.

"I've never even seen a car like this up close, much less ridden in one. This is so cool!" she said excitedly. I laughed as she eagerly played with all the buttons and bells and whistles in the vehicle after I assured her I didn't mind. "Scary how quickly I could get spoiled hanging out with you. Between your amazing apartment and this thing. Just wow."

"Well, you deserve the best."

"Whatever," she said with a laugh.

"You know, I could always buy you some jewelry. A diamond necklace, a bracelet, whatever you want. Might be a nice touch to show people you're really my serious girlfriend. You could keep that stuff of course. You know, when this is all over."

I was surprised at how sad it made me to think of a time when this was all over. When I wouldn't see Lyric every day anymore. That would kinda suck.

"Oh, I don't know. That kind of thing really isn't my style."

"I guess I get that. You're not exactly high maintenance. I am, that's for sure. At least I am now. I swear, I don't mean to be," I said with a laugh. "It's not like I was spoiled growing up. Average middle class and all that. But now that I make a ridiculous amount of money, I've developed finer tastes, I suppose."

I pushed the end of my nose up to show my snobbery. Lyric laughed.

"So what? You're into fine wine and things like that now?"

"Nah. Not wine. But craft beer, yeah. I used to drink cheap beer all the time before I made it to the big leagues, but now it's like I can't stand the stuff. Now I like all the crafty, hoppy stuff they got on draught. And I've got a weakness for electronic gadgets. Like, I'm the first in line when the newest phones come out and all that. I'm spoiled rotten, but at least I *know* I'm spoiled if that makes any sense."

"It does," Lyric said. "You buy lots of expensive stuff, but you don't take it for granted."

"Exactly," I said, feeling relieved that she didn't actually think of me as a snob. "Damn, I know a lot of women who sure would have taken advantage of our arrangement," I said, shaking my head. "I'd be buying jewelry and high-end shoes every day of the week for those types. They'd have no problem emptying my wallet."

"I don't know. Medical school is pretty damned expensive," she said, sounding worried.

"But it's a helluva good cause."

"True. I can't argue with that."

"You wouldn't want to be *frivolous* or anything," I teased, using the same word she'd used to describe my life's work.

"Brady. That's not what I meant."

I laughed. "I know. Just givin' ya a hard time."

She laughed and then resumed playing with the buttons in my car.

"You ever been here before?" I asked when we arrived at the steakhouse I'd chosen for lunch.

"No, I don't think I have."

"It's a cool place. Classy, but not too fancy where you have to get super dressed up. Saturday nights you can barely get in, but this early we should be good."

We got seated right away at a nice table in the corner. It was good that it wasn't too crowded, but that meant there was less of a chance of me being recognized and photographed with my "girlfriend."

After we put in our food order, I gazed across the table at Lyric. Funny how this felt more real than any other date I'd been on in a long time. Most of the time when I went out with a girl, I threw lots of money around on drinks and dinner in the hopes the evening would end in sex, which it usually did. When it came to a lot of women, the drinks and dinner weren't even necessary. They just wanted to go to bed with a celebrity. "Dating" Lyric was an entirely different experience and, except for the not having sex part, it was way better.

"Brady, I have to say that I had so much fun at the game last night," she said with an excited smile. It was like she'd been waiting all morning to tell me that good news.

"Yeah?"

"Oh, yeah. I had a blast. I wasn't sure what to expect. But it is a lot different being there than when you're just watching the game on TV."

"You have no idea how happy I am to hear you say that," I said, feeling relieved. "I was so afraid it would end up being one of those boring games."

"So you admit that sometimes baseball games can be boring?"

"Not to me, they're not. But I get how some games are more

fun for fans than other ones. Like low-scoring games where both pitchers are amazing and it's hard to get anybody on base. For hard-core baseball fans, that can be fun. Like if a pitcher is tossing a no-hitter. That means nobody gets a hit off him the entire game. Very, very hard to do, and it's fascinating to watch. Then there's a perfect game, which is really rare. That means the pitcher didn't allow anybody to get on base for any reason. Didn't give up any walks, no hits, no reaching base on error, no hit by pitch. Nothing. Those are real edge-of-your-seat nail-biters, but to the casual viewer, it might seem boring."

Lyric smiled as I spoke. Damn, I loved how she always seemed to be genuinely listening when I prattled on about baseball.

"So I was glad that last night had lots of runs and stuff to keep the crowd on their feet. That's the kinda game you hope for when you're trying to get somebody interested in the game. Had it been a pitcher's duel, I might never have gotten you to set foot in a baseball stadium ever again."

"Oh, I would definitely go again. Even if the game itself had been boring, I like watching you play."

"Yeah?" I asked, feeling hopeful.

"Yeah."

I reached over and took her hand in mine and said quietly, "I'm doing this in case anybody here knows who I am and is watching us. That, and I kinda like touching you. Hope that's okay."

Lyric laughed softly. "Yep, it's okay. I kinda like it, too."

Unfortunately, I didn't get to hold her hand as long as I would have liked to since the server arrived with our drinks. We'd both ordered unsweetened iced teas.

"There ya go," the server lady said with a smile. She was a pretty girl in her early twenties. "Food should be arriving shortly."

After she walked away, I watched as Lyric put a packet of sugar into her tea and stirred it.

"One sugar. Just like your coffee," I observed.

"Yeah. So?" she asked curiously.

Chuckling, I said, "I guess sometimes I worry I might have to pass a relationship test like they say you do when you marry an immigrant. You know, to make sure the marriage is real. So I try to pay attention to stuff like this. Coffee, one cream and one sugar. Unsweetened tea, one sugar and some lemon."

Lyric laughed as she finished twisting her lemon into her drink. "And you're lemon only for tea. And coffee black, right?"

"Right."

"And you always smell your coffee before you drink it."

"I do?"

"You do," she said with a smile. "Every time."

"So this is what it's like," I said.

"What what's like?"

"Having a girlfriend. An especially sweet one who notices how I smell my coffee."

She blushed, and I hoped I hadn't made her uncomfortable. I was just really touched that she'd noticed little things about me. I felt like I noticed everything about her.

"What, you never had a girlfriend before?"

"I have, but it's been a while."

"Oh, right."

"Right what?"

"I've read the articles about you, Brady," she said wryly. "You have quite the playboy reputation. You know your way around the ladies, from what I hear."

"You read stuff about me?" I asked with a grin. I was loving that she seemed kinda into me.

"Hell yeah, I read about you. I had to make sure I knew

what I was getting into. For all I knew, you'd been arrested for beating up your past girlfriends," she said quietly. "I wasn't gonna move in with you until I knew at least something about you."

"Oh."

"I mean, I know you wouldn't do something like that. I know now, anyway. But I had to look you up. Had some second thoughts when I discovered the origin of your nickname, I'll tell you that." She laughed before sipping her tea.

"Fair enough," I said. "So yeah, I guess I do like to have my fun with the lady baseball fans and such."

"Cleat chasers, to use your lingo."

"Yes. What about you? I assume you have no boyfriend at the moment. Or if you do, he is pretty understanding."

"Nope. Nobody special. Not for a while now. I dated a biologist for a while, but we broke up more than a year ago."

My stomach tightened at the mention of her dating some other guy. I was surprised at how intense my literal gut reaction was. Not only did I hate the idea of some other guy being with her, I knew there was no way I could ever compete with some super-smart biologist.

I saw our server approaching with our food. "Oh my God, I can smell that from here," I called to her. "That smells amazing!"

She smiled nervously as she set down my plate in front of me. Her hand slipped a bit, and some of my fries fell off my plate.

"Oh, I—I'm sorry!" she said, looking horrified.

"No worries. Little bastards can't get far from me," I said, nabbing the fries and putting them back on my plate next to my steak. I popped one of the escapees into my mouth to show there were no hard feelings. "See? No harm done."

The server smiled gratefully at me. Then she carefully set Lyric's smaller steak and baked potato platter in front of her.

"Thanks," Lyric said. "Wow, you can hear it still sizzling. This looks awesome!"

"Is there, um, anything else I can get you?" the server asked. After we both shook our heads, she headed off.

"What was that all about?" Lyric asked. "She seemed so normal earlier."

"I can tell you exactly what happened. Or at least what I figure happened."

"What?" she asked, intrigued.

"She's not a baseball fan so at first, she had no idea who I am. I guarantee one of her coworkers tipped her off and now she knows I'm famous."

"Ohhh. That makes sense," Lyric said, before taking a bite of her steak. I rather enjoyed the sensual moan she let out. "That happen a lot?"

"Kinda," I said with a shrug. "I feel bad when people get nervous around me. I'm just a person, after all."

"I'm so glad you're not a jerk about being a celebrity."

"Yeah," I said, gazing off in the direction our server disappeared. "That's the messed-up part. I'm famous enough that I could make her life a living hell. Isn't that sad? She might be nervous because I'm a known ball player, or she might be afraid that if she screws up, I might yell to see the manager or whatever. That's the thing about being a celebrity. You can do some pretty awful things and get away with it. Believe me, I've seen it. And it sucks."

"I bet," Lyric agreed.

"But then you also get to meet cute little guys like your birthday pal last night."

"Oh my gosh, wasn't he the sweetest?" she said, her eyes opening wide. "He was my little baseball buddy the whole game. I'm doing what I can to let people know we're together and all that, so I told the family sitting next to me that you were my boyfriend. Hayden was so excited!"

I laughed and nodded.

"His parents seemed pretty impressed about it, too, I'll tell you that. Then there were these super bitchy girls behind me who kept accusing me of lying about it."

"Really?" I asked after swallowing my bite of steak. "What the hell?"

"Oh, they were so awful. I tried to ignore them, but they kept using vulgar language in front of the kids," she said, shaking her head.

"That sucks. That seriously pisses me off." I stabbed my steak with my fork. "I hate when rude fans ruin the game for other people. You know, the ushers are really good about dealing with that sort of thing. If it happens again, you can let them know. Usually, they'll come talk to the people and ask them to watch their language. If it keeps up, they can toss them out of the place."

"Good to know," she said. "Oh, I didn't tell you the best part. I swear, I'd forgotten all about those mean girls when I called you over. You really made that kid's day, Brady. Thanks so much for doing that."

I swallowed hard as I looked into her eyes. All she had to do was look at me like she was gazing at me right now, and I'd do pretty much anything she asked of me.

"My pleasure," I told her.

"But *dude*, when you looked at me and said 'See you at home, hon'? Oh my God, the looks on those girls' faces. I thought they were gonna *die*." Lyric threw her head back and laughed joyously. "It was just so perfect because I didn't say anything to defend myself, but then you came along and did it without me asking. Seriously, you can wait a lifetime for a moment as sweet as that."

Grinning at her, I said, "I'm glad to be of service. Damn, if I'd known, I would have said more."

"Believe me, you didn't have to." Leaning in close to me,

she said in a husky voice, "By the looks on their faces, they really believed I was going straight home to your bed. The sheer jealousy in their eyes ... like they just knew I was gonna go home last night and have glorious sex with you all night long."

My mouth went dry hearing her talk like that. Though I'd found Lyric Rivers quite attractive since the day I'd first laid eyes on her, now I realized how much I actually *wanted* her.

I wondered if she would ever go for the idea of being friends with benefits. I couldn't have sex with anybody else while we were supposedly madly in love, and she broke up with her last boyfriend more than a year ago. It would make sense for us to satisfy each other's needs, right?

Lyric graced me with a lovely smile, and I immediately abandoned the idea when I saw what was in her eyes. *Trust.* She'd already said how much she appreciated my gentlemanly manner, and I knew she liked that I asked permission before kissing her. What would she think if I floated the idea of having sex? She might think I was being a total creep. Worse, she might feel like I was treating her like a whore or something. The mere thought made me shudder. I never wanted her to feel that way. I wanted her to feel safe with me.

"So you know, I got a road trip coming up," I said, eager to get my mind off sex with Lyric. At least while she was right in front of me. There was plenty of time to have imagination-sex with her when I was alone in the shower.

"Oh yeah, I saw that on the schedule. Florida and then Cleveland, right?"

"Right. Enjoy having the apartment to yourself."

"I get the place to myself all the time as it is since you're out most nights."

"True. I really liked having you at the game last night."

"You did? I wasn't even sure you remembered I was coming."

"Of course I did. The whole game I was very aware you were watching. I wanted to do good, you know?"

"Were you actually nervous?" she asked, looking fascinated.

"Yeah," I said with a laugh. "You know, the one time you were there to see me in action, and I didn't want to mess up."

"You were great, Crush," she said.

"Thanks."

"I'll try to watch some of the away games on TV. Unless you think it'll make you nervous," Lyric said with a wink.

"Not at all, Doc. In fact, knowing you're watching might just inspire me to do better."

She laughed. "Ah, yes. Your girlfriend, the wind beneath your wings." With that, she lifted her iced tea glass to toast mine.

More than you know.

CHAPTER 11

rady

THE FIRST GAME against Florida was rough. I went 0 for 4 and committed a throwing error. We ended up losing 7-2, which was not a great way to start a road trip. I kinda hoped Lyric hadn't seen the disaster of a game.

"Wanna go drown our sorrows?" Tyler asked in the visitors' locker room after the game.

"Nah."

"What?" he asked, eyes wide.

"I told you, man. I haven't given up on playing for Baltimore yet, and I gotta show them I'm not an irresponsible drunk anymore."

Tyler slung his gym bag over his shoulder, and we headed out the tunnel toward the players' parking lot.

"I'm not saying you have to get wasted and trash a hotel room. Just have a couple of drinks is all. Been a bad night."

I already felt myself starting to cave. Dealing with a tough loss was so much harder when you were sober. Then I pictured myself wearing a Bay Birds uniform and standing on the field at Old Bay Stadium. The thought helped center me. I was about to tell him no again, but I got distracted by fans screaming my name once we got outside.

A bunch of diehard Florida fans were standing around the parking lot, yelling for their favorite players. The lot was surrounded by a tall fence that kept people from messing with the cars and protected the players from the masses. Some of the Florida guys stopped to chat with people, while others just got in their cars and headed out.

"Brady! Brady!" came the voices of several women and kids. I was in a bad mood and didn't feel like talking to anybody after my performance tonight, but I just couldn't walk away from the kids. I headed over toward the fence with Tyler just behind me. It was a bit awkward, though, since it wasn't like anybody was clamoring for his autograph. Back in Richmond, sure, baseball fans knew who he was. Here, not so much.

"Just a few autographs, okay guys? I'm kinda tired," I said as I reached over the fence to grab a ball that some kid's dad passed over to me. His son, who looked about five years old, literally started jumping up and down as he watched me sign it. I chuckled, feeling slightly better already. After signing programs, balls, and baseball cards as quickly as I could, I turned to go.

"Gotta go, guys. Sorry!" Groans went up from the crowd. Unfortunately I couldn't get to everybody, or I'd be there all night. I felt bad, but I had to draw the line somewhere. Besides, it was better than never signing stuff, like some players do.

"Hey, Brady, wanna go grab a drink somewhere?" an attractive redhead asked me.

"Don't think so. Sorry."

Tyler made a face and muttered, "Go for it, man."

"I told you, Ty. I have a girlfriend," I said, loud enough for the fans to hear. Tyler rolled his eyes. He knew I was dating Lyric, but he didn't think it would last. He'd never known me to be serious about a woman for long. I took my phone out of my pocket to check on the status of the Uber I'd called and saw I'd missed a text from Lyric.

Tough game. But you still looked great out there, Crush.

She punctuated her text with a heart emoji. I knew it was really just a friendship text, but seeing as she used her private nickname and included the heart, it would certainly look romantic to an outsider.

"See?" I said, holding up my phone for Tyler to read.

"Aww, ain't that sweet," Tyler said dryly. "Crush?"

"That's what she calls me," I said proudly.

Tyler groaned. Then he turned to chat up the redhead. Sometimes I wondered if that guy would ever get laid if it wasn't for me.

I texted Lyric back during the ride back to my hotel.

What are you still doing up?

I knew she sometimes caught the beginnings of games on TV, but she rarely stayed up long enough to watch the whole thing.

Studying. What else? But I'll have you know I unmuted the TV every time you were up to bat.

Sorry I didn't give you anything worth watching, I responded.

Not true. You look sexy when you're mad lol. But I am sorry you had a rough night. Tomorrow will be better.

Thanks. Now go to bed.

I wished I was home in bed with her.

Staring out the window at the Miami traffic, which was bad even at this time of night, I thought how nice it was of Lyric to text me. Usually after a rough game I'd go get drunk with Tyler and then bring some girl back to my hotel room and bang her senseless. Both those things were enough to put me in a better mood. The one thing I'd never had after a bad night was somebody to commiserate with. Hell, most of the women I fucked hadn't even watched the game. But Lyric had. And it meant a lot to me.

Once I got to my hotel room, I got bored pretty damn quick. My bad mood was back. It wasn't all that late yet, and I wasn't tired. It usually took a long time to wind down after a game, whether we won or lost. With no booze and no women, I wasn't quite sure what to do with myself.

Well, I could think of *one* thing I could do with myself, but given how horny I was, that wouldn't take long. Still, it might relieve some of my tension and help snap me out of my shitty mood. Though it felt more than a little pathetic lying on the bed and rubbing one out all alone in a hotel room, it was better than nothing. Closing my eyes, I pictured having sex with Lyric. *Lyric.* Not the redhead from the parking lot, and not any of the countless other women I'd been with that always worked nicely in situations like this. I couldn't help it. Lyric Rivers was gorgeous, and lately, most of my sexual fantasies revolved around her. My favorite fantasy was picturing her face as I pleasured her. Her eyes wide, mouth open as I gave her a powerful orgasm while I rammed into her as hard as I could. The sound of her voice screaming my name as she came.

Yep. It didn't take long, but I definitely felt better. After I cleaned myself up, I looked around my hotel room. Still bored, still sober. This whole acting like a responsible human being thing was gonna be harder than I'd thought. Though I was less physically tense, I still wasn't tired enough to try to sleep.

I wondered if my brother was awake. He had a nine-to-five job, but he was still kind of a night owl. I texted him to see if he was up. A few minutes later I got a response.

Yeah. Why?

Instead of responding to his text, I called him via video chat. He answered right away, looking worried.

"You okay?" Eric asked.

"I'm fine. I'm just bo*rrr*ed."

"Oh," he said with a laugh. "Why aren't you balls deep in some rando?"

"You kiss our mother with that mouth?"

"It's a fair question," he said. Eric was not the type to sleep around, but he was fascinated by the fact that I did.

"Well, I'm kinda seeing someone back in Richmond. I may be a manwhore, but I'm not a cheater."

"Is this the dark-haired girl with the pretty blue eyes?" Eric asked. "I've been seeing pictures of you together lately. People have been speculating that you might have a girl-friend, but I didn't believe it for a second."

"Well, believe it."

"No kidding? Damn. How did that happen?"

I shrugged. "I dunno. We just hit it off right away."

"How did you meet her?"

"She dumped hot coffee all over me."

"Shit, what did you do to her?" he asked, sounding shocked.

I burst out laughing. "She didn't do it on purpose. It was an accident."

"Su*rrr*e, it was," Eric said. "She probably did it to get your attention, Mr. Crusher."

"No, she had no idea who I was. For real, she had no clue."

"I thought everybody knew who you were, hotshot. What, she live in a cave?" he asked before crunching on a piece of popcorn from a bowl on his desk.

"No, she lives in the library. She's in college."

Eric made a face. "Dude, how old is this jailbait?"

"Don't freak out. She took a few years off after high

school so she could save up for college, so she's my age. Her name is Lyric Rivers. She's pre-med. Or pre-health, whatever it's called. She's prepping to go to med school, and it's a ton of work. Doesn't exactly have time for sports."

"You're dating a future doctor?" Eric asked, looking surprised.

"I know," I said, feeling my stomach tighten a bit. "You wonder what she's doing with a dumb fuck like me."

"I didn't say that. I just wondered what you have in common with a non-sports fan when your whole life is baseball."

"Yeah," I said, suddenly feeling miserable. "It was kinda stupid to think a smart chick like her could ever go for a guy like me."

"What are you talking about? She obviously did go for you. She's your girlfriend."

I stared at my brother through the screen, wondering if I should just tell him the whole truth. He would never blab my secret. That much I knew for sure. I would trust my little brother with my life. But if I told him, he might tell me I was out of my mind. Worse, he might tell me it would never work and Baltimore still wouldn't want me.

"What's going on in that brain of yours?" Eric said, squinting at me suspiciously.

"I'm trying to decide if I want to tell you the truth about something."

"You gotta tell me now, dickhead. Otherwise I won't let it go until I figure it out anyway." He casually popped another piece of popcorn into his mouth. Eric was super smart. Knowing him, he *would* figure it out.

I sighed. "Okay, well you know how Baltimore passed on a contract for me?"

"Yeah," Eric said solemnly. He knew how much that news had broken my heart.

"Well, they mainly shot me down because of my reputation for being a partier. Unstable. A heavy drinker and all that."

"Right," he said, nodding.

"So I'm trying really hard to clean up my reputation, you know? Show them I can behave like a good little boy so they will let me come and play with them."

"Which explains why you're currently sober and alone in your hotel room and talking to me instead of drunkenly banging some woman," he said matter-of-factly.

"Correct. And it also explains why I'm paying a beautiful young woman to live in my apartment for the season and play the part of my devoted girlfriend to show everybody that I've settled down."

Eric's hand, full of popcorn, froze halfway to his mouth. I honestly wasn't sure if he was shocked or if his screen had frozen. Slowly, he put the popcorn back in the bowl.

"You hired a hooker?" he asked incredulously.

"She's not a hooker," I said way louder than I'd meant to.

Startled, Eric jumped in his seat. Then he held up his hands in mock defense. "Shit, calm your balls, dude."

"Sorry. It's just … It's nothing like that. Really. I'm not even exactly paying her directly. I'm just paying for the rest of her college and all of her medical school."

Eric whistled. "Wow, that's a lotta money. So she's a high-*priced* hooker."

I glared at him fiercely and he laughed. I knew he was trying to get a rise out of me.

"I'm just kidding, man."

"I know," I said, still wishing he was here in person so I could punch him.

"So this was all just supposed to be pretend, but now you like her for real," Eric said, quickly cutting to the core of what I'd been trying to deny to myself since this whole thing started. "That's why you looked like you wanted to choke me when I insulted her."

"I often want to choke you for so many reasons."

"You like her, don't you Brady?"

"What difference does it make? She would never go for a guy like me."

"Sure she would. I hear you're quite the catch."

"Yeah, to shallow girls. Not a smart one like her."

"You don't know that. Do you two get along well?"

"Yeah, we do. I can honestly say I love talking with her."

"Just talking with her?" Eric asked in disbelief.

"We try to be seen in public when we can. You know, to make it believable that we're a real couple. And when we do that, it's, like, a lot of fun, you know? She's a real sweetheart."

It felt weird and kind of icky to be baring my soul to my little brother like this. I hated feeling vulnerable, and there was a good chance Eric might laugh in my face.

"Are you sleeping with her?"

"I wish."

Eric did laugh at that. "It is so strange to hear you say that. You never have a problem getting pussy."

I winced at the idea of thinking of sex with Lyric as "getting pussy." To be fair, it was probably shitty of me to think of other women that way too. I guess I never really thought about it.

"The last thing I want to do is make her feel like sex is supposed to be a part of this deal. We have to be convincing in public, like kissing and all, and I've tried to ease her into it. You know, kissing her at home with her permission so she can feel more comfortable."

Eric nodded thoughtfully.

"It was hard to convince her to go for this whole scheme to begin with. Lyric really needs the money, but she's not comfortable with all the attention she's getting. And she really hates lying."

"She sounds like a good person," Eric said sincerely.

"She is. She really is."

"You're an asshole, Brady," he said bluntly, like only a little brother could get away with. "But you're a good guy, too. There's no reason Lyric couldn't go for you for real. Just let her get to know you. She's not into you just because you're a famous ballplayer, and that's a good thing. If she didn't jump at this weird opportunity right away, then she's not into you for your money, either. I mean, getting you to pay for med school and stuff ... that's a lot different than her wanting a fancy car or expensive jewelry."

I smiled as I thought of Lyric playing with the buttons in my car, not interested in the way she looked in it and not caring about diamond jewelry.

"Well, whatever happens, I just hope it's enough for Baltimore to think I've settled down and changed my ways."

Eric chuckled. "If you're not careful, you're gonna wind up actually becoming the person you're pretending to be."

"Can you imagine?" I asked, shaking my head.

"Not really."

"Me neither."

Eric let out a small sigh, and I noticed he looked tired.

"Past your bedtime," I said.

"Eh. I'm okay."

"Spare me the pity. I'll be fine here all by my lonesome self. Go to bed."

"Okay. I will."

"Is work okay?" I asked him.

"Yeah. Yeah, it's good."

"I'm proud of you."

"I know, Brady," he said with a laugh. He knew how much

I worried about him being known as Eric Keaton, Brady Keaton's Brother instead of his own person. "Talk soon."

"Cool," I said before signing off.

Sighing, I lay back down in bed. Eric was good about not making this any more awkward than it already was for me, and it was nice having somebody to talk to about all this craziness. I was falling harder for Lyric than I wanted to admit to myself, and I was glad at least one other person knew how I felt.

It had only been a day on the road, and I already missed her. I wondered if she missed me at all.

CHAPTER 12

$\mathcal{L}$yric

I SETTLED in to watch the game, or at least some of it, in the living room. I really hoped the game would go better for Brady tonight. It was always tough to watch him struggle when he was having an off night. Everybody had bad days in the office, but there usually weren't thousands of people watching them. I shuddered at the thought.

My heart thumped in my chest when it was Brady's turn to bat. The nice thing about watching him on TV was I could stare at him all I wanted, and he would never know. He was obviously a physically attractive man, made even more obvious by the screaming women everywhere he went. Even when the Dominoes weren't the home team, the fans went crazy for him. But honestly, I found him more attractive because of the person he was. The way he treated the fans, waitstaff at restaurants, and especially the way he treated me. This fake-girlfriend thing could have been a real nightmare, but instead, I felt like the luckiest woman alive.

And every day I was more and more physically attracted to him. I was usually so busy that I barely had time to think about sex, but now it felt like I thought about it all the time. Every time I looked at Brady, my sexual fantasies became stronger and more vivid.

All I would have to do is ask.

Though I knew it was true, it was still a terrible idea. We were supposed to be just friends. I really cared for Brady, and adding sex to the mix could make things messy really quick. Besides, even if I was bold enough to ask to add "benefits" to our friendship, what if he turned me down? I'd never be able to look him in the eye again, never mind convincing people that we were in love when we were in public.

Nothing could be gained by sleeping with Brady.

Well, nothing besides earth-shattering physical pleasure beyond my wildest dreams.

Biting my lip, I moaned out loud. I had no doubt in my mind that Brady would be utterly *masterful* in bed. His physique was nothing short of masculine perfection, and I was confident he knew his way around a woman's body.

Dear God, the things he could do to me.

For the first time, I started to question whether or not I would be able to stop myself from floating the idea of being friends with benefits with Brady. Though part of me was worried he might say no, I highly doubted that he would. The man had a healthy sexual appetite. Apparently, so did I. Who knew? I guess it just took meeting a devastatingly handsome man to make me rethink my whole "sex requires a serious commitment" rule.

Sometimes I felt like I was slipping out of control when I was with him. Like I didn't quite trust myself not to say something stupid, which was unusual for me. My default setting was overthink everything to death. I wasn't quite sure what I might do the next time he "practiced" kissing me. It was kind of scary.

But also exhilarating.

I stared at Brady as he stood at the plate, my hormones in overdrive. The man was never more desirable than when he was playing baseball. He lunged at the first pitch as he sometimes did, but this time it paid off. Launched that ball right the hell out of the park, he did. I jumped off the couch, cheering as I watched him round the bases. Funny how steady he kept his face when I knew he was yelling and punching his fist in the air on the inside.

Laughing at myself, I settled back down on the couch. Who would ever have figured me for a baseball fan? Naturally, I was a Brady fan more than anything, but it was more than just the way he set my lady parts afire when I watched him. There really was something great about rooting for the home team, as the old song went. Richmond was a lovely city, and it was fun to watch the Dominoes fans get all riled up and excited for their team. It genuinely made me feel good—proud, even—when they won.

My cell phone rang, and a surge of guilt washed over me when I saw it was my mom. Damn.

"Hey, Mom! I swear I've been meaning to call you."

"It's okay, honey," she responded. I could hear the smile in her voice, which made *me* smile. "Just callin' to check in. How ya doing?"

"Doing pretty good. I'll be glad when this semester is over. I am so not gonna miss that physics class."

"Yeah, that does not sound like a good time to me. But I'm sure you'll do great with it. How goes the MCAT studying?"

One of Brady's teammates made it to first base on a solid hit, and I had to suppress a shout. It took me a second to rewind in my head and remember what my mother had just asked me.

"Oh, um. Well, depends on the day. Sometimes I feel ready for it, like I know I'm gonna nail it. And then other days I feel like I have no idea what I'm doing."

"That's understandable, Lyric. But I know you're gonna crush it."

The word "crush" made me smile. God, I was so goofy sometimes.

"Are you ... Are you dating anyone these days?" she asked.

I was surprised at the question. Though sometimes she worried about me being alone so much, my mom was not the type to pressure me about finding a husband and giving her grandchildren.

"Um well, kind of," I said.

"You don't have to tell me about it if you don't want to," she said. My heart squeezed at the sadness in her voice. She clearly wanted me to confide in her. "It's just, well, Kate Miller forwarded me this article in the news. It said you might be dating some ballplayer?"

Okay, now I felt truly terrible. I closed my eyes, cursing myself for being so insensitive. My parents weren't sports fans, so I figured they wouldn't know what was going on. Leave it to my mom's nosy friend Kate Miller to blab. I knew I had to tell my mom at least some of what was going on before she found out any more.

"Yeah, I am dating a baseball player. Sorry. I should have told you about him sooner. You know how I am. I get so wrapped up in my school and all that."

"Yes, I sure do know," Mom said. She sounded worried, but less offended, which was a start.

"It's so crazy. His name is Brady Keaton, and he plays for the Richmond Dominoes. Idiot that I am, I had never heard of him. He's a famous celebrity, and I had no idea who he was when we met. He's very nice, Mom. I think you would really like him."

"That's great, Lyric. You do sound happy."

I *was* happy. For now. Scary to think how I might feel months from now when this was all over. When Brady and I would probably still be friends but no longer roommates. Which reminded me. I needed to tell Mom about that before nosy Kate Miller found out first.

"You should know ... I am living with him."

"You are?" she exclaimed. My mother was no prude, and I knew she didn't object to me shacking up on principle. She was likely worried that it was awfully fast, which it was. I'd never lived with a guy before, even the ones I'd dated far longer.

"I know. It all happened kind of fast, but I'm loving it. We just decided it made a ton of sense. He lives in a nice apartment not far from my school, and it beats the hell out of living with a bunch of noisy college girls. I have so much quiet time to study. He's not here now, so I've got the place to myself. He's in Florida and then he's off to Cleveland."

"That's good, I guess?" she said uncertainly.

"Don't get me wrong. It's not that I don't miss him." I felt a small piercing sensation in my heart when I realized how true that was. "It's just nice to have some alone time once in a while. But really, we have so much fun together. He's even turning me into a baseball fan. I went to my first game the other night. I couldn't believe how much fun it was!"

"Hard to picture you at a ballgame."

"Right? But I went and had a blast. He's a great guy, Mom. He's super supportive of my schoolwork and knows how important it is. He even calls me 'Doc,' which I love."

My mother laughed. "That's cute. Well, I hope I'm able to meet him soon."

I winced, but I knew it was unavoidable since my parents

lived close by in Alexandria. I felt horrible for lying to my mom about my relationship with Brady, but at the same time, I knew it would break her heart if she knew the truth. She was already worried about me moving in with him so quickly. If she knew I'd done it for the money, knowing her she would berate herself for not being able to provide for me and my schooling.

"Brady's busy with his schedule and all, but I'm sure that can be arranged."

"Great! I'll let you go for now. Love you, little girl."

I closed my eyes and smiled. No matter how old I was, I would always be my parents' little girl. And I wouldn't have it any other way.

"Love you too. Promise I'll call you soon."

After ending the call with my mom, I told myself I needed to go to bed soon.

But the game ended up being quite the nail-biter, and I wound up watching the whole eleven innings.

The Dominoes lost 9-8.

I wished it had been a home game so I could have hugged Brady.

CHAPTER 13

L yric

I woke up to go to the bathroom and heard noises in the living room on my way back to bed.

Brady is home.

My heartbeat sped up, and I was once again struck by how much I had missed him while he'd been away. Feeling groggy, I picked up my cell phone from the nightstand to see it was only 11pm. Though I knew I should wait until morning, I really wanted to see him.

I walked back into the bathroom and smoothed down my hair, going for the casually messy but not insane hairdo of someone who just got out of bed. I also rinsed my mouth with mouthwash. Dressed in sweatpants and a sweatshirt, I figured I was decent enough.

Brady was sitting on the couch when I walked in, and I thought about clearing my throat to let him know I was there without startling him.

Once I got a closer look at him, I was horrified to see that he was crying. My heart seized in my chest, and I forgot all about trying not to scare him.

"Oh my God, Brady. What happened?"

His entire body jumped at the sound of my voice, and he clutched his chest like I'd given him a heart attack.

"Sorry, sorry!" I said, rushing over to him. "I heard noises out here and ... Brady, are you okay? What's wrong?"

To my relief, he laughed as he awkwardly wiped his eyes. "No, no. It's nothing. It's, you know, totally stupid," he said, sounding flustered. I'd never seen him look embarrassed before. "It's just ... the movie." He gestured weakly at the television.

My first instinct was to laugh with relief that nothing terrible had happened, but I couldn't bear the idea of him thinking I was laughing at him. "Oh, thank God. I thought somebody had died."

"Nothing like that." He still seemed so uncomfortable. Such a shame that men weren't allowed to cry without being embarrassed.

"Want me to sit and cry with you?"

"Y—yes, please," he said with an exaggerated sob as he wiped his eyes.

I did laugh at that, and Brady grinned at me. "I missed you, girl."

To say I was surprised that he said it out loud would be putting it mildly. Until then, I had no intention of fessing up about feeling the same way.

"I missed you too."

"Is it okay if I give you a hug?" he asked.

"Of course." I sat next to him on the couch. He wrapped his arms around me and squeezed me in a chaste but warm and comforting hug. My body tingled all over at his touch. After he let go, I said, "I'm glad you're back safe."

"Didn't mean to wake you up. I didn't mean to scare you, either. Sorry about that," Brady said, glancing uncomfortably at the television.

"What are you watching, anyway?" I asked.

"*Field of Dreams.* Happened to catch it toward the end on TV."

"Oh. I've never seen it."

Brady drew in a deep, loud gasp. "You've never seen it?"

I laughed. "Why are you surprised? Until I met you, I wasn't into baseball."

He shook his head and muttered, "Can't believe I let this girl in my house and she ain't never seen *Field of Dreams.*"

I laughed again, and I saw the amusement in the corner of his eyes.

"I ought to sit you down and force you to watch it start to finish right now."

I shrugged. "Okay by me."

"Really? It's awfully late."

"Yeah, but I'm wide awake now. Would take me a while to fall asleep anyway. Go ahead. Start it over."

"Cool," Brady said, his brown eyes lighting up. Damn, he just got cuter by the minute. "Ya want some popcorn?"

"Sure, why not?"

Getting up, he said, "My brother was eating popcorn last time I video chatted with him, and I've been craving it ever since."

"Shouldn't be hard for you to get. Aren't peanuts and popcorn a staple at the ballpark?"

He chuckled adorably. "Yep, I suppose so."

I walked over to the kitchen as he made the microwave popcorn, and soon the scent of buttery goodness filled the room. "How's your brother doing?"

"Doing pretty good. I told him about you."

"Did you now?" I asked curiously.

"Yep. He wanted to know why I was all alone in my hotel room, and I told him it was because I had a beautiful girl back home." He punctuated his words with a flirtatious wink. It was only too easy to believe he was really my boyfriend in moments like this. Hanging out with him felt so natural.

"I guess you normally bring girls back to your hotel after a game?"

Brady shrugged. "Yeah, sorta."

Though I was well aware of Brady's womanizing ways, it still hurt to think about it. It was sweet how he downplayed his bed-hopping when talking to me. Like he was trying to be respectful.

"I told my mom about us, too. Well, I sorta had to."

Brady grimaced. "Saw the pictures of us, did she?"

"Yeah. I feel bad. She sounded hurt that I hadn't told her I had a boyfriend, and she was definitely concerned about us living together."

"She the old-fashioned type?" Brady asked as he dumped the popcorn from the bag into a bowl.

"No, not at all. It's more of a safety concern."

"Oh, I see."

"It's not like me to move in with a guy so quickly. So she worries."

"And she most likely looked me up on the Internet, which probably didn't exactly soothe her anxiety."

"No doubt. It's okay. I told her how great you are and that she had nothing to worry about. She trusts my judgment, so it's all good."

I grabbed a Diet Coke from the fridge as Brady headed to the living room with the popcorn. Sharing the popcorn gave me the perfect excuse to sit next to him on the couch, which was nice.

"Lyric," he said sternly, but I knew that tone. It was his "pretending to be deadly serious" tone.

"Brady," I said, matching his tone.

"I have seen this movie a million times and I have never, not once, made it through without tearing up. You have to promise not to make fun of me."

I smiled. "I promise."

Narrowing his eyes, he said, "I feel like I should have you sign a non-disclosure agreement. Because if you *ever* tell *anyone*—"

"I would never do that, Brady. Really," I said sincerely. "Honestly, I'm surprised you didn't make me sign anything for this whole deal."

"I guess I just trust you," he said with a smile. "Just like you apparently trust me not to renege on our deal about my paying for school."

"I do trust you," I said, realizing how crazy that was. He *could* just walk away and leave me with nothing. Somehow, I knew deep in my heart that he was trustworthy.

We settled in to watch the movie, and I was surprised at how good it was. The only thing I knew about *Field of Dreams* was that it was about baseball. That, and of course I knew the famous "If you build it, he will come" line. It quickly became clear that you didn't have to be a big baseball fan to enjoy the film, but I could understand that the love of the game added another dimension to it. Just knowing Brady, I knew the stirring music that swelled when Ray Kinsella stood on the field affected him differently than it did me. Plus, I could see it in his eyes when I discreetly glanced at him.

The movie featured many ghosts of baseball past, namely the team that came to be known as the Black Sox after it turned out they had been paid off to lose the World Series. It was never proven that "Shoeless Joe" Jackson had helped to throw the game, but he'd been punished just the same. It was heartbreaking when Joe, played by Ray Liotta in the movie, said that getting thrown out of baseball was like having a part of him amputated.

Brady watched the screen intently at that part, his jaw tight. Clearly, he felt the same way about baseball. It was deeply a part of who he was.

Joe went on to talk about the smell of a baseball glove and the way the crowd would rise to its feet for a run. With deep emotion, he said how much he loved the game. That he would have played for nothing.

"I feel the same way," Brady said quietly as he stared at Shoeless Joe Jackson. "I'd play for free."

"Especially for Baltimore."

He turned toward me and said, "Yeah."

I took his hand briefly and squeezed it, and he smiled at me. He didn't tear up at this part of the movie, but I could tell he was fighting it. Such a beautiful thing to witness, how somebody could love anything as much as Brady Keaton loved baseball.

We sat together and watched the rest of the story unfold. It was lovely and powerful to see the tale of long-broken dreams finally come true. I especially loved the part about "Moonlight" Graham, the doctor who had once dreamed of being a pro ball player. When the main character, Ray, said it was a tragedy that the man had never gotten to fulfill his dream, Doc Graham disagreed. He said the tragedy would have been if he'd never become a doctor.

"Oh, I love that," I said.

"I knew you would," Brady said softly.

We gazed into each other's eyes, and it felt like I was looking directly into his soul. Maybe it was all the emotions the film had stirred up.

And maybe it wasn't.

"This part," Brady said a bit later. "This speech is so great."

He turned up the sound slightly as James Earl Jones gave

a beautiful speech about baseball and how, no matter what happened in the country and in the world, baseball had marked the time. It was stunning.

"Wow," I said softly.

"Yeah. He says it so much better than I ever could." Brady did tear up a little at that part.

Just as I had turned to watch him during the emotional parts about baseball, I felt him turn to look at me when the doctor saved the child's life toward the end of the movie. Brady knew my dreams every bit as much as I knew his.

Toward the end of the movie, Brady wiped his eyes. It was the part where Ray got to play catch with his dad, who had died long ago.

"Did your dad ever play catch with you?"

"Yeah," Brady responded. "All the time. He ... he always believed in me. Even when I didn't believe in myself."

"Good," I said. My eyes were watering too. Because of the movie. Because of Brady. Because of everything that had happened since the moment I met my favorite baseball player, who was fast becoming my favorite *person*.

"I'm glad you showed this to me," I told him.

"Thanks for not making fun of me," Brady said, his eyes still slightly red.

"I would never do that, Crush."

Brady smiled when I used my special nickname for him.

"I feel like I'm learning a lot from you," I said.

"About baseball?"

"About everything."

He eyed me curiously.

"I rarely watch movies. And—hear me out, now—I always thought it was kinda silly to cry over movies. Or television shows or books. But I feel like I get it now." I paused a moment, trying to gather my thoughts. "Those kinds of things might be make-believe, but they reflect real life. The characters are fictional, but they remind you of real people and, maybe I'm getting too philosophical here, but it's like movies and TV shows do reflect the human condition. You're not crying over the actors and the pretend parts they're playing. You get emotional, whether it's laughing or crying or whatever, because what you're watching touches something inside of you. Something real."

Blushing, I averted my gaze from him. "I don't know. I guess that's kinda stupid. I'm overthinking stuff because it's late and I'm tired."

"It's not stupid, Lyric," Brady said firmly. I looked at him and he smiled gently at me. "You said it perfectly. It always bothers me when people say *Oh, it's just a TV show* or *It's just a movie*, because there's a lot more to it than that."

"And baseball's not 'just a game,'" I said. "Not to all the fans and the families and friends who gather together to watch and root for the home team."

That got a huge grin from Brady. "Yeah. Exactly." After I was quiet for a moment, he asked, "What's wrong?"

"Nothing. I just … I feel like I should call my parents and tell them I'm sorry for not taking their music more seriously. In a weird way, I feel like I understand them better."

"That's very cool, Lyric. Very cool." Gazing at me with concern, Brady said, "You're tired."

"Yeah. I guess I'd better go to bed." I stood and said, "I'm glad you're home, Brady."

"Me too."

I could feel him watching me as I headed back to my bedroom.

CHAPTER 14

rady

LYRIC RIVERS WAS one hell of a woman. She was all I could think about as I drove back to my place after the game. Though it was only a few blocks away from home, I usually took my car to the park for games. Fans were often waiting outside for the players, and I couldn't very well have them follow me on foot and see where I lived. We'd lost tonight, so I should have been in a shitty mood, but I wasn't. All I could think about was the girl back in my apartment, despite the fact that she was probably fast asleep, and I wouldn't get to see her until tomorrow.

It felt like every second I was with her I was more and more into her. Though I'd long ago lost count of how many women I'd been with physically, not one of them had spent more than two minutes talking about baseball with me. Sure, they were excited that I was a famous baseball player, and they certainly appreciated the physique that went along with being a professional athlete. But not one of them gave a damn about how I felt about the game. Or how I felt about anything else, for that matter.

Enter Lyric. Not only did she talk to me about baseball without her lovely blue eyes glazing over with boredom, but she'd spent two hours last night watching *Field of Dreams* with me in the middle of the night. And she had actually *watched* it, rather than just humoring me. No. Lyric didn't just watch it. She understood it. I felt like she understood *me*.

When I got home, I was thrilled to find her wide awake and standing in my kitchen.

"Well, look who's still up," I said, unable to hide my enthusiasm.

"Unfortunately," Lyric said wryly, but she said it with a smile.

"Another test tomorrow?"

"Yep."

"Good times." I set down my gym bag.

"I was just finishing up a snack. You hungry?"

"Nah, I'm good," I told her. She finished cleaning up in the kitchen, then walked into the living room.

"Sorry, I'll get all this stuff out of your way," Lyric said, gathering up her books and papers from school. I grinned when I saw the TV was still on, though it was on mute.

"You were watching the game?" I asked.

"Yeah." She smiled and shyly tucked her hair behind her ear. "I usually try to have the game on in the background when I can."

"Cool."

"Sorry you lost. You were robbed, Brady. Oh my God, I was yelling at the TV."

I laughed. I'd hit a long fly ball that nearly made it out of the park for a two-run homer, but the center fielder nabbed it with an impressive catch. "Well, thanks for your support."

"Anytime," she said as she stacked her things on the floor next to her bookbag to get them off the coffee table. She knew I liked to put my feet up when I was watching TV and unwinding after a night game.

"You done studying for the night?"

Lyric sighed deeply. "I don't know. I'm tired, but I don't feel prepared for this test for some reason. I should keep going, but I'm not sure I can. I'm like ... mentally tired more than physically tired, if that makes sense."

"Of course it does. You should probably get some rest. You'll probably feel better about everything in the morning."

"Maybe," she said, leaning wearily against the living room wall. I watched her thoughtfully for a moment. "What?" she asked, sounding a little self-conscious.

"You look just like you did when we first met. Very pretty and very tired."

"Oh," she said with a sweet smile.

As I looked into those beautiful blue eyes, I felt my impulsive nature start to take over. Ignoring the blaring warning signs in my head, I walked over to her.

"Would it be inappropriate of me to ask if we could practice kissing again?"

Lyric's eyes flew open wide. She was clearly stunned at my question. I held my breath as I waited for the answer.

"No. No, I think that would be okay. It's been a week since you've been away." She swallowed hard. "Practicing is a good idea."

"A very good idea," I said, my heart thudding in my chest. Wasting no time, I lowered my head and pressed my lips against hers. A soft moan escaped those luscious lips of hers, which sent my libido into overdrive. I'd been aching to touch this woman ever since I left Richmond a few days ago, and she'd occupied every one of my sexual fantasies the whole time.

Pressing her against the wall, I kissed her harder. Her moans grew louder, and the most delicious image of spreading Lyric's legs and fucking her against the wall filled my head. Dear God, I'd never wanted anyone or anything as badly as I wanted this gorgeous woman right now.

My tongue explored her mouth, and my right hand began to slide down her chest toward her breasts. It was at that moment I somehow managed to regain a tiny bit of my senses back.

Fuck, what the hell am I doing?

I pulled back as if I'd been stung, and Lyric blinked in confusion.

"Oh my God, Lyric, I'm so sorry. I—I didn't mean to be so forceful like that."

This sweet woman had always trusted me, and I'd let myself get carried away with her. Lyric was not some cleat chaser who was good for an easy lay, and I hoped like hell I hadn't made her feel like she was. I was afraid I'd made her feel like a high-priced hooker, like Eric had said.

"It's okay, Brady. Really."

I stared into her eyes, worried I would see discomfort or worse, terror. Instead, I saw desire. Or at least I thought I did. It's not like I was thinking clearly right now.

"No, it's not all right. I'm so sorry, Lyric. I swear, I didn't mean to be so rough."

"I'm *fine*, Brady. I'm not a little girl, you know. You don't have to be delicate with me."

"I know but I also shouldn't be overstepping any boundaries here," I said nervously. We hadn't set any official boundaries, but still. I was pretty sure fucking her against the wall wasn't in the original plan. "It's just, I know it's no excuse, but it's been a while since I've had sex. I guess I'm not used to that."

"I understand. It's been a while for me, too," she said, sounding as sexually frustrated as I was.

"Like how long?" I blurted out.

Lyric blushed deeply and looked away.

"Sorry, sorry. I shouldn't have … You don't have to answer that."

Without looking up, she said in a quiet voice, "You know, we could always … since we're both … and we can't, you know, with other people …" Lyric trailed off, still not looking at me.

"Are you suggesting we could be friends with benefits?" I said much louder than I should have. I was just so excited about the idea of having sex with her, I could hardly contain my enthusiasm.

"No. I—I just … Forget I said anything," Lyric said, clearly embarrassed. She hurried away from me and toward her bedroom to escape.

"Lyric, wait. Please!" I called after her, and for once, I wasn't thinking with my cock. I couldn't stand for her to be ashamed of voicing out loud what we'd both been thinking. It was kinda fucked up how women weren't allowed to admit they got horny too, sometimes. "Please, come back."

Sighing, she trudged back. Her face was red, and she looked like she was near tears. It tore me up to see her looking like that, and all I wanted to do was fix it as soon as possible.

"Lyric, come here." I opened my arms, and she went into them while avoiding my face. I hugged her briefly and released her so I could look at her. Wearily, she leaned back against the wall. I waited to speak until she lifted her face. "I want you to know that I have been incredibly, insanely attracted to you since the moment I laid eyes on you. Given our, you know, crazy circumstances, I wanted to always be very careful. The last thing I ever wanted was for you to feel like there were any kind of physical expectations that came along with this deal."

Lyric nodded, and the color drained from her face, but in a good way. She no longer looked like she wanted to die of shame.

"You are an amazingly desirable woman, Lyric Rivers, and I've done my best to be a gentleman around you. But that hasn't always been easy."

I watched her pause and swallow hard again, like she was gathering her courage. Then she said, "I appreciate that. But there are times when I don't want you to be a gentleman around me."

"Good to know." I dipped my head to kiss her again. Her body relaxed against mine as she wrapped her arms around my neck, and she eagerly kissed me back. My earlier vision came roaring back, and it was tough to fight the urge to rip off her clothes and take her against the wall. Judging by her desperate kisses and the moans of desire from her throat, Lyric was totally into this. Had it been any other woman, I would have taken her right then and there.

But this wasn't any other woman. This was Lyric.

Forcing myself to pull back, I said, "I'm not sure we should do this." My rock-hard cock protested angrily in my pants, like my body couldn't figure out why I wasn't inside the woman already.

"Why?" Lyric asked in a breathy, frustrated voice. I could see the sexual need in her eyes, and this side of her was *hot*. "There's no reason we can't satisfy each other's *needs*, Brady."

Good God, the way she said "needs" made me feel like not fucking her senseless would be downright cruel. She wanted this. She was practically begging for it. So why in hell was I about to say no?

"There is nothing in the world I want more than to fuck you so hard you won't be able to do anything but scream my name," I said through clenched teeth, my muscles tight. It took every ounce of restraint I had to keep control, and *restraint* was not something I had much of in the first place.

A soft whimper escaped her lips; she was practically drooling.

"Then do it," Lyric whispered.

"I want to, Lyric. More than I can possibly say. I know a thousand percent that it's what I want, but I have to make a thousand percent sure it's really what *you* want."

"And me practically throwing myself at you isn't enough?" she asked. She sounded so vulnerable, and it was killing me. A moment ago, she was blushing like a schoolgirl, and now she was asking me to have sex with her. That made the whole restraint idea so much harder.

"Look, I sleep around a lot, and I get the feeling you don't," I told her bluntly. "I don't want you doing anything you might regret just because we got caught up in the moment."

Her pretty blue eyes softened, and relief swept through my body. She was starting to understand that I wasn't rejecting her advances. I was trying to protect her.

"You're right. I'm not usually one to have casual sex. But I'm a grown woman, and I'm allowed to change my mind," she said in a sultry, seductive voice that threatened to destroy my defenses completely.

"True," I said. My resolve was weakening by the second, and the flash in Lyric's eyes told me she damn well knew it.

Restraint, restraint, restraint. No amount of glorious sex is worth hurting her. She is not some cleat chaser who'll be gone in the morning.

Having sex with Lyric could change everything between us. She was still gonna be living with me for the next few months, and I knew I would never forgive myself if she regretted being too impulsive. Lyric was well aware of my reputation with the ladies, and the thought of her feeling like a notch on my belt was unbearable.

"We can't do this now. We need a cooling off period."

"What?" she asked.

"We're both too ... hot right now and not thinking clearly."

Lyric sighed impatiently.

"Twenty-four hours," I said, knowing they would be the hardest hours of my life in every sense of the word. "Let's wait twenty-four hours, 'til this time tomorrow night. If you still want to have sex with me, I promise I will make it worth the wait."

Lyric swallowed hard, considering my words.

"It's not that I don't want you, Lyric," I said, hoping she could hear the truth and the desperate need in my voice. "I just can't bear the thought of hurting you. You want this now, but you might regret it tomorrow."

She nodded, but said, "I really don't think I would."

"But this way we can know for sure."

Lyric groaned and leaned against the wall. How I hated that look of frustration on her face. It went against everything in my nature to leave a woman sexually unfulfilled. I liked to have my fun with women, but I was not a selfish lover.

"Twenty-four hours, Lyric. In exactly one day's time, one spin on the Earth's axis, we can do anything you want if you haven't changed your mind."

"Brady, you are being incredibly stubborn. Not to mention kind of a martyr," she said irritably.

"I don't mean to be like that. Really. It's just, I don't know, sometimes women get all emotional when it comes to sex, and I don't ever want to do anything that might hurt you."

"I doubt most of the women you sleep with feel that way."

"Exactly. You are not like those women."

Lyric sighed. She knew I wasn't wrong.

"Look, there's nothing wrong with having sex for fun. But that's not really you, is it? Be honest. Have you ever had sex with a guy when you weren't in a committed relationship?"

"No. I haven't. But then again, until now, the opportunity never came up. I know you have women beating down your door in every city that has a major league baseball team, but I don't exactly have a line of men begging to sleep with me."

God, I hated how hurt she sounded when she said that. Lyric was incredibly desirable to me, and not just because she was pretty. She was smart, which was sexy as hell. And she was so kind the way she took care of that birthday kid at the ballpark, and she never complained, no matter how many fans interrupted our meals to ask for autographs.

The dejected look on her face was nearly enough to weaken my resolve completely. I could deny myself gratification for a day if it meant protecting her feelings. But what if turning her down now was just making her feel rejected?

No. All the more reason to wait a day. Lyric was vulnerable and seemed kind of down on herself at the moment. There was a good chance she might regret having sex with me now because she was seeking comfort.

One day. I could make it one day.

Still, it took everything I had not to scoop her up and carry her to my bedroom so I could make her feel like the deliciously desirable woman that she truly was.

Tomorrow. If she was still game tomorrow, I would make her feel sexy, desired, and beautiful, not to mention completely and utterly sexually satisfied.

"The only reason there isn't a line of men desperate to be with you is because they can't find you. You're always hiding in the library with your pretty nose in a book. Guys stare at you all the time, Lyric. You just don't notice."

It was true. Even though most people stared because they recognized me, I definitely caught guys checking her out. I hated when guys looked at her, so I tried not to think about it. I tended to assume that every guy who wanted Lyric was probably a helluva lot smarter than I was. Definitely more her type.

"That's nice of you to say, Brady," she said, clearly not believing a word I said.

"It's true. I feel like punching guys when I see them checking you out," I said without thinking,

"You do?" Lyric asked, sounding shocked.

"Well, yeah," I said, quickly recovering from nearly confessing my feelings for her. "I don't want any creeps perving on you."

"Oh. Well, that's sweet of you. You're really sure you want to wait until tomorrow?"

"I don't *want* to," I said, trying not to whine. "But I think it's the right thing to do. Tomorrow, Lyric. If you still want me, I'll be all yours. You can do anything you want with me."

She still looked a tad rejected, which made my chest ache.

"I have to say, I do admire your restraint."

Cupping her face, I said firmly, "Lyric, you have no idea how much restraining I've had to do every time I'm near you."

She swallowed, and I hoped she could hear the need in my voice and see it in my eyes.

Even the word "restraining" was getting me hot, conjuring up all sorts of images of handcuffing Lyric to the bed while she eagerly anticipated me having my way with her.

"I really need a cold shower right now," I said.

I knew damn well it would actually be a warm shower,

with me picturing what Lyric's face would look like while she was having an orgasm. Just thinking about it made me feel like I was going to explode.

"Tomorrow," I grunted, then kissed her a little too hard on her mouth before heading toward my bathroom.

I heard Lyric chuckle softly behind me.

CHAPTER 15

$\mathcal{L}$yric

HE DIDN'T SAY NO, he just said not yet.

As I got ready to go to bed, alone, I felt more sexually frustrated than I had ever been in my life. Still, if all went according to plan, by this time tomorrow night I should be sexually satisfied. I moaned out loud, imagining I'd barely be able to walk after a good hard pounding from Brady "the Crusher" Keaton.

I winced a bit, thinking about how I'd practically thrown myself at him. But I knew he was used to much more forward behavior from his many female admirers. And yet, I was pretty sure mine was the only sexual offer he'd turned down.

No. He hadn't turned me down. He merely said we should wait, and that was because he cared about my feelings, not because he didn't want to have sex. Just before he'd headed for the shower, Brady had looked like he was about to explode, which made me feel better. Not that I wanted him to be uncomfortable, but I needed to feel he desired me at least a little bit. I knew I was nowhere near as sexy as the women he was used to sleeping with, but right now it was me or nothing.

The next morning, I stood for a long time with my hand on the bedroom door handle, unable to go out and face Brady. I still hadn't changed my mind about wanting to have sex with him tonight, but it would still be rather weird to face the man who'd technically rejected my advances last night.

"Good morning," Brady said when I walked into the kitchen where he was sitting at the counter.

"Good morning." I grabbed a mug and helped myself to the coffee he had made. In fact, I took the carafe the second the coffeemaker dinged. Brady hadn't even gotten any yet.

He got up to get the coffee creamer, and then he picked up the sugar bowl. He brought both to me.

"Thanks," I said, quickly fixing my coffee just the way I liked it.

He selected his favorite mug—the really big one with Baltimore Bay Birds logo emblazoned on it—and poured himself a cup. I smiled as I watched him smell the coffee before he drank it.

Laughing, he said, "You're right. I do sniff my coffee."

"Every single time," I said with amusement.

"You sleep well?" he asked.

"I guess."

"Same," he said, making a face. "Wasn't easy settling down after you got me all fired up last night."

"Tell me about it," I grumbled.

Brady grinned at me. "So, have you changed your mind about tonight?"

"Hell no," I said, feeling bold. I gestured at his body. "I need to get me some of that."

He laughed heartily. "Love it. I *love* it!"

"What about you? Have you changed your mind?"

"Of course not. I've wanted to sleep with you since the second I laid eyes on you. The coffee was still burning my chest when I first had naughty thoughts about you."

"Really?"

"Hell yeah. There is no way I'm ever gonna change my mind, but no pressure, okay? For real. You still got eleven hours and twelve minutes to make a decision."

"But who's counting?" I said.

Brady mouthed the word "me" as he pointed to his chest, which made me laugh. It felt good to know he wanted me, even if it was probably only out of sexual desperation. I didn't believe his story about wanting me when we first met, but I enjoyed hearing him say it anyway.

After breakfast, I had to head out to class.

"Good luck on your test," Brady said as I slung my backpack over my shoulder. Winking at me, he said, "Hope you can concentrate."

"Me too," I said, resisting the urge to avoid his gaze. "See you tonight."

He groaned. "Gonna be a looong day 'til then."

"Wouldn't be so painful if you'd let me take care of you last night," I said in a singsong voice. I heard a louder groan from him as I shut the door.

Walking to school gave me a few minutes to think, clear my head. Unlike deciding to be Brady's fake girlfriend, I didn't have any back-and-forth feelings about this particular decision. Not anymore. There were definite risks, but I had every intention of plowing forward anyway. To put it simply, having sex with Brady "The Crusher" Keaton was a once-in-a-lifetime opportunity, and even Goody Two-shoes me wasn't about to pass it up. So crazy to think there were literally thousands of women out there who would give anything to be *in* my Goody Two-shoes right now. All those screaming fans, those mean girls who had sat behind me at the ballpark, all those ladies drooling over Brady as they watched him play ball. Most of them would never get the chance to go to bed with him.

And then there was the most important reason of all to have sex with him. The way I craved Brady's touch. I loved the way he engulfed me in his warm hugs after we'd been apart for a while. I loved the way he sometimes put his hand on my back when we were walking in public. Even though he was probably doing it to make sure people knew we were together, but it was hard to care. It just felt so damned good.

I couldn't help it. I loved being close to him, and sex was about as close as two people could get. Brady had a point that I might regret sleeping with him. For once, I decided to put that worry off for another day. Down the road when he was playing for Baltimore, I could bury my head in my medical school studies and try to forget that amazing time when I got to be Brady Keaton's girlfriend.

Putting Brady out of my head when I reached the campus, I focused on my physics test. It was by far my hardest class and I hated it, mainly because it seemed to have so little to do with medicine. But it was a requirement for my major, so I just had to get through it. No matter what, I would not allow Brady—or any man for that matter—to distract me from my goal of being a doctor.

* * *

THE TEST WASN'T AS bad as I had expected, and I was fairly confident I did okay on it. During a break between classes, I grabbed a bite to eat and then I had biochemistry class. My brain was pretty fried by the time I was done, and it felt good to breathe in the fresh air as I walked back to Brady's apartment. It was the middle of May, and it was getting warmer and brighter all the time.

Brady wasn't home when I got there, which wasn't unusual. During the day, he often went to the stadium to work out or he went to lunch with his friends on the team. It was just as well. I was nervous about tonight, and it would be good to have some time alone to mentally prepare.

I'd promised myself I wouldn't be another one of his one-night stands, but technically, this wouldn't have to be just a one-time thing. As long as we were supposedly together, he couldn't risk being caught with any other woman. Since the baseball contract stuff wouldn't happen until the fall, we'd be living together until then. If things went well tonight, we might end up having a lot of sex over the next few months.

Sounded like a good plan to me.

As much as I wanted more with Brady, he just wasn't the settling down type. He was the pretend to settle down type. I'd known from the beginning that this was a temporary situation, and when it was over, it would be over. Most likely, I was setting myself up for a huge fall by getting too close to him. That was a worry for future me. Current me just wanted to be with him as much as possible while I still could. I could overthink the hell out of it later when all I had left were the memories of having incredible sex with him.

Game time was 7:05 tonight. As usual, I had the ballgame on the TV while I studied.

It was torturous sitting through the game; I was a bundle of nerves and excitement. In the ninth inning, the Dominoes were down 6-3 with two guys on base. Though I would never want Brady's team to lose, I dreaded the thought of them tying the score and heading into extra innings.

I'm not rooting against you boys. But if you're gonna lose, please do it in nine innings.

They did lose, and I felt guilty for feeling so relieved. I wondered if even Brady had been secretly hoping they would lose so he could get home faster.

The minute the game ended, I jumped up from the couch. Unless he stayed around signing autographs, Brady would be home within the hour.

Since I owned no lingerie and not even a matching bra and panty set, I decided on the next best thing. I wore my oversized Richmond Dominoes shirt and panties and nothing else. My plan was to stand against the same wall where we'd kissed last night. That way, we could get right down to it the second he walked in the door.

This was downright sexually aggressive for me, and definitely out of my comfort zone, but Brady was worth it. I knew how much he would enjoy seeing me in a baseball shirt, and I wanted to make sure he knew I was totally cool with this. He'd seemed so hesitant last night, which was sweet, but it didn't get me laid. Greeting him dressed like this would hopefully convince him I was one hundred percent on board with this. He'd promised that we could do whatever I wanted tonight, and as far as I was concerned, the sooner we got started, the better.

Nearly an hour had passed after the game, and I started pacing nervously around the apartment. I gasped out loud when I finally heard his key card in the door. Rushing over to the wall, I did my best to try to look cool for when he opened the door. My insides were a jangled mess, so it wasn't easy.

After tossing his car keys into the bowl by the door, Brady's jaw literally dropped when he saw me. Staring, he slowly lowered his gym bag to the floor. I had to bite the inside of my cheek to keep from smiling; this was just the kind of reaction I'd hoped for.

"Are you wearing underwear?" was Brady's first question.

"Just panties."

He sucked in his breath and walked over to me, eying me up and down.

"You. Look. Incredible."

"Thanks. You like my shirt?" I asked, turning around so he could see the Keaton 8 on the back.

His eyes flashed with joy. "When did you get that?"

"Bought it at that game I went to."

"I love it, Lyric."

"Good. I don't have any fancy underwear or anything, so I figured this was the next best thing."

"Yeah," Brady said, practically drooling. "I take it this means you haven't changed your mind."

"Nope."

"Thank God," he said, and then in one swift move, he scooped me up off my feet.

I cried out in surprise and flung my arms around his neck. Holding me tight, Brady charged toward his bedroom.

This is definitely going to be worth the wait.

All of his earlier hesitation had disappeared. He'd been given the green light, and now he was going full steam ahead. *Awesome.*

Brady kicked the door open like he was a hero firefighter in the movies, and it sent a thrill of excitement and desire rippling throughout my entire body. He carried me to the bed, laid me down, and quickly straddled me. Gazing down at me, his eyes blazed with desire.

"I would have understood, you know. If you'd changed your mind. But I am so goddamn glad you didn't, because I can honestly say I've never wanted any woman as badly as I want you right now."

The crazed look in his eyes almost made me believe he found me as sexy as all those women he'd been with. Deep down, I knew he was just hard up. He hadn't had sex since the day we met, and he was desperate. Any meal was delicious to a starving man.

Brady slid his hands underneath my shirt, closing his eyes and groaning when he reached my naked breasts. I arched my back to give him better access, reveling in the feel of his large hands massaging my chest. He caressed my nipples with his thumbs, sending a tingling bolt of sheer sexual need that traveled straight down from my breasts to the spot between my legs. His hands gripped the bottom of my shirt and he yanked it off me.

He took a moment to admire me as I lay there clad only in my white cotton panties. "*Goddamn*, you look good," he said, his eyes traveling up and down my body.

Though he was still fully clothed, I admired his broad chest. I knew what he looked like shirtless from his magazine photos, but now I wanted to see the real thing.

"I want to see you, too," I said, tugging at his T-shirt.

"Anything you want, Doc," he said, grinning as he pulled his shirt off with one hand.

Drawing in a sharp breath, I said, "Wow." As expected, the guy was *ripped*. "The magazine pictures don't do you justice."

"Saw those, did you?" he asked in a teasing voice.

I nodded. "Part of my research before I moved in with you."

Brady gave me all the time I wanted to admire his chest. He even flexed his muscles for me. Had anyone else done that, they might have looked like a cartoon character showing off, but Brady's muscles were huge and bulged impressively when he flexed.

I reached out to touch his arm and he moved toward me. Running my hand up and down his arm and shoulder muscles, I said, "You are so *strong*."

Brady smiled, seeming genuinely pleased with the compliment.

"I want to see the rest," I said, lowering my eyes to his jeans.

"Done," he said, unbuckling his pants. His willingness to obey my commands was such a turn on. Exciting how he seemed willing to do anything I asked, even little things like removing one item of clothing at a time.

My heart raced with excitement at the thought. I wasn't exactly the sexually adventurous type, but it was thrilling to think of all the ways this athletic man could satisfy my needs.

At last, Brady was completely naked for me. I stared at his cock, finding it every bit as huge as I'd expected. My breath came in short gasps; I was literally panting at the idea of having his huge penis inside of me.

Again, he allowed me all the time I wanted to admire his manhood. While I stared at what he had to offer between his legs, he reached over to his nightstand and grabbed a condom. I watched as he slowly put it on, wide-eyed at the way he struggled a bit to stretch the latex over his girth. When he was done, I lifted my gaze back to his eyes. Wasting no time, he grabbed my panties and yanked them off me.

Planting his palms on the mattress near my head, he kissed my mouth as he straddled me. I threw my hands around his neck as his lips devoured mine. He shifted his body slightly so his cock pressed firmly between my legs.

Oh dear God, I need this man inside me right now.

His kisses were divine, deep, passionate, and slowly driving me out of my mind with desire. His cock was so close to where I needed it.

I knew all I had to do was ask. Tell him what I wanted, what I needed, and he would do it. My body was practically screaming at my brain to just say the words out loud.

Still kissing me, Brady gently pushed my hair out of my

face. It was at that exact moment, with that simple, tender gesture, that I knew I was safe with him. I could say anything I wanted. He wouldn't make fun of me or make me feel pathetic or desperate.

"Brady, please. Give it to me. *Now*," I pleaded.

Moving his lips from my mouth down to my neck, he murmured, "Anything you want, Doc. *Anything*."

He grabbed his cock to position himself at the perfect spot between my legs and then rammed into me. I was so slick that he filled me up completely in one, delicious thrust.

Crying out with sharp pleasure, I arched my back, allowing him to penetrate me even deeper.

"Yes! Yes!" I screamed as he slammed in and out of me.

"Oh God, Lyric," Brady grunted in my ear.

Selfishly, I'd been so focused on my own pleasure that I'd nearly forgotten his. Judging by the ecstatic expression on his face, Brady was having as much fun as me. God, we were good together. Moving in perfect rhythm, each thrust felt more pleasurable than the last.

Thank God I hadn't let my stupid inhibitions keep me from this incredible experience. Having sex with a professional athlete was like ... well, there was *nothing like* having sex with a professional athlete. Brady was massive, and having him on top of me, inside me, was the most exhilarating experience of my life.

"Lyric," he said softly, meeting my gaze as he made love to me.

And suddenly it didn't matter that I was having incredible sex with a celebrity ballplayer. Brady was so much more than that. He was my best friend and the man I adored. And sex with him would have been thrilling even if he'd had an average body.

"Tell me what you need," he said. I could see he was struggling, holding back for my sake. He needed to come, but he wanted to take care of me first.

"Finger me, Brady," I said, knowing I needed more direct stimulation to my most intimate spot. He slipped his fingers between my legs, rubbing my clit while still pumping in and out of me. My eyes rolled back in my head as the already intensely pleasurable sensations doubled, tripled, even. "Faster, Brady. Oh God, faster."

I grew quiet for a moment, only seconds away from total sexual release. The bed squeaked rhythmically, and Brady and I both panted heavily in anticipation as we rocked each other's worlds.

"Crush, ah!" I screamed when I reached my long-awaited peak.

"Attagirl," Brady said, and I was acutely aware of him watching me as I rode wave after wave of pure, orgasmic bliss. Oh, how I loved the intimacy of it all. His cock and fingers stroking my most intimate spots while he watched me during the most private and pleasurable moment a woman could experience.

Then it was my turn to watch Brady lose control. Closing his eyes, he pounded me harder and harder. Letting out the sexiest guttural sound, he came with tremendous *force*. How delightful to watch his face go from fierce concentration to utter relief.

"Oh my God," he groaned as he rolled off me. Brady took only a few seconds to recover, then he reached for me, pulling me close.

"Mmmm," I said, melting into his arms.

This might only be a friends with benefits thing, but I was deeply grateful that Brady took the time to hold me afterward. I would have felt cheap and used if he'd just gotten out of bed right away.

After cradling me for a few minutes, he let go and turned on his side to face me. "You good?"

He gazed carefully into my eyes as if scanning for signs of discomfort, or perhaps regret. He genuinely looked worried.

"I'm good. More than good. That was incredible. Probably even more incredible since you forced me to wait so long."

Brady chuckled, and I saw relief in his eyes.

"You were amazing, Crush," I said, noting that familiar softness in his gaze when I called him by that name.

"You too. We should do that again sometime," he said hopefully.

"Give me some time to recover," I said with a laugh. "But yeah. I'm definitely up for another round."

"Cool. You better get some rest."

"Yeah," I said.

With tremendous mental and emotional effort, I managed to get out of bed. I bent over to pick up my baseball shirt, and I heard Brady groan with approval. I bit my lip to keep from laughing, since it was no accident that I'd bent over like that in front of him.

I slid the shirt over my head but clutched the panties in my fist instead of putting them on.

"Sweet dreams, Crush."

"You too, Doc."

I headed off to my room, knowing the bed would feel cold without him.

CHAPTER 16

rady

Now that I'd slept with her, Lyric was dearer to me than ever before. Usually, it was the opposite. The thrill was pretty much gone after I slept with most women, and I was ready to move on to the next one. Such a strange feeling to think now that I'd been inside of her, I wanted *more* of her. The idea that I might want to have a real girlfriend was a new experience for me.

Lyric walked into the kitchen, and seeing her literally took my breath away. I stared at her for a moment, still adjusting to the intensity of my reaction. Funny how I'd been so worried about her emotional state after having sex; it never once crossed my mind how sleeping with her might affect *me*.

"Good morning, Doc."

"Hey, Crush," she said with a smile.

"Hope you got some sleep last night."

"I did," she said. "Turns out fabulous sex is great for a good night's rest."

I took the creamer out of the fridge and set it down next to the sugar bowl for her.

"So, this lack of underwear thing," I began, raising my eyebrows.

"What?" she asked with a delightful little giggle.

"First of all, I want to make it abundantly clear that I am a huge fan of you greeting me at the door with no bra."

"Okay, good," Lyric said as she prepped her morning coffee.

"But is your lack of fancy bras and panties because you don't have the money? Or do you just not like that sort of thing?"

She shrugged. "I dunno. I don't have anything against nice underwear. But if I won the lottery, I can't say it would be the first thing I would run out and buy."

"I'm asking if I'm allowed to buy some of that stuff for you. You don't even have to wear it for me or anything. I like spoiling you, but you won't let me buy you jewelry and stuff."

"Sure. I guess that would be okay."

"Text me your sizes. Unless you wanna pick out stuff yourself."

She smiled before sipping her coffee. "You can surprise me."

"Cool."

"Thanks, Crush. That's really thoughtful of you."

Though I didn't want to stare at her, I found it hard to tear my gaze away. She was just so pretty. That, and now I knew what she looked like naked. I also knew what it felt like to hold her close in my arms, and not just for a quick hug. Sex with her had been incredible in every possible way. Relieving my pent-up sexual frustration was only the beginning. I couldn't get over how right it felt to finally take her to my bed.

I had another multi-day road trip with the team pretty soon, and I knew I was gonna miss the hell out of her. I wanted to spend as much time with her as possible before I went.

"I know this is last minute, but do you want to go to the game today?" I hated how needy my voice sounded, so I tried to recover. "I was thinking, if you came to batting practice before the game, I could talk to you a little while you're in the stands and I'm on the field. You know, make it clear you're my girlfriend and all that."

I watched her think for a minute, probably going over her study and volunteer schedule in her mind. Since it was Saturday, I knew she didn't have class, but she often had other things going on.

"Yeah. Yeah, that should work. I've got final exams coming up," she said with a grimace. "Which is super stressful. But taking the afternoon off isn't a bad idea."

"Cool! I mean about coming to the game. Not about your stress level."

"Well, we did discover a way to decrease my stress," she said in a seductive voice that made me want to scoop her up and charge back into my bedroom with her. "Having terrific sex helped clear my head, which is great for studying."

"Does that mean I have an even better chance of getting laid during exam week?"

"Maybe so. As long as I still have enough time to study between sex sessions."

I groaned, leaning against the counter. "You kill me when you talk like that."

Her chest heaved as she drew in a breath. "What time is batting practice?"

"It's at 12:30. Why?" I asked, my cock stiffening. "Need a study break already?"

"Maybe," she said. The hunger in her eyes made me feel like I was the greatest lover in the world. It was like she'd gotten a taste of me and wanted more.

"Think we have time for a quickie?"

"Let's make time." She put down her coffee cup so fast, the liquid sloshed from the sides.

Needing no further invitation, I rushed over to her and crushed her mouth with mine. Even though she was wearing a bra this time, I could still feel her hard nipples poking through. I loved how much Lyric *wanted* me. Lots of women wanted me, but who the hell cared? The only woman I wanted was her.

Instead of picking her up, I grabbed her hand and pulled her to the bedroom. With none of the finesse of last night, we ripped off each other's clothes. Time was of the essence, after all. As soon as we were both naked, I grabbed a condom and got myself ready.

Pushing her down on the bed, I straddled her, ready to ride her hard until she screamed in ecstasy.

"No," she said.

"What? Oh God, am I hurting you?" Sometimes I forgot how big I was, and she was rather petite.

"No, I just wanna be on top," she said, blue eyes flashing with excitement.

"Oh, hell yeah," I said, gripping her shoulders and flipping her so she could straddle me.

She giggled happily, then bit her lip in a way that made me nuts. Lyric lowered herself onto my cock, and we both moaned once I was inside her again. She arched her back, a motion that thrust her breasts forward. She rode me hard, her dark hair falling back, eyes closed as she cried out with pleasure. It seemed every time we fooled around, she became more and more uninhibited. It was awesome.

As thrilling and pleasurable as it was having Lyric in charge, it made it almost impossible for me to keep control.

"Oh God, Doc," I said. "You feel so good, I'm not gonna make it much longer."

"Okay," she said, her breath coming in gasps. She ground herself against my cock in a steady, rhythmic motion to maximize her pleasure. "Ah, ah, ah ..."

It was so hot to watch her chase her orgasm that I nearly exploded myself. Then she threw her head back with one final, "Ah!" and I knew she'd reached her peak. Grunting, I reached mine only seconds later. I hadn't thought my second orgasm with Lyric would be as intense as the first. But I was wrong.

"Damn, girl. That was *hot.*" I said in a vast understatement.

"Yeah," she said, breathing heavily. She climbed off me, collapsing by my side.

"You're a wild woman, Lyric. I've never seen you like that before."

She smiled. "I guess I just feel safe with you."

"I sure do love hearing that," I said, pulling her close and holding her. I was sorely tempted to gently stroke her hair, but somehow that seemed too intimate. That was ludicrous, of course, considering the woman had just ridden me like a racehorse. Still, we were supposed to be friends with benefits, and not real lovers.

Lyric's stomach growled, making her giggle.

"Oh, shit. You haven't eaten yet. Come on, let's get you fed."

"Sounds good to me," she said, getting out of bed and putting her clothes back on.

"And remind me to give you my credit card in case you

want more food later at the ballpark. Shit is so expensive there."

"Thanks, Crush. I appreciate it."

"You're welcome, Doc."

After we got dressed, we stood there a moment. I reached over and pulled her into a hug. As usual, her body relaxed, melting into mine.

"You're the best, Lyric. The *best*."

* * *

WE TOOK my car to the stadium, and I dropped off Lyric at the front.

"Gates should be open by now, and your ticket will be at will call."

"Thanks," she said, looking freaking adorable with her dark hair swept up in a ponytail and wearing her Keaton 8 T-shirt.

Lyric gave me a hug before getting out of the car. I loved that we no longer had to fake intimacy, and it wasn't just about the sex. We were genuinely fond of each other, and it showed.

I watched her walk toward the will call window, admiring her cute butt in her tight jeans. And of course that shirt conjured up naughty images of her wearing it with no bra underneath.

Once she'd disappeared inside the gate, I drove over to the player's parking lot. Lyric and I had discussed our plan on the way to Dominion Park. She would watch batting practice—BP in baseball speak—from her seat. Then at some point she would walk over and talk to me while I was on the field. Fans often gathered around the edge of the stadium during BP, trying to get autographs. Second only to the player's parking lot, it was one of the best ways to get the players' attention. I would sign some autographs, but more importantly, I would give Lyric special attention and make it clear we were an item. That was bound to get my teammates attention, since they'd never known me to be serious about any woman. If we were really lucky, the media on the field would take notice as well.

I smiled as I slung my gym bag over my shoulder and walked through the tunnel from the players' lot to our locker room. Though I knew Lyric was uncomfortable attracting too much attention, I relished the idea of doting on her in public. I wanted to let the fans know she was my girlfriend, especially after what happened last time with those awful girls in her section. If I lavished attention on her before the game, the fans would treat her like a queen.

I hit a bunch of long balls during practice, not like that was hard to do. Unlike during the game, the pitcher wasn't trying to strike me out. He was helping me to perfect my swing.

I was acutely aware of Lyric's eyes on me the whole time. I found it comforting to know she was there, cheering me on. That, and I loved showing off for her. I was proud of my powerful swing, and I hoped she was impressed. Batting practice was the perfect opportunity to show off without it affecting the actual game.

As promised, Lyric wandered over to the edge of the stadium, as close as fans could get to the field while remaining in the stands. I waved at her, and she smiled and waved back. Even that small gesture got her some attention from the fans that had gathered hoping for autographs. I heard murmurs ripple through the group as they realized the dark-haired beauty wearing my shirt actually knew Brady "The Crusher" Keaton personally.

I strutted over, keeping eye contact with her. Once I reached the group of fans who had been waiting patiently, I started plucking some baseballs from eager fans and signing them. As always, I went to the kids first. After I'd taken care of all the little guys, I signed a few programs, photos, and baseballs for the adults.

One of them happened to be a very attractive adult female fan. She wrote her phone number on her program before handing it to me.

Chuckling, I said, "Sorry. I'm spoken for."

I briefly signed my name on one of the glossy pages and handed it back to the woman. Then, as if to prove my point, I turned to Lyric.

"Hey, baby," I said, though I kinda regretted it. "Baby" sounded artificial, especially since I didn't think I'd ever called her that before. "Doc" would have been better. She was standing a few feet away from the on-deck circle, where batters practiced their swing during the game when they were up next at the plate. It was a good spot because there was a dip in the railing there for some reason, which allowed her to get closer to me.

"Hey, Crush," she said with a smile that lit up her eyes. My body tingled all over when she looked at me like that. It was fun having a shared secret that only we were in on.

Tenderly stroking her face, I said, "You should take my credit card and get a baseball cap. Your skin is so fair, I don't want you to burn."

"Probably a good idea. Thanks."

Lowering my voice, I said, "I'm gonna kiss you, okay?"

It seemed weird to ask her permission, considering we'd had sex twice in the last twenty-four hours. Still, I was wary of doing anything in public without asking.

"Okay," she said, her eyes still smiling. Yeah. She was cool with it, and I was proud of how well she was handling all this attention.

I had to stretch a bit to reach her lips, but we made it

work. Several hoots and wolf whistles came up from the crowd, and I felt her lips tremble with laughter while still pressed against mine.

"Mission accomplished," I mumbled after breaking off the kiss. She nodded, still giggling a bit. Then, on a sudden impulse, I said quietly in her ear, "I'm gonna say I love you, okay?"

"Okay," she said in a breathy voice.

After pulling away from her, I said, "See ya later. Love you, Doc!"

"Love you too!" Lyric called out to me, being the good sport that she was.

Louder murmurs came up from the crowd. They were clearly surprised at the notion that Brady Keaton was in love.

As I strolled away from the stands, my heart suddenly seized in my chest. I almost froze in place, but I forced myself to keep walking and act as if everything was normal and I hadn't just had a life-changing epiphany.

Oh dear God, I am in love.

It wasn't until I'd said the words out loud that I realized it was true. I was in love with Lyric.

Still walking, I turned around to glance casually at her. She was finding her way to her seat a few rows behind home plate, and the fans were already talking to her. Most likely, they were peppering her with questions about me. Lyric laughed graciously as she spoke to them. She was so sweet and patient.

Fortunately, I turned back around to watch where I was going only seconds before I would have slammed into the opposing first baseman who'd been shagging balls during practice.

"Sorry, man," I mumbled. Shit. I had to get myself together. Get my head in the game.

It wasn't easy, but I managed to compartmentalize my

feelings and focus on the game. Having Lyric in the stands actually helped in that regard, since I didn't want to look stupid in front of her, nor did I want to embarrass her in front of the fans. I could just imagine fumbling balls in the infield all night and swinging at bad pitches, leaving Lyric to have to deal with fans booing me.

All in all, I had a good night. Got on base twice, though I didn't get to drive anybody home or cross the plate myself. I winced a bit when I saw Lyric featured on the jumbotron twice during the game. I knew that was no accident. No doubt the media guys up in the booth had seen us together during BP and knew we were together. In fact, I wouldn't be surprised if she even got featured on television. It wasn't unheard of for TV announcers to feature players' wives and family members during the broadcast.

Champ that she was, Lyric had smiled and waved when she saw herself on the jumbotron. Seeing her up there had sent a renewed wave of affection and love for her through my whole body.

I had fallen in love with my pretend girlfriend. That was *so* not supposed to happen. Now what the hell should I do?

The Dominoes won by a score of 5-2. At the end of the game, I looked over and saw Lyric standing and cheering with the rest of the fans. Though I knew her enthusiasm was real and that she genuinely wanted the team to win, I wished she was cheering me on as my actual girlfriend. The woman in my life. Hell, for the first time ever, I actually pictured a woman as my *wife.*

That revelation hit harder than the first one. How could things have changed so fast in my life?

Was it humanly possible that Lyric might ever feel the same way about me? That was the bigger question.

For about two seconds, I thought about carefully broaching the subject of wanting to be more than friends, but I abandoned the idea just as fast. It might completely fuck up what we had, and I was not about to risk losing Lyric from my life.

Sighing like a lovesick teenager, I took one last look at Lyric before disappearing into the dugout.

CHAPTER 17

$\mathscr{L}$yric

AFTER YESTERDAY'S GAME, Brady and I became an overnight sensation. Though I'd never been particularly close to my college roommates, I got several texts from Kerry and Jill telling me that the local news reporters had been talking about us on their morning show. Apparently, the TV sportscasters covering the game had noticed us together at batting practice and had watched me during the game. They'd even referred to me as "The lady in Brady Keaton's life."

I physically shuddered to think I'd been on television without my knowledge. The jumbotron had been strange enough. That hadn't seemed so terrible, though, since I figured it was just for people at the game, and it was all in good fun. Besides, I was proud of Brady and had no problem cheering publicly for him. Being on the sports broadcast and now the local news was a bit much.

Brady had left for his west coast trip before I woke up, so

I didn't get to say goodbye. I wondered if he knew what was going on, and how we were the talk of Richmond right now.

I smiled when I saw Brady had thoughtfully prepared the coffeemaker for me so all I had to do was press the button. While it brewed, I scanned the Richmond Dominoes magnet schedule that was posted on the fridge. Just as I'd thought, most of the games wouldn't even start until 10:35pm because the team was in California. Past my bedtime, so I probably wouldn't get to see much of the series.

The schedule also had the media information on it, meaning you could see what channel would show the game. Most of the time it was the local sports network. When I happened to glance at yesterday's game on the magnet, I froze.

Yesterday's game had been a *national* broadcast, not a local one.

Feeling a bit dizzy, I wandered into the living room and turned on the TV. It was already tuned to the cable sports channel. *SportsCenter* was on, though it was currently on a commercial break. By the time I retrieved my coffee from the kitchen and came back, the show was on.

I sat on the couch and breathed in my coffee, just as Brady always did. It smelled delicious, and I smiled as I thought of him.

I drew in another deep, steady breath as watching *Sports-Center* confirmed my fears; Brady and I were national news. Setting down my coffee on a coaster on the table next to me, I reminded myself that this was good news. At least Brady would be thrilled. The Baltimore owners were bound to catch wind of this. Everybody knew we were a serious item now, and they would see us together more and more over the next few months. That would do wonders for Brady's reputation and give him a great shot at playing for Baltimore.

Tears sprang to my eyes. *Happy* tears. The idea of Brady

achieving his lifelong dream filled me with joy. I could deal with the media attention if it helped him. It was worth it. *He* was worth it.

Because I loved him.

Hearing him say "Love you, Doc" yesterday had really thrown me for a loop. It was all part of the act, of course. He'd warned me ahead of time that he was going to say it. I wished he hadn't told me in advance, and then I could have at least fantasized that he might have meant the words. That he did have those feelings for me, and he'd accidentally confessed them to me. Brady wasn't known for his impulse control, after all.

But that's not what had happened. His profession of love was pre-planned. If nothing else, it had felt good to be able to say the words out loud myself.

I knew I was wading into dangerous territory. We were having sex now, and our relationship was quite public. When we were out together, displays of affection would be expected. And Brady was genuinely affectionate with me when we were in private. He frequently hugged me, was always good about holding me after sex, and he seemed fond of me as a friend. We did care about each other; the line between make-believe and reality was getting blurrier by the minute.

Was it possible his friendly affection for me had blossomed into love?

There was no way to tell without flat-out asking him, and that sure as hell wasn't going to happen.

I went back into the kitchen to make breakfast. All alone, I found myself missing his good humor and warm, playful smile.

* * *

STRANGELY ENOUGH, I liked the way the hospital smelled. That weird mix of cleaners and antiseptic was oddly inviting —it smelled like excitement and adventure. I was thrilled to be working toward my dream of becoming a doctor, and volunteering at the hospital as often as possible made me feel like I was inching closer to it all the time.

"Hi, Lyric," Dr. Bennett said when I walked into her office. Her door was almost always open, literally and figuratively. She was the best mentor ever, because even though she was incredibly busy, she always had time for me. I had talked to some volunteers who worked with other doctors and knew that wasn't always the case.

"Hey, Dr. Bennett," I said, sitting down in the chair across from her desk. She was clearly in the middle of working on something on her computer, so I kept quiet for a minute.

"Okay," she said, turning her attention to me when she'd finished typing. "The next stop on your hospital tour will be emergency medicine."

"Oh, cool," I said with enthusiasm.

"Yeah, it really is. That's where the action is for sure. It will be quite a different experience from cardiology."

"I bet."

She looked at me curiously, her dark brown eyes unusually inquisitive. "Lyric, can I ask you something?"

"Sure."

"You don't have to answer if you don't want to."

"Uh-uh," I said, laughing nervously. "Should I be worried?"

"Of course not. My apologies, but I have to ask. What is *up* with you and Brady Keaton?"

I laughed again, no longer feeling nervous, since her question had nothing to do with my performance here at the hospital.

"Oh, that."

"I was watching the game on TV, and I practically fell out of my chair," Dr. Bennett said, her eyes wide.

I moaned. "Yeah, I heard they showed me during the broadcast. I didn't know you were a baseball fan."

"Oh, I love it. It's hard to get to any games because of my crazy work schedule, but I catch the games on TV when I can. It's always fun talking about the Dominoes with patients, too. If they've got the game on when I'm doing my rounds, it's a nice way to connect with them."

That was the special connection people had to baseball that Brady had been trying to explain to me. I remembered how he said games were something for patients to look forward to when they got out of the hospital. It never once occurred to me that sick people might be watching the game during their stay here.

"So is he your man, or what?"

I supposed the answer was "or what," but I wasn't about to spill the truth to my boss.

"Yeah, kinda. He's my boyfriend." Technically, he was my boyfriend, even if it was only temporary. We were living together, sleeping together, and I was in love with him.

"*Damn,*" she said, obviously quite impressed. I would rather have her be impressed with my college grades or medical performance, but I admired her so much that I would take anything I could get from her.

"Yeah," I said with a smile.

"How did that happen? I mean, how did you meet him?"

I explained what I had done to him at the coffee shop when we first met, which got a hearty laugh out of her. Once again, I reveled in getting such attention from my personal heroine.

"He's good to you, though, right?" Dr. Bennett said. "He treats you well?"

"Oh yes, definitely. He's a real sweetheart."

"Good, good. That's what I want to hear." She paused for a moment and then asked, "Have you met any of the other players on the team?"

"No, not yet. It's all rather new. And he's so busy. They're on the road right now."

"Oh, that's right. They're in L.A., and then they play Seattle."

Wow. She really *was* a fan.

"Right."

Dr. Bennett eyed me curiously, like she wanted to ask a bunch more questions. However, after a brief pause, she changed the subject.

"Anyway! Back to work. Let's go get you oriented in the ED."

She got up and we headed over to the Emergency Department. After she introduced me to the doctors and nurses there, she went back to her office.

Being in the ED was quite an experience. It was a busy few hours, and time flew by. We had some heart patients, most of whom were taken to triage right away to rule out heart attacks. They were sent back to the waiting room once the doctors were confident they weren't in immediate danger. We had an adorable three-year-old who had broken her arm after falling off a swing. Seeing her cry broke my heart, but her smile once she was all fixed up with a brightly colored cast was incredibly rewarding. I still wasn't interested in pediatrics as a discipline, but I could see the appeal of it for sure.

Things really got wild when they brought in a shooting victim. It was like on television, with everybody rushing around. My job was to observe, learn, and stay the hell out of the way. The doctors managed to stabilize him by the time my shift was over. I really hoped the guy would make it.

I was beyond exhausted by the time I got home. I washed

up and collapsed into bed; my last thoughts before falling asleep were of Brady. He had such a late game tonight, and I hoped he wasn't too tired with all the traveling and the time difference.

I wondered if he was thinking of me too.

CHAPTER 18

rady

I STARED at the hotel television in awe. The rumors about me and Lyric had been in overdrive since the game on Saturday. It was Monday morning, and we were still big news.

I'd ordered a late breakfast from room service. Sitting at the small table in my suite, I ate and caught up on the sports news. *SportsCenter* wasn't normally known as a source of celebrity gossip, but today it certainly was. Turned out the cameras had caught me kissing Lyric after batting practice. I'd totally forgotten that the game was being broadcast nationally, so my little plan to get attention had worked out way better than I could have hoped. I grabbed my phone and looked up the Richmond news, and there had been a brief mention about Brady Keaton's girl. Next, I searched up the usual gossip sites that had always given me tons of attention in the past. Between the sports news and local news mentioning us a little and the gossip rags talking about us a lot, Lyric and I were everywhere.

It was crazy the way people were talking about us like we were some royal couple. Well, maybe not exactly like a royal couple, since only one of us was famous. It was more like when a movie star suddenly married a civilian that nobody had ever heard of, and people reported on it like it was a fairytale romance.

I barely tasted my bacon and eggs as I looked for clips from the local Richmond television news on my computer. Apparently, the sports reporters had spoken to some of the fans who had been sitting near Lyric during the game. One of the reporters said the fans had given Lyric a "rave review," saying how sweet she was and how happy she seemed to cheer me on. The guy said Brady's "mystery girl" seemed to be "down to earth" and "very nice."

Thank God the public seemed to like Lyric already. Not that I cared so much about what people thought, but it would have been unbearable if the media had trashed her. She had a hard enough time with *positive* attention.

Lyric.

I wondered what she was doing right now. I wondered if she missed me. I hoped she was doing okay with everything blowing up in the media. She watched *SportsCenter* fairly regularly now, which I loved. She said she always liked to see if they mentioned me. Between that and the Richmond news, she must be aware of what was going on. As much as I wanted to call to check on her, I knew she was probably in class by now.

Later on, during BP at the stadium in Los Angeles, I wasn't surprised when a local reporter wanted to interview me. Not only did that happen all the time, I knew the TV station had more than just sports in mind today. We started with the usual banter about batting lineups, and we talked about my difficulties with the L.A. starting pitcher. The dude had a fierce cut fastball that I had a tough time connecting with.

With the business portion of the interview out of the way, Chuck Miller, ace reporter, carefully introduced the subject of the girl I'd recently been spotted with.

"So Brady," the reporter with the frozen-in-place TV-anchor hairdo began, "You've always had a reputation for being quite the devil with the ladies, but rumor has it there might be a special woman in your life."

I grinned. Having spent all morning thinking about how I was going to respond when directly asked about Lyric, I was ready with all my talking points. This was Chuck Miller's lucky day because he was about to score the inside scoop.

"Oh yes. There is definitely a special lady in my life."

Chuck's eyes grew wide, and he held his tongue, waiting for me to continue.

"Her name is Lyric Rivers. She's a medical student. Well, she's currently majoring in pre-health studies in college, and then she's gonna go to medical school to become a doctor. Don't ask me what a gorgeous, super-smart girl like her is doing with a schmuck like me, 'cuz I got no idea."

It was so much fun building Lyric up like that on television. Every word I said was true of course, and I relished the chance to say nice things about her publicly. Giving this interview might do wonders for my chances with Baltimore, but it was funny how that didn't seem to be all that important at the moment. Fake relationship or not, it felt good to talk about Lyric as my girlfriend.

"How long have you been seeing her?" Chuck asked, keeping his tone even. He was probably bursting to ask many more questions, but he likely knew damn well how quickly celebrities clammed up if you weren't careful how you approached them.

"A few months now. Been kinda keepin' it on the down low for a while. Unlike a lot of women, Lyric's a little shy about getting lots of attention." That was true, and I knew saying it would make her even more endearing to the public. As I spoke, I realized the royal couple angle made more sense than I thought. I was the prince, and she was kinda like Cinderella or Snow White or any of those other poor girls. Only in the financial sense of being poor, though. Lyric was a strong, smart woman who needed no rescuing from a prince.

I really wanted people to see her as the heroine in our story.

"Lyric is amazing. I haven't really talked about her in the media until now because I wanted to respect her privacy. I'm only talking about her now because the word's out. Still, she's really not the flashy type, and dating somebody famous can be a little uncomfortable for someone like her," I said to the reporter.

"I can understand that," Chuck responded. He stared at me as if willing me to keep talking.

"Lyric has been good for me. She keeps me grounded. As everybody knows, I used to party and drink a lot. Sometimes got myself in trouble, but she helps me realize that's not a great way to live." I paused for a moment, worrying that I was making Lyric sound like a nag or a buzzkill. "Being with her is so much better than staying out late and partying. Never thought I would want to settle down, but ..."

I trailed off, and it was an effort to keep from laughing at Chuck's carefully controlled expression. I could see he was exploding with excitement at my revelatory interview. I was just glad I'd gotten out the words "settle down" on the air. Hopefully the Baltimore owner would hear that and it would get him thinking about me as a prospect.

"Lyric changed all that. I'm in love with her," I said with a shrug like it was no big deal.

"Really?" Chuck said with enthusiasm.

"Yup," I said. The interview had gone perfectly as far as I was concerned, and there was no reason to press my luck. "Well, it was good talking to you. I better go practice my swing if I want any chance at the killer cut fastball. Take it easy!"

I handed him back my mic and took off so fast that Chuck couldn't have caught me if he tried. Not without tripping over microphone wires and whatever else he was tethered to.

I wound up glad that tonight's game had started so late on the east coast and Lyric probably hadn't seen any of it. Definitely not my best showing; I really did struggle against that nasty fastball. Falling back on my bad habit of impulsiveness and swinging at the first pitch, I went 0 for 4 and we lost 7-0. It did suck that it was also too late to call or text Lyric so she could commiserate with me. She was always great about reassuring me after a rough outing.

After the game, I just couldn't bear the idea of going back to my hotel room alone.

I was stressed out and wide awake, and I knew a drink or two would help me unwind and decompress. So when Tyler asked me to go out with him, I caved and decided to go. He was pretty surprised since I'd been turning him down so often lately. By now he knew I was serious about my girlfriend and wasn't about to go whoring around like I used to. I figured a couple of drinks wouldn't hurt, as long as I didn't get out of control.

Tyler and I went to the bar at the hotel so we wouldn't have to worry about getting a ride back when we were done. That, and he could just take whatever girl he managed to pick up back to his room. I felt better immediately after having a drink. Really did take the edge off after a bad night. Several women approached us. Well, they approached *me* and, as usual, they went to Tyler when I turned them down. I was sure to make it abundantly clear that I was off the market because I had a sweet girlfriend, whom I loved.

It was such a rush to be able to say those words out loud. *I love my girlfriend.* I felt like a cheesy romantic comedy hero who was in love for the first time and wanted to shout it from the rooftops. Supposedly, women loved when guys made grand romantic gestures, like writing some lovey-dovey message in skywriting or serenading them with some love song. Thinking of Lyric and how much she hated that kind of thing made me smile. So many women would have milked this fake relationship thing for all it was worth. They sure as hell would have taken me up on my offer to buy them jewelry, and might have used their status as the girl-friend of a celebrity to smite all their enemies. Not my Lyric.

Wow. The phrase *not my Lyric* had a double meaning there, didn't it? She wasn't my Lyric. Every time I got caught up in the euphoria of being in love, which was an entirely foreign feeling to me, the reality of the situation came crashing down on me.

This wasn't real.

We were only pretending to be in love. At least, she was pretending. I was a man who was actually in love, playing the part of a man who was only pretending to be in love. Just thinking about it gave me a headache, so I took another healthy swig of my beer.

Watching Tyler get steadily drunker while he hit on several women at once was somehow not as much fun as it used to be. Sitting at the bar and having a drink was kinda nice, and I wasn't sorry I'd gone out or anything. But party-ing, if that's what this was, had lost some of its appeal. It wasn't hard to figure out why.

I missed Lyric. I would much rather be at home with her.

Watching TV. Talking. Having sex. Honestly, it didn't matter what we were doing. It was just fun being with her.

"You okay, dude?" Tyler asked. It took me a second to realize he was reacting to the huge sigh I'd just let out.

"Yeah, fine. Just miss my girl I guess."

Tyler shot me a look like I'd just spouted an alien conspiracy theory. Though he had no idea that my relationship with Lyric was just a plan to try to get to Baltimore, I didn't think he was really convinced that I was in love. Not that I could blame him. He'd known me a long time and had seen me fuck my way through dozens of cities, all across the country.

"Think I'll call it a night," I said wearily.

"You sure you're all right?" Tyler asked.

"Yeah. I'm cool. See ya on the field."

Tyler nodded, still looking concerned. It was cool to have a friend in my corner, but I realized that what I really needed right now was to talk to my brother. Not only was he good about discussing my problems rationally while busting my chops about them at the same time, I trusted him with my life. Eric already knew about my fake-girlfriend plan, and I knew I could talk to him about the plan going awry. Namely, that I had accidentally fallen for my partner in crime.

Unfortunately, it was far too late to call Eric now. Though I didn't know the exact time, it was late here on the west coast, so it was even later in Maryland where he lived. At least tomorrow was a day game. I'd have time to video chat with my brother after the game and before the team headed for Seattle.

* * *

THE NEXT DAY, the media was still talking about me and Lyric. Unfortunately, they were also talking about the picture

173

some jerk snapped of me at the bar with one of the women who had approached me. In the photo, I was smiling and laughing and looking like I was having a grand old time with this gorgeous woman.

Great.

What was really annoying was that I distinctly remember laughing with that woman while telling her that I was spoken for and extolling Lyric's virtues. The paparazzi always did love getting pics of me with women, and I should have realized they would redouble their efforts now that I was in a serious relationship. There was no better scoop than a scandal, and they would love to catch me cheating on my girlfriend. Bastards.

I hoped Lyric wouldn't be too upset if she saw the pictures. Or did I? I would have been crushed if I thought she was with some other guy. Though I didn't want her to get hurt, I did want her to care.

If nothing else, I knew I had to quit going to bars for a while. I had no way to stop women from approaching me everywhere I went, but it looked slightly less suspicious if people snapped photos of me at the ballpark or at the airport talking to women than in a bar. Out in the open in broad daylight, it was hard to make the case that I was running around on Lyric.

After the day game, which we won 8-7, I did get a chance to talk to my brother. I packed my stuff at the hotel as quickly as I could since the bus would arrive soon to take the team to the airport.

"Hey," I said to Eric when he answered my video call.

"Hey, hey," he said with a grin. He was outside with his computer this time, since it was early evening where he was. "What's up?"

I paused, only now realizing I had put zero thought into

how to begin this conversation. Normally, we would shoot the shit for a few minutes before getting into anything real.

"Helloooo! Don't have all night here," Eric said, waving at me with his beer.

"Oh yeah. You look real busy."

He chuckled and nodded. "Good point."

"Unfortunately, I *am* busy. Got a flight to catch."

"That's what I thought. I figured you'd be on the bus by now."

"It'll be here soon."

"Okay, so you are calling me now because ..." Eric said, taking a chug of beer.

"Maybe now isn't the best time."

"Brady. What already? Just spill it."

I hesitated again, and my brother groaned with annoyance. "Okay, I'm gonna go out on a limb here and guess this has something to do with the high-priced hooker you hired."

"Dude, you fucking call her that again and I will break your face the next time I see you."

"Nailed it," Eric said in a singsong voice. "Knew you were all tied up in knots over her. I saw you sucking face with her on *SportsCenter* of all places. I tune in for the sports news and I get celebrity romance gossip. What the fuck is up with that?"

"Yeah. We're officially an item in the media now."

"So your devious plan is working," Eric said, raising his beer to me.

"Yeah. I guess so," I said, still trying to figure out how to get to the point.

"But now you're in love with her," he said bluntly. I stared at him and he laughed. "I figure that's the only reason you're calling me all flustered. Besides, it's pretty obvious the way you look at her."

"Really?"

"Yeah. It's weird."

"What do you mean 'weird'?"

"I've just never seen you look at a woman with anything but lust before. That, and I saw your on-field interview this afternoon."

"You did?" I was surprised that Eric had seen the L.A. interview. "It was just a local news thing in California."

"Yeah well, it got picked up by plenty of other places already. You said you were in love with that girl. I know that's supposed to be part of your plan to get to Baltimore, but you meant what you said. I can tell."

"Really?"

"You're a horrible liar, Brady. Remember when we spilled paint all over the living room rug?"

I nodded, laughing. When we got caught, I had stumbled through some ridiculous lie about a bird flying in the house and knocking over the paint. My parents hadn't even seen the carpet yet, but they could tell by my face that I had been up to no good.

"We had sex," I told Eric now that the hardest part of this conversation was over. I hadn't denied that I was in love with Lyric, and that was all Eric needed to know the truth.

"Damn, really?" He started to smirk, and I held up my hand to shut him up.

"I swear to God, if you call her a hooker—"

"I won't, dude," Eric said, and this time he wasn't kidding. Now that he knew for sure I was in love with Lyric, he wouldn't call her names ever again. "But how did that happen? Was it planned, or did you guys just get carried away one night?"

"It was planned, and it was her idea."

Eric scoffed.

"You find it so hard to believe Lyric would want to sleep with me?"

"Of course not. Everybody wants to sleep with you." I heard the hint of jealousy in his voice. "But from how you describe her, Lyric seems pretty level-headed. Like she's focused on her future career and all that. I just thought, ya know ..." He trailed off, and it seemed like he was trying not to offend me with his words.

"You figured she was just in this for the business part of the deal."

"Well, yeah. So I'm surprised she let it get personal like that. You know how women get when it comes to sex."

"I know. Believe me, I thought an awful lot about that. Dammit, I would've been fine with sleeping with her as soon as she moved in, but I swear I never made a move on her. We had to make this whole thing convincing, so we had to practice kissing and all that so we'd look believable."

"So you started making out, and the next thing you knew you were on top of her."

"No! I swear, that is not at all how it went down. For the longest time, even when I went to hug her, I asked her permission. It was important to me that she be okay with everything. Lyric is not like any other woman I've ever met," I said. Wincing, I glanced at the time on my cell phone. I was gonna have to wrap up this conversation and haul ass to make the bus on time.

"Yeah, I don't even know her, and I still know what you mean. Lots of women would be all over the media attention, grabbing their fifteen minutes of fame with you. Lyric doesn't seem like she's exactly mugging for the camera. Every time they showed her on TV at the game, she was joking around with the kids in her section."

"That's my Lyric," I said with pride. Or at least I *wished* she was my Lyric. "So anyway, it really was her idea to be friends with benefits. I can't sleep with anybody else while I'm supposed to be dating her, and she has needs too. So she suggested we have sex, and I made her wait a full twenty-four hours before we did it, just to make sure she was okay with it. I would have felt horrible if she'd regretted sleeping with me."

"Wow. I gotta hand it to you, Brady. That is pretty cool of you." Eric seemed genuinely impressed by my restraint.

"I didn't want her to get all gooey and emotional after we had sex, but now I'm the one who's all fucked up over it."

"You're screwed, bro."

"Thanks, asshole," I said. "So glad I called for your advice."

"You really want my advice?" he asked. He sounded surprised, even touched.

"I do. And make it snappy because I gotta roll."

"Do you have any idea how she feels about you?"

"She definitely likes me. I mean, we really are friends, and we talk about real stuff. Lyric didn't understand how I felt about baseball at first, but she does now. Like, she gets it. She gets *me*."

"That is pretty cool. But you don't know if she thinks of you as more than a friend."

"Right. Not a clue."

"Okay," Eric said, putting down his beer and leaning forward. "For the moment, I wouldn't say anything to her. If you tell her you love her and she doesn't feel the same way, shit will get awkward real fast. And if you still plan on trying to make it to Baltimore, you'll be stuck in a bad, weird situation for months. I would just give it time and see how it plays out. But ..." Eric's voice took on an ominous tone of warning.

"But what?"

"But I know you. You're not known for your impulse control. Knowing you, you'll blurt out your feelings anyway."

I sighed heavily, knowing he was right. I definitely tended

to let my emotions get the best of me, and in a weak moment, I just might tell Lyric I loved her.

"Dammit. I really gotta go," I said.

"Okay. Seriously, Brady. I hope it works out. It's not like you to be so nuts over a girl, so she must be really amazing."

"She is, Eric. You have no idea."

"Good luck in Seattle. And think about what I said. There is a possibility that Lyric has feelings for you too, and everything will be fine. But you can still get together after you've signed a contract in Baltimore, so there's really no reason to mess with shit at the moment."

"Yeah. You're probably right. I appreciate your advice and your unusual lack of ball-busting while you gave it."

Grinning, Eric said, "You have no idea how much restraint that took. Later, asshole."

Chuckling, I said, "Later."

I snapped my laptop shut and shoved it in my bag. Grabbing my other stuff, I rushed out the door to where the bus was probably already filled with my teammates. At least I'd have a bus ride and a flight to give me some time to think about what I should do.

Though I knew Eric was right that I should play it cool, I also knew how hard it would be to not tell Lyric that I was in love with her.

I set my phone to airplane mode—for the time being, I could avoid calling or texting her. But once I got back home and saw her again, there was no telling what I would do.

CHAPTER 19

yric

I HAD INTENDED to look my best when Brady finally returned from his road trip. I'd missed him terribly, and I had hoped he'd take one look at me upon his return and scoop me up and take me to the bedroom. I'd had delicious fantasies of him working out all his pent-up sexual frustration on me. My plan had been to wear makeup, style my hair a bit, and dress in the sexy underwear he'd ordered for me and had shipped to the apartment while he was gone.

Instead, I was a crying, sobbing mess when he got home. Good thing I hadn't put on any makeup, because it would have smeared all over my face. I was so upset, it was hard to care what I looked like, even when I heard his key card in the lock as I sat on the couch. He arrived home at about 7pm from what was probably a long day of travel.

Dropping his car keys in the bowl near the door, Brady stood and stared at me for a few seconds.

"Jesus Christ, Lyric," he said with alarm. He rushed over and sat down on the couch next to me. "What the fuck happened? Who do I have to kill?"

Wiping my eyes, I smiled weakly at his sweet attempt to avenge my nonexistent enemies.

"Nobody. They're already dead."

"Oh God, Lyric. Who died?" He sounded panicked, and I felt terrible.

"No, no. Sorry. It's okay. Nobody I knew personally. Just a really bad day at the hospital."

"Oh. Oh, I see," Brady said, relaxing only slightly. He let out a soft breath, but he was still physically tense. "I'm so sorry, Doc."

Fresh tears filled my eyes, this time due to Brady's tenderness. Sometimes I forgot how much this guy really understood me. Lots of people would have said *Oh, is that all?* once they realized that it wasn't my mom or a close friend who had died. Brady never minimized anything I was going through. Ever.

"Want me to sit and cry with you?" he asked with a gentle smile.

I laughed softly, remembering that I'd asked the same question in the same way when I had caught him crying over *Field of Dreams.*

"Yes, please."

He gently rubbed my back as I tried to compose myself. I cleaned my face up as best I could with a tissue.

"I'm sorry I'm such a mess. I was hoping to be more put-together by the time you got back. I only just now got back from the hospital after several hours of trying not to break down 'til I got home."

"Must have been really bad," Brady said, still massaging my back.

"It was." Swallowing hard, I recalled in vivid detail all the horrible images of this afternoon's tragedy. "You know how I've been working in different departments at the hospital as part of my program?"

Brady nodded.

"Well, I've been working in the Emergency Department recently."

"I guess that's a whole different experience from what you've been doing so far."

"Yeah," I said quietly. "I thought I was ready for this. All this time I've spent studying and preparing to be a doctor."

"But it's tough to prepare for experiencing the real thing. Seeing real patients."

"Exactly! I mean, it's great when they get better and you send them home."

"But they don't all make it," he said somberly. "What happened, Lyric?"

I fought to keep my composure as I spoke. In barely a whisper, I said, "It was a sixteen-year-old girl."

"Damn." Brady shook his head.

"I can't ... I just can't get over the fact that this young girl was alive and breathing this morning. And now she's just *gone*."

Brady patiently waited for me to continue. He could see how hard it was for me to talk about this, so he gave me the space I needed.

"It was all so sudden. In the middle of the goddamned afternoon. She was driving home from school, and she got hit by a drunk driver."

Brady drew in an audible breath.

"They tried so hard to save her," I said, my voice quavering. "You wouldn't believe how long they try to revive you in the hospital. Not like on TV when they pronounce the patient dead after a few minutes of trying to resuscitate them. Hard to know how long this was, but I think they worked on her for a half hour or more."

"And you had to stand there and watch the whole thing. That must have been really stressful."

"Yeah," I said, struggling to find the words to express how horrible it was. "Of course, I know these things happen. Every day. I mean, that's what I'm signing up for as a doctor. I just ... I just never realized it would be this hard. It was all such a shock. I thought I could handle it, but ..."

Brady stopped rubbing my back and took my hand instead. He gazed at me with quiet concern.

"You just can't imagine what it's like to—" I stopped, unsure of how much detail I wanted to burden him with.

"To what?"

"It's just so awful, Brady."

"Tell me."

"You can't imagine what it feels like to stand back helplessly and watch as an innocent sixteen-year-old girl lies on that table and slowly turns from a living person into a dead body."

He drew in another deep breath and let it out. "Wow. That's brutal."

"Oh, Brady. I'm so sorry to hit you with all this heavy stuff when you're barely in the door. You must be exhausted from your trip."

"Don't worry about me. I'm just glad this happened today when I was home to be here for you. Not that there's really anything I can do."

"Believe me, Crush," I said, noting the smile on his face when I called him that. "You're doing plenty. I had no idea this kind of thing would hit me so hard."

"It affects you because you care. You wouldn't be human if it didn't, Lyric."

"I guess. But I'm supposed to be able to handle it. If I'm

gonna fall apart every time a patient doesn't make it, maybe I'm not cut out to be a doctor after all."

Sharp pain squeezed at my heart when I said those words out loud. I felt like all my dreams were tearing apart at the seams.

"Of course you're cut out to be a doctor. This was your very first experience with this kind of thing. Though you don't ever want to get so tough that you don't care when you lose a patient, it won't always be this hard. Over time, this kind of thing will get easier."

"I don't know what to think."

He let go of my hand and gently caressed my face, looking me in the eye. "They're not all gonna die, Lyric. Some of them are gonna have happy endings. Happy endings that you helped give them. You think you want to go into oncology, right?"

"Right," I said, astonished at how Brady always remembered important things like that. I'd never known a man to sincerely listen to me the way he did.

"Think of all the end-of-chemo parties you'll be a part of. You know how people post those happy videos online?"

"Yeah. They always make me cry."

He grinned. "See? Sometimes these will be happy tears." He gently wiped away the tears from my eyes with his thumbs.

"I know you're right, Crush. It's just that …" I struggled to be brave enough to finish the sentence.

"That what? You can tell me."

I nodded, knowing I could tell him absolutely anything. "I'm scared to death that I can't do this."

Brady opened his mouth to protest, but I couldn't believe any reassurances right now. I was in a bad place.

"You don't understand how unbelievably *hard* this is. I get good grades, but it's always a struggle. I have to work so hard and study all the time to be able to keep up. And this is only college! I can't begin to imagine what medical school will be like. That is, if I even get *into* medical school. Your grades have to be close to perfect, you're expected to do all this extra-curricular stuff, and you're even supposed to conduct scientific research on the side to show you're serious. And the MCAT! I'm supposed to take that next month, and I still don't feel ready. You gotta score at *least* 500 to—"

"Just take it one step at a time, Lyric," Brady said in a soothing voice. "All of that sounds completely overwhelming. No wonder you're stressing out. But I'm willing to bet every single med student in the world breaks down crying once in a while. Doesn't mean you can't do it."

His words made sense, but I didn't know what to believe anymore.

"I don't know if I can do this. I really don't."

"Well, it's not like you have to decide anything right now. Maybe you should just try to relax. Do something to take your mind off everything for a while."

My body tensed, and I hoped he wouldn't suggest sex to relax me. I was incredibly vulnerable right now, and him wanting to go to bed with me would feel like he was taking advantage of me.

"Do you feel like watching some TV? We can find something fun to watch. *No* medical shows."

I smiled, feeling my muscles relax.

"Unless you're too wiped out and you just want to go to sleep," he said, watching me carefully.

Gazing into his eyes, I was reminded all over again why I had fallen in love with him. I should have known better than to think he would try to pressure me into sex right now. He never pressured me to do anything ever.

"I don't think I could sleep too well right now. TV sounds good."

"Cool," Brady said, reaching for the remote. He turned on the TV, which was on the sports channel. He chuckled. "Been watching sports news while I was gone?"

I laughed. "A little. I usually watch to see what they're saying about you, but now I need to see what they're saying about me."

Brady winced. "Yeah. News about us has really exploded over the last week. You doing okay with all that? The last thing I want to do is add to your stress."

I smiled at him. "Don't worry. I'm doing okay. And this is good news, right? Word is out about us. All I have to do is play the doting girlfriend, and sooner or later the Baltimore team will notice how you've changed and settled down."

"Hope so," he said. "We'll see."

"Oh, I love this movie!" I said while Brady was flipping channels.

Brady chuckled. "Me too. It's a classic."

Tommy Boy was one of my favorites. No matter how many times I watched it, it still made me laugh.

"I'm surprised you like it," he said.

"Why?"

"I dunno. It's kinda frivolous, don't ya think?" Brady said, nudging me playfully.

I laughed. "Yeah, it is. But it's just so damn funny."

Luckily, we'd caught the movie toward the beginning. The film helped take my mind off the tragic events of the evening. Watching Chris Farley in the movie did remind me of how fragile life could be, though, considering he had died at a relatively young age.

Brady and I laughed together as we watched, often saying the lines out loud. When my dark thoughts intruded and I let out a deep sigh, he noticed right away.

"You okay?"

"Yes, I'm okay. I can't help feeling bad. I'm sitting here

laughing at the television while that girl's family was completely torn apart tonight." My voice was unsteady as I spoke, the tears threatening to spill.

Brady turned to me and said, "And that's what makes me think you're gonna be a terrific doctor. It's horrible what happened, and my heart breaks for everybody affected by that poor girl's death. But feeling terrible isn't gonna change things. The fact that you can come home and somehow put it out of your mind for a little bit means you'll have the strength to walk back into the hospital tomorrow and help more people."

I considered Brady's words for a moment and then nodded.

"Over time you'll get more hardened to this kind of stuff. Hopefully not so much to the point where you no longer care what happens to your patients, but enough that you can ... what's that word? Compartmentalize. You find a way to put it out of your mind so you can go on to the next person who needs you."

"How'd you get so wise, Crush?"

Chuckling, he said, "Honestly, I have no idea. Not like I've thought a lot about stuff like this. I'm just saying what I think."

We watched the rest of the movie, which ended with a touching moment where Chris Farley's character gazes skyward and asks his late father to send him a little wind for his boat sails. Then a soft breeze blows, ruffling his hair and gently moving his boat across the water.

I dabbed my eyes with a tissue. Laughing at myself, I said, "Oh my God, I'm crying over *Tommy Boy*. I really am a mess."

Brady smiled at me. "I think it's kinda sweet."

"Thanks."

As the credits rolled, he pulled me close and wrapped his arms around me.

"Everything's gonna be okay," he said.

"I wish I could believe you." After he released me, I straightened out my hair and tried not to think about how awful I must look. "There's just so much to think about. I have final exams this week at school. Then I have the MCAT in a few weeks. And between that and what happened at the hospital, I'm just questioning everything. I honestly don't know if I can do this, Brady. It's like I don't know what I want anymore. I thought I had it all figured out, but—"

"I know it's overwhelming, Lyric." He looked worried as he scanned my face. "You've had a really tough day. I think what you need more than anything right now is a good night's sleep."

"You're probably right."

He smiled. "You're a hard worker. A tough cookie. You got this, girl."

"We'll see, I guess," I said weakly. "You need to rest, too. I haven't even given you a chance to breathe since you got home."

"S'okay," he said with a shrug.

"Get some rest," I said, leaning over to give him another hug.

"You too."

I could feel his worried eyes on me as I stumbled, emotionally and physically exhausted, toward my bedroom.

CHAPTER 20

$\mathcal{L}$yric

I DID MANAGE to get some sleep since I was too exhausted to overthink my life anymore. I woke up feeling rested but *restless* at the same time. Thoughts of that young accident victim weighed heavily on my mind. I simply could not fathom what that family was going through.

Compartmentalize.

I reminded myself that there was nothing I could do for that family, but there were other patients at the hospital who needed me. Well, not really—I was still mainly an observer since I was in training to eventually help patients. The idea of actually treating and healing patients seemed abstract and far away. The teen girl's dead body was real.

Tears sprang to my eyes, and I wiped them away. I was a long way from being able to compartmentalize things.

I showered and got dressed, making sure to look a lot more presentable than last night. Though I still wasn't in the mood to have sex, I put on the fancy underwear anyway. Somehow, it made me feel more attractive. After I fixed my hair and put on some makeup, I wandered into the kitchen to search for Brady.

There was no sign of him except for the pot of coffee he had brewed. As delicious as it smelled and as much as I needed a cup of coffee, I needed Brady more. He wasn't in the living room, and I knew he wasn't in his bedroom either, since he'd left the door open and the room was empty.

Damn.

Maybe he'd gone to the stadium to work out or something. He'd been so comforting last night, and I could have used more of his reassurance this morning. With a heavy sigh, I headed back to the kitchen to grab some coffee. And that's when I saw him.

Brady was sitting out on the patio, staring into space. Though it wasn't unusual for him to be sitting out there, he was always playing on his phone. Not now. He just stared.

I opened the sliding door carefully, trying not to startle him.

"Hey. You okay?"

"Good morning," Brady said. His mouth smiled, but his eyes looked serious. "Just out here thinking."

I took a seat in the chair next to him. The air was mild, and a soft breeze blew.

"What are you thinking about?"

"Last night. And what happened at the hospital," he said, his expression grim. "I've done that."

"Done what?"

"Driven drunk."

"Oh," I said. No wonder he looked so somber.

"I can't tell you how many times I've driven home after being on a bender. Used to laugh about how I couldn't even remember driving home." Brady shook his head. "That coulda been me last night. I could've been the one on the slab. Worse, I could have been the one who hit that girl. Good Christ, I could have *killed* someone."

I nodded, holding my tongue. It had always pissed me off when people joked about driving drunk, but I saw no reason to say that out loud and rub salt in Brady's wounds. In fact, it also made me mad when people joked about drinking too much in general. Partying once in a while was fine, but I hated it when people were irresponsible. I could never say it without sounding like a total buzzkill, but college drinking really infuriated me. College was incredibly expensive, and it truly was a privilege to attend. Yet somehow it was considered a rite of passage to get blackout drunk and cut classes. I knew there was more to life than studying and getting good grades, but college was supposed to prepare you for life. If you were fortunate enough to get a college degree, you'd likely always have an easier time getting a job in the real world. While some of these rich kids were drinking away their education that was paid for by their parents, countless other people were working really hard at minimum wage jobs and dreaming of a better life.

As I thought about what happened in the ED last night, it occurred to me for the first time that the owner of the Baltimore team might have been right to turn Brady down. At any moment, he was one drunken accident away from getting hurt and ruining his career.

"It's never too late to change," I said softly.

I could've been the one on the slab. Chills ran down my spine as the gravity of his words hit me. God knows what Brady got up to when he was on the road. It could so easily have been me receiving the phone call that the one I loved had been killed in an accident.

"I swear to God, I will never be reckless like that again," Brady said.

"Good. At least something positive came out of what happened yesterday."

"Yeah. Yeah, you're right. Though it shouldn't have taken a tragic accident to get through my thick skull," he said bitterly. "It's like, you know things like that can happen, but you never think they will happen to you."

"Exactly."

Turning to face me, he asked. "How are you doing?"

"I feel more rested if nothing else. Other than that, I still feel confused and scared and unsure about everything."

"You know what I think you should do?"

"What?" I asked, hoping he had some good advice for me.

"I think you should talk to that doctor lady you admire so much. What's her name again? Dr. Barrett?"

"Dr. Bennett."

"Yeah. Her. I know how much you admire her. She was once a med student, too. Maybe she can tell you about how she felt the first time she saw somebody die."

A ripple of relief went through me. I adored Dr. Bennett, and she was a kind and compassionate mentor. If anybody understood what I was going through, it was her.

"That is a great idea."

"Cool," he said with a grin. He seemed happy to have come up with something that might help me. For the umpteenth time, I marveled at how Brady listened when I spoke and even remembered things I talked about. He knew how much Dr. Bennett inspired me.

"Did you have any coffee yet?" I asked. Brady shook his head. "Want me to bring you some out here?"

"Yeah. Yeah, that'd be cool. Thanks, Lyric."

"Sure thing. I'm glad you're back, Brady. I missed you."

Brady grinned widely. "I missed you too."

* * *

THE ANTISEPTIC SMELL of the hospital wasn't so exciting anymore. Now, it struck me the way it must hit the loved ones of patients. Like a mix of fear, anxiety, and loss. That teenager's family would likely never forget the way this placed smelled on that horrible day when the girl had taken her last breath.

My eyes were welling up already, destroying what little confidence I'd managed to build up this morning. Fresh dread filled my stomach, my body heavy with the stark realization that maybe I just wasn't meant to be a doctor.

Fortunately, Dr. Bennett was sitting in her office when I stopped by to see her. I wasn't sure I would have been able to face the Emergency Department again without talking to her first.

"Good morning, Lyric." She briefly glanced up from her computer and did a double take when she saw my face. "Are you okay?"

Shaking my head, I said, "Not really."

Dr. Bennett got up immediately and walked over to shut her office door behind me. Then she sat back down at her desk, scooting her chair forward. I knew how busy she was, and it meant a great deal to me that she was clearly giving me her undivided attention because she knew I was upset.

"What's going on, hon?" she asked, her dark brown eyes filled with concern.

"It's just ... everything, I guess. I'm feeling completely overwhelmed with school and with the MCAT and everything, and I'm starting to question if I can really do this. If I'm, you know, really meant to be a doctor."

Dr. Bennett smiled warmly. "I don't think I've ever had a med school volunteer go through this hospital who didn't say that very thing."

Vivid memories of what happened at the hospital came

crashing down around me again. Tears falling, I managed to say, "I watched somebody die here yesterday."

"Oh, Lyric," she said with deep compassion. She handed me the tissue box from her desk so I could wipe my eyes.

"Car accident. She was only sixteen years old."

Dr. Bennett nodded thoughtfully. She waited for a moment to see if I wanted to say more.

"It's always hard the first time that happens, no matter what the circumstance," she said. "And it's much worse when it's a young person. I'm so sorry you had to see that."

"But that's part of the job! I should be able to handle it."

"And you will be able to handle it. It's never easy, but it does get easier. Be gentle with yourself, Lyric. Think about it. What kind of monster would you be if you saw somebody die suddenly and you just walked away like nothing happened?" She shook her head. "I sure as hell don't want a doctor like that. You're completely shaken up because you *care*, Lyric."

"I guess I know that. I just didn't expect it to hit this hard. I should have been prepared for it. Death is gonna be a big part of the job, especially with oncology."

Dr. Bennett smiled softly. "Have you decided on oncology?"

"I haven't decided anything. I don't even know if I want to be a doctor anymore."

Hearing those words from my own mouth tore my heart apart. I'd wanted to be a doctor for as long as I could remember, and now it felt like I wasn't sure of anything anymore. Not wanting to see Dr. Bennett's reaction to my confession, I glanced out her office window. Looking out at the tall buildings of downtown Richmond, I thought about all the office workers out there doing normal jobs where nobody died during the workday.

When I finally forced myself to look back at my beloved

mentor, she was still watching me with gentle compassion. Not even a hint of surprise on her face.

"Do you think you're the only one to sit in that chair and say that?" she asked.

"But a lot of med students do quit, don't they?"

"Some do," Dr. Bennett said. "You need to do what's best for you, Lyric. But I don't think you're gonna quit. I think you've got what it takes to make it as a doctor."

It took all the self-restraint I had not to burst into tears. If anyone else had said that, even Brady, I might not have believed them. But Dr. Bennett was my personal heroine, and she knew what she was talking about. If she believed in me, maybe I had a chance.

"Every individual has to figure out what works best for them as far as coping with the emotional trauma of this job," Dr. Bennett continued. "So all I can do is offer some advice on what works for me."

I nodded eagerly, still feeling as if my dream of being a doctor was hanging by a thread.

"I think the hardest thing for me to get over was the guilt of just going on with my day after tragedy struck."

"Exactly!" I said, remembering how terrible I felt for laughing at a movie while that girl's family was dealing with the unthinkable.

"You have to remember that putting the bad things out of your mind is what enables you to move on to the next patient who needs you."

"That's what Brady said."

Dr. Bennett's face flashed with interest. I had nearly forgotten how excited she was that I was dating a famous Richmond Domino. Ever the professional, she plowed forward.

"It's true. You will not have the emotional stamina to treat the next patient if you allow yourself to remain in a dark place after you lose a patient. There will simply be no time to grieve."

Nodding thoughtfully, I did my best to take her words to heart.

"And the good news is, you don't have to grieve. Nor should you. Being devastated when someone dies is normal and expected. What feels *abnormal* is picking yourself up, dusting yourself off, and moving on like nothing happened. But as a doctor that is what you can and must do. For your sake and for the patients who need you."

Dr. Bennett stared directly into my eyes as if willing me to understand what she was telling me.

"The hardest part for me was learning to give myself *permission* to move on. I could be holding the hand of a grieving mother one moment and then down the hall laughing with my coworkers five minutes later. It took quite some time for me to not feel like a monster when I did that. So let me save you some time, Lyric. I hereby give you permission to move on as quickly and efficiently as you can from this tragic loss."

"That does make sense," I said. I let out a deep, heavy sigh.

"Tell me what you're thinking right now."

"I'm thinking I'm still not sure I can do this."

Shrugging, Dr. Bennett said, "Of course you're not."

"And I'm thinking that I cannot begin to imagine being the one to deliver the news to the family. All this time I spend studying at school with so much to learn and the MCAT and everything, sometimes I forget that part of the job." Swallowing hard, I said in a small voice, "Somebody had to go out into the waiting room and tell that girl's family she didn't make it."

I grabbed another tissue and dabbed at my eyes.

"You're right, Lyric. And that will always be the toughest part of the job. But hear this," she said, leaning forward and making sure I looked her in the eye. "It *matters* how you tell the family. As a doctor, you are going to have to tell the family bad news. If you're an oncologist? I'm so sorry, Mr. Smith, but it seems your cancer has come back. Mrs. Jones, the surgery was not as successful as we had hoped. I would advise that you get your affairs in order."

That now familiar sense of dread filled my stomach once again. It was unfathomable to think of having to say those words to patients.

I don't think I can do this.

"You will be there for some of the worst moments of people's lives, Lyric. They will never forget the day they heard terrible news, and they *will* remember how you spoke to them. It makes a difference if you speak to them with kindness, dignity, and respect. I might somehow find the energy to smile and laugh throughout my day after delivering terrible news, but you can bet your life it won't be within the earshot of the patient. Kindness. Dignity. Respect."

A flash of uncharacteristic anger crossed my mentor's face.

"Funny how people tend to assume that people in a so-called caring profession are all kind and compassionate. Believe me, girl. That's not always the case. A friend of mine went in for an ultrasound when she was pregnant. It was supposed to be just a routine follow-up, so she didn't have her husband with her. The doctor took one look at the ultrasound and just said 'Oh wow. This baby's dead!'"

I gasped audibly, covering my mouth with my hand.

"I know!" Dr. Bennett said, eyes blazing with anger. "The rest of the appointment, that jerk was just blasé about the whole thing. Like it was no big deal. Now. Can you imagine how much my friend's pain was magnified by his cruel indifference?"

I nodded slowly, my heart broken for that mother.

"It *matters how you talk to people*, Lyric. You won't be able to save everyone. But you will be able to ease their pain by being compassionate. Kindness. Dignity. Respect."

After keeping silent for a time, I said, "I still don't know what to do."

"Of course you don't," she said with a smile. "Even one of my classic pep talks won't fix everything right away. You know I will support you no matter what you decide, Lyric. My advice for the moment is to keep on keepin' on. You've come this far. Don't make any rash decisions now, while you're still so upset."

"Thank you, Dr. Bennett. This really was helpful."

Leaning back in her chair, Dr. Bennett sighed wearily. "Lyric, I owe you an apology."

"What for?" I asked. I couldn't imagine anything she might have done wrong. She was perfect as far as I was concerned.

"Normally, I sit down with my volunteers and have a talk before they work in the ED. Sometimes, their stint will be uneventful. A few broken bones, maybe a heart attack in an elderly patient, things like that. And sometimes, you get a night like you had. I'm so sorry I didn't prepare you better."

"It's fine, really."

"No, it isn't. I was distracted, and it was unprofessional of me."

She looked at me like she wasn't sure if she should say more. But then she did.

"The truth is, I was distracted by what we were talking about that day."

I wracked my brain, but I could not recall what we had been discussing before I went to the ED. My head was so full from studying, it was hard to remember anything else.

"Your boyfriend?" she added, still sounding apologetic.

I burst out laughing, and Dr. Bennett's face finally relaxed.

"Oh, right. Of course. It's okay. Really."

"You guys are big news these days," she said.

"Yeah, I know," I said dryly. "It's weird. I'm not used to all the attention."

"Hell, it probably won't hurt your med school applications any to be famous."

"Really?" That thought had never occurred to me.

"Well, they're not gonna let you in on fame alone, but you know how schools are. They love to brag about famous alumnae."

"I guess that's true."

Dr. Bennett still had that look on her face like she wanted to say more. This time, she kept her mouth shut.

Giggling, I asked, "What do you want to know? I know you're dying to talk about him."

"I am. And I'm sorry," she said with a laugh.

"Don't be sorry." Though I was known as "Brady's girlfriend" at the ballpark and all over the media, Dr. Bennett treated me like a potential doctor first. The rest was all in fun.

"Well ..." she began cautiously, "I guess I want to know ...
"

"You want to know how he is in bed," I said, my face suddenly flaming hot.

"Yes. You don't have to answer that if you don't want to."

Though it was a little embarrassing to talk about, my heart soared at the way my mentor talked to me like a colleague and a friend.

"Brady's, you know, *amazing* of course," I said.

"Mmmph!" Dr. Bennett said with approval, slapping her hand on the desk. "I knew it."

"But he's also surprisingly gentle. Brady's six-foot-whatever, so he's a lot bigger than me. And it's like he's always careful not to hurt me and all that. He's just ... wonderful."

"That's great, sweetie. You know what I say. As long as he treats you well, he's okay in my book."

"Thanks. For everything."

"You're welcome, Lyric. You've got this. You really do."

"I hope so."

Drawing in a deep breath, I stood up and tried to mentally prepare myself for another day in the ED.

rady

Sitting out on my patio, I sipped my morning coffee and pondered what to do about Lyric. She was incredibly stressed out these days, and I wished like hell I knew how to help her. She was questioning her call to be a doctor for the first time in her life. Though I knew next to nothing about anything medical, I could totally understand how that must feel. Ever since I was a little boy, I'd wanted to be a professional baseball player. If I suddenly had a change of heart? Jesus. I don't think I would know who I was anymore.

Lyric had final exams coming up. Then, in early June, she would finally take that awful MCAT that was causing her so much headache. Though she was still unsure about the whole doctor thing, she was plowing forward for the moment. She said it would be crazy to skip out on the MCAT at this point. Might as well take it and see how she did.

Since I didn't have any answers, I figured all I could do

was love her and support her while she did what she had to do.

Trouble was, Lyric didn't know that I loved her. She knew I cared about her as a friend, of course. I'd managed so far not to blurt out my true feelings. For once, it wasn't even that hard to control my impulses. Lyric had enough going on in her life. If it turned out that she had fallen for me, too, everything would be great. If not, my love for her would be awkward and uncomfortable, adding yet another complication to her life. That was the last thing she needed right now.

I looked up as the sliding door opened and Lyric stepped out onto the patio with her coffee.

"Good morning, gorgeous!" I said with a grin. Lately, I'd avoided calling her Doc because I didn't want to upset her. "Did you sleep well?"

"Yeah, I did," she said, though she still looked tired. "I've actually been up for a while. Tried to get some studying done before breakfast."

"Before coffee? Why would you do such a thing?"

"I like a challenge, I guess," she said, toasting me with her mug.

"You got enough challenges going on right now. I'm worried you're burning yourself out."

"You're sweet, Crush. I appreciate your concern."

"Lyric, I want you to know," I began carefully. Shit, when she looked at me with those sad eyes, it was tough not to tell her I loved her and take her in my arms. But I reminded myself it was not good to mess with her fragile emotions right now. "I will totally support you, whatever you decide about being a doctor and all that. You know that, right?"

"Of course. You've been an incredible friend through all of this."

I winced inside at the friend-zone language but plowed ahead anyway.

"Just so you know, if you decide not to continue with your education or whatever, it's okay to call off our deal."

Her pretty blue eyes went wide. "Oh my God, I hadn't even thought about that."

"Yeah, that's what I figured. It hadn't occurred to you since you got so much going on, but I want you to know that it really is okay to back out of the whole thing. If it, you know, doesn't really fit your needs anymore."

She set down her coffee cup and took my hand in hers. Good God, it felt good to touch her. Since I'd been home, all we'd done so far was hug each other. But that was okay. Lyric clearly needed the "friend" part now much more than the "with benefits."

"I wouldn't dream of backing out of our agreement, no matter what happens. Brady, I want to help you play for Baltimore. I know how much it means to you. It's important to you, so it's important to me. My dreams are up in the air right now. But you? You know what you want, and I will do everything in my power to help you get it."

Right now I was doing everything in my power not to lean over and kiss the woman that I loved more than life itself. Somehow, I managed to restrain myself.

"I'm already worn out from studying today," Lyric said, rubbing her temples.

"I'm sure you are. Wish there was something I could do to help."

"Maybe there is."

"Really? Name it."

"I could use a study break."

"Okay," I said, waiting for her to tell me what she needed.

"You could help ... *relax* me."

Dim bulb that I was, it took me a few seconds to catch her meaning.

LINDA FAUSNET

"Ohhhh," I said at last. "Are you sure that's what you want?"

I searched her face, wanting to make sure she wasn't suggesting sex out of any feelings of obligation to me.

"Rolling around with you in the bedroom always did help me study better afterward."

Groaning, I said, "You had me at rolling around in the bedroom."

"Thanks for being patient and not, you know, pouncing on me the minute you got home. I appreciate you taking care of me while I've been such a mess."

"Not much I can do, but I try."

"I know," she said softly. "Right now there's plenty you can do to make me feel better."

Abandoning her coffee, she stood up and headed straight toward my bedroom. I scrambled to my feet and practically ran after her.

Lyric flopped down on my bed and looked at me expectantly. The woman I loved was lying on my bed waiting for me to ravish her. Life did not get much better than this.

I grabbed a condom from the drawer and set it on the bed for easy access. As sexually frustrated as I was from being away from her for so long, I still took my time. Caressing her face, I gazed into her eyes and wished I could kiss all her worries away. If nothing else, I could at least take her mind off everything for a while.

Though I'd managed to resist saying the words "I love you" so far, it was entirely possible she might figure out how I felt just by the way I touched her. Lyric was well aware of my former playboy reputation, and I was sure she realized I wasn't this tender with all those other women.

I kissed her longer than was really necessary for foreplay because I had really missed touching her while I was away. Though she hardly seemed to mind my mouth leisurely exploring hers, her nipples were rock hard and she was breathing heavily. If I wanted to distract her from her current stress and worries, I needed to give her the good, hard pounding she needed. And deserved.

Pulling off her shirt and then snapping off her bra with superior expertise, I quickly rid her of her jeans and underwear. With hunger in her eyes, Lyric grabbed my shirt and pulled it over my head. She ran her hands over my chest, admiring my muscles. Once she was done staring at my pecs, she tugged at my belt. To speed things up, I got out of bed so I could pull off the rest of my clothes. I picked up the condom and dramatically tore it open with my teeth. It felt a little silly, but women seemed to love when I did that.

Sure enough, Lyric let out a soft groan as she watched me work the condom onto my rock-hard cock. Then she flung her legs open.

"Good God, Lyric," I said, eagerly accepting her X-rated invitation. I practically jumped onto the bed, still mindful of her petite frame.

I rammed into her, and the sight and sound of her throwing her head back and crying out in ecstasy was even more pleasurable than the blissful sensations emanating from my cock as I thrust in and out of her.

"Oh God, I needed this," she moaned. "I need *you*, Crush."

"I need you, too D—" I managed to stop myself before I used the "D" word. Not what she needed to be thinking about right now. "My gorgeous Lyric. You have no idea how bad I need you."

I felt the sharp pain of her nails digging into my back, which was an exciting reminder of how much she did need me right now. My only job was to give my girl a mind-blowing orgasm. Trouble was, my own release was well on its way. That happened when you were having sex with a beautiful woman after being away from her for far too long.

Without warning, I pulled out of her. I had my mouth between her legs before she even had a chance to protest the loss of my cock in her.

Fisting the sheets, she cried out, "Crush! Oh, God!"

Swirling my tongue in circles across her most intimate spot, the sound of her screams was truly, well, *lyrical*. After standing by helplessly watching her stress level rise with each passing hour, it was gratifying to finally do something to make her feel good again.

"Yes, yes," Lyric said, her voice nearly a whisper as she clutched the sheets harder. I could tell she was close. Then she let out the most delightful cry when she reached her peak.

I couldn't even give her any time to recover because I was about to explode. Ramming back into her, I pumped in and out of her, desperate for my own sexual relief. Lyric was panting and her nails were digging into my back again. That, combined with her sweet cries of, "Crush! Crush!" pushed me over the edge.

Grunting, I came hard, momentarily forgetting not to press all my weight down on her. She groaned a bit when I collapsed on top of her, so I rolled off as quickly.

"Feel better?" I asked. Cocky, I knew. The answer was obvious.

Lyric responded with a sexy moan, running her fingers through her luscious dark hair.

Chuckling, I said, "Glad to hear it."

"Crazy how much fabulous sex helps clear my mind. I'm thinking you should probably fuck me senseless on the morning of the MCAT."

"You had me at fuck me senseless. I'm always happy to oblige, sweet Lyric."

Her soft smile told me she liked it when I called her things like sweet Lyric. I took that as a good sign.

"I guess I better get back to studying for my final exams," she said, those damned worry lines already back on her face.

I leaned over and kissed her on the forehead. "Everything's gonna be okay, Lyric. I promise. You got this."

She let out a soft sigh as she gazed into my eyes. "Thanks, Crush. It helps when you say things like that. It really does."

"Cool," I said with a grin. Putting my hands behind my head, I enjoyed the show of watching Lyric bend over to pick up her scattered clothing.

CHAPTER 22

 yric

I finished my final college exams last week, but even though school was done for the year, it wasn't like I had much time to breathe; I still had the evil MCAT to contend with. Since I'd started grappling with the notion that maybe I wasn't meant to be a doctor after all, everything had become so much harder. School was always tough, but dreaming of the future had always powered me through. Now I didn't know what to think or how to feel, but I still had to slog through all the work. Too late to back out now. After the test from hell was finally over with, I might have some room to think and hopefully figure things out.

Brady had been absolutely amazing through it all. He was my rock, forever cheering me on while supplying me with a steady stream of orgasms. And he was busy with his own life. Being a professional athlete took its toll, and baseball seemed to have an especially grueling schedule. Football games were only like once a week or so, but MLB had very few days off between April and September.

The Richmond Dominoes were really heating up, and there was already talk of postseason play. Brady was giddy as a schoolboy whenever anybody mentioned the playoffs or the World Series, and I loved seeing him so happy. Winning the World Series was on par with playing for Baltimore according to him, so it was a huge deal.

On the day of the MCAT, Brady was up bright and early to support me. Though we'd frequently joked about having sex on the day of the test, he didn't mention it. Crush rarely suggested sex, nearly always following my lead. I didn't know whether to be comforted by his chivalrousness or offended that he clearly found it so easy to control himself around me.

Then again, many times he felt like he was losing control during sex, which I found both exciting and flattering. Once I'd made it clear I wanted to do it, Brady was all in. Taking the lead, tearing off my clothes and all that. It was wonderful, but I couldn't help wishing he would initiate sex once in a while.

But not today.

"I thought I wanted to have sex before the MCAT, but now I just feel like I'm gonna throw up."

Brady didn't look disappointed that he wasn't going to get laid after all. Mostly, he just looked worried.

Looking up at me from where he sat on the couch, he said. "You're gonna do great, Lyric."

"God, I hope so," I said, rubbing my temples and trying to psych myself up for a grueling test that could determine my future. "I've been so stressed out lately, trying to figure out what I want to do for the rest of my life, but the truth is that decision might be made for me today if I flunk this test."

Brady laughed, which took me by surprise. He'd always taken my worries so seriously.

"I'm not laughing at you, Lyric," he said quickly. My expression must have shown how upset I was. "It's just the idea of you flunking this test is ludicrous. You are crazy smart, and you worry about every test you take. Yet you always nail them. I wish you believed in yourself as much as I believe in you."

He got up from the couch and wrapped his arms around me. "You've been prepping for this test forever. *You got this.*"

"Thanks, Crush," I said, squeezing him tight and hoping some of his confidence would physically rub off on me.

"Got coffee all ready for you," Brady said after releasing me.

"Thank God." I followed him into the kitchen.

"Make sure you eat a good breakfast," he said. "I wish I could be here when you get back, but I'll be at the ballpark. How long is this test again?"

"The actual test time is seven and a half hours."

His eyes flew open comically wide, making me laugh.

"I know," I said. "I need all the coffee I can get right now."

"I hope you get some breaks during all that time."

"Yeah, we do."

Brady leaned against the counter, eying me curiously.

"What?"

"I am amazed by you," he said quietly.

"Why?"

"If you sat me down in a room and told me to write down everything I know, I don't think it would take seven and a half hours. And yet, you know enough super hard medical and science stuff to fill all that time. You're amazing."

"Thank you," I said, feeling a lump in my throat. I always worried so much about getting good grades that sometimes I forgot to take the time to be proud of how hard I was working. Everybody in pre-health worked their asses off, and sometimes it took talking to somebody outside of the medical world to make you realize how tough you really were.

"You could talk for way more than seven hours about everything you know about baseball," I told him. "You'd ace any test on that."

"Yeah, I guess so," he said with a grin. "Hmm. So I guess you could say the MCAT is like the playoffs in the medical world?"

"You could say that."

Brady headed into the living room to watch TV while I made my breakfast. My stomach was a quivery mess, yet I had to force myself to eat a substantial breakfast to sustain me through the grueling day ahead. In a way, I was relieved when it was finally time to go. I could hardly stand the stress anymore.

I walked into the living room, and Brady stood up right away.

"Thanks for getting up so early, Brady. You didn't have to do that. You must be exhausted."

Shrugging, he said, "I'm fine. Really. Just wanted to see you before you left."

He stood there gazing at me for a moment. Then he said," Can I give you a kiss for luck?"

"Of course," I said with a smile. It had been a long time since Brady had asked for permission to kiss me.

Just before he put his lips on mine, I realized this was the first time he had ever kissed me when it wasn't either for practice, public show, or foreplay.

Brady's kiss was soft, sweet and, well, *loving*.

I told myself not to read too much into it. He was my friend—a friend I frequently had sex with—and he was providing loving support because today was important to me.

Murmuring in my ear, he said, "*You. Got. This.*"

"Thank you," I whispered, feeling genuinely bolstered by his confidence and support.

* * *

THE ACTUAL TEST was given at a professional center located in Richmond. As far as I could tell, the center existed exclusively for professional exams like the MCAT. The test was comprised of four sections, including Biological and Biochemical Foundations of Living Systems; Chemical and Physical Foundations of Biological Systems; Critical Analysis and Reasoning Skills; and Psychological, Social, and Biological Foundations of Behavior. The MCAT was designed to test not only medical and scientific knowledge, but also to determine reading and comprehension abilities.

Without question, sitting for that exam was one of the most exhausting and challenging experiences of my life. The entire day was like a microcosm of my journey so far to becoming a doctor. I had moments of exhilaration when my knowledge and training kicked in and I felt confident in my abilities, and despair when I'd get a bunch of questions in a row and felt clueless and downright stupid. There were times that made me smile, and I definitely shed many a silent tear of frustration and fear.

When the test was over at last, I was too exhausted to feel relieved. It was hard to wrap my mind around the fact that I would never have to study for the MCAT again. Still, I knew there would be plenty more taxing tests to come.

That was, if I still wanted to be a doctor.

I nearly fell asleep on the Uber ride home. It wasn't until I made it back to Brady's apartment that I realized how hungry I was. Since there was no way in hell I was going back out today, I ordered a pizza. I ate more than half of the thing before passing out on the couch.

I woke up with a gasp, having no idea where I'd fallen asleep or what time it was.

"Hey, hey," came a gentle voice. "It's okay. Sorry to wake you. I didn't know you were out here."

Brady's dark brown eyes gazed at me with concern. He smelled like sweat and dirt and grass. The smell of baseball. The scent of *Brady*.

"Oh, hey," I said groggily as I tried to get my bearings. "Did you win?"

"Yeah, yeah. We won. Who cares? How are *you*?" he asked.

Laughing softly, I said. "I'm okay. I survived if nothing else. Oh my God, look at this mess."

I had left the pizza box out with only a few slices left, plus a bunch of empty soda bottles and dirty napkins.

"Don't you worry about that. I'll clean it up. Let's get you to bed."

Before I even knew what was happening, Brady picked me up in his arms and carried me to my room. After tenderly laying me down on the bed, he smiled and said, "The day I met you. You looked so tired, I remember thinking I wished I could tuck you into bed so you could get some rest. Now I can finally do it."

"Thanks, Crush," I mumbled. Though I was moved to the point of tears by his tenderness, I was still too exhausted to speak much.

The last thing I remember before falling asleep was his sweet kiss on my forehead.

rady

THE NEXT DAY I was relieved that Lyric looked well-rested and happier than she'd been in a long time. She'd been worried about that awful test for so long, it must have been incredible to have that weight off her back.

"Good morning," she said as she walked into the kitchen.

"Good morning, sweet Lyric." I still missed calling her Doc. I honestly believed she'd come around and remember all the reasons she'd dreamed of becoming a doctor and she would regain her confidence, but I still didn't want to put any pressure on her.

"I mean, is it still morning? I don't even know."

"Yeah. It's 11am. I just got up too."

Opening the fridge, she said, "The question is, breakfast or lunch? Ooh, I've got leftover pizza. I forgot."

"You're not one of those weirdos that eats cold pizza, are you?" I asked.

"'Fraid so."

"*Blech.* More for you."

"Thanks for cleaning up last night. Didn't mean to leave you with all that mess."

"No problem. How you feeling?"

"Better. Much better." Lyric took a bite of her cold pizza. "Hard to know how well I did. Some parts I know I nailed, other parts not so much."

"How long 'til you get the results?"

"About thirty days or so. It sucks because I don't have a minute to waste once I get the numbers. If they're not terrible, then I have to start applying to medical schools ASAP."

I hated that she still looked so unsure of herself, but I hoped she'd feel better once she got the test results back. I had every confidence she'd crushed that exam, and getting a good score might make her feel better about going to medical school.

"It is so bizarre not having to study anything for once. Like you go from killer college exams to the mother of all killer exams, the MCAT, and then nothing for a while."

"You got plans for today?" I asked.

"Not a one."

"You can always come to the game," I blurted out. "No, wait. Forget I said anything."

"You don't want me to come to the game?" Lyric asked, pretty blue eyes opened wide.

"No, no. Of course I do. But I figure a baseball game is probably not number one on your list of things to do the minute you finally get a chance to breathe."

"I'd love to go. It'll be fun. What time's the game?"

"It's 7:05. But seriously, don't feel obligated. I won't be offended."

"I want to go, Crush. Really. It's been a while since I put in a public appearance for you anyway. Besides, I like cheering for you. You sure you can get a ticket at the last minute like this? You boys are on fire lately, and I know you've been selling out the place lately."

"I'll make it happen. But only if you're sure."

"I'm sure," she said with a pretty smile. "Oh and by the way, I keep hearing all this stuff about the MLB All-Star Game coming up. Fans can vote on that, right?"

"Yeah."

"I wanna vote for you. How do I do it?"

"It's real easy. You can vote online and they have ballots at the ballpark too."

"You're pretty popular, you know," she said happily. "Do you think you'll make the team?"

"Dunno. I have before. Last year."

"Oh," she said. "So I guess it's not that big a deal."

"Wrong," I said vehemently. "It's a very big deal. One of those childhood dreams coming true kind of things. It's amazing and awesome and it will never get old. I love it, I love it, I love it, and I hope like hell I get chosen again."

Giggling, Lyric said, "You're so cute when you get all excited about this stuff."

"If I do get picked, you can come with me to the game if you want. It's in mid-July. They have it in a different ballpark every year, and this year it's in Washington, D.C. so it's not that far. Hey, if you do go, I could show you around Baltimore while we're there. It's only a couple hours away."

I suddenly felt stupid for getting so carried away. I hadn't even been selected for the All-Star roster yet, and Lyric hadn't even agreed to go.

"I would love that, Brady. To go to the game and see Baltimore with you. Oooh, I hope you get picked."

She sounded almost as excited as I was. Reason number one billion for why I was hopelessly in love with her.

"Me too! It's a huge honor. It really is. Not only for me, but I get to represent my team, play for the American League, and all that. The winner of the game determines which league will get the home field advantage during the World Series. And you get a special jersey with your name on it. And they sell jerseys for fans, too. I can get you one and you can wear it to the game!"

Lyric laughed. "You're awful damn sexy when you get all excited, Crush."

She looked me up and down for a moment. I knew that look by now. She *wanted* me.

But then she turned away for some reason.

"You okay?" I asked.

Turning back, she said, "Yeah, sure. Why?"

"What's on your mind?"

"Nothing," she said, unconvincingly.

"Come on. You got something cooking in that brain of yours. What is it?"

Sighing, she said, "Okay. It's just that … sometimes I feel like I'm the only one asking for sex. I mean, I know this isn't like a real relationship or anything."

Those words hit me like a bullet to the heart. But she was right. I had no real claim on her.

"But I guess I feel like if I didn't bring it up, we'd never do it. Makes me feel pathetic. Needy. Like you don't find me attractive or whatever."

"Holy hell, is that what you think?" I asked, hopping up so fast I made her jump. Rushing over to her, I put my hands on her shoulders.

"Lyric Rivers, I want you. Bad. Like, all the time. Every single second of every single day. It's just that I never want you to feel pressured or obligated to be with me given our arrangement. I never want you to feel like, you know …"

"A high-priced hooker?"

I laughed at that. How funny that she used the same phrase my brother had.

"Well yeah. That, and you've been under so much strain with everything else you got going on, I didn't want to put any more pressure on you. So I let you take the lead. If you need a sexual study break, I'm *always* down for that. But if you're too tired and overwhelmed and don't have the energy, I understand that too. It can be hard to tell the difference between those moods, so rather than proposition you, I wait for you to let me know what's what. Make sense?"

Lyric nodded, gazing into my eyes while I still gripped her shoulders. "Yes. I guess it does."

I could still see the uncertainty in her eyes, and I hated that she questioned for one moment how much she turned me on. My job was to remove all doubt from her mind.

"You know," I said, my eyes boring into hers with deep intensity. "There's something I've wanted to do to you ever since you greeted me that time standing against the wall wearing that Dominoes shirt and not much else."

"Really?"

My eyes heavy with deep lust, I nodded slowly.

And that's how, moments later, I found myself banging her against that very wall, just like I'd fantasized. I'd been pleased to find she was wearing the black lace bra and panty set I'd bought for her. Not that she was wearing them for very long since I ripped her clothes off pretty damn quick.

"Crush, Crush!" Lyric cried out as I gave it to her harder and faster than usual. It was as if I wanted to prove with every thrust how goddamned insane she made me.

Slinging my arm around her neck while I pounded her against the wall, I was sure to make eye contact with her. Through gritted teeth, I said, "Don't you *ever* think for a *second* that I don't want you, Lyric."

Panting, she nodded. I was a little afraid I was being too

rough with her, but she seemed to love it. She was stronger than she looked, and she'd proved many times she could take a good hard pounding.

I reached down between her legs to stroke her clit and finish her off, delighting in the way she threw her head back when she came. Lyric seemed unable to form actual words during that critical moment. Instead she cried, "Cru— Crus — Oh—AHH!"

I kept sliding my cock in and out of her while stroking her. We came at almost the same time.

"Lyric," I said through clenched teeth as my body spasmed in a powerful orgasm.

Seconds after we'd both finished, I asked breathlessly, "Believe me now?"

Laughing and nearly out of breath, she said, "Yeah, I do."

Then she nuzzled my neck, and I wrapped my arms around her while I was still inside her.

Now you finally know how much I want you. Maybe someday I'll be able to tell you how much I love you.

CHAPTER 24

yric

BRADY WAS off on another road trip with the team, and the apartment felt strangely quiet. It was always quieter when he was away, but I was usually too busy with studying to notice. Though it was a relief to finally get a mental break, bizarrely, I actually missed my schoolwork. Being a pre-health major was tough to be sure, but I did enjoy the challenge of it. I loved learning and reading about science and medicine, it was just hard having to remember so much all at once. It was a good sign that I missed my studies, I supposed.

The weirdest thing was to go from being utterly overwhelmed to just ... nothing. At least nothing to do at home. I still worked at the hospital a lot, which was good. I enjoyed working with the patients and most of the doctors. Like any other job, some bosses were great and some were jerks. So far, nothing too traumatic had happened since that horrible night in the ED.

There had been several deaths, but they had hit differently. I'd been getting experience in the Intensive Care Unit and, unfortunately, many of those patients were on death watch. When their time came, it was still sad, but not unexpected. They were mainly elderly patients, and there was a lot less chaos when they passed. Though I knew telling their families was undoubtedly still difficult for the physicians, it wasn't the heart-wrenching shock of a sudden accident victim.

Through it all, I thought about what Dr. Bennett had said. That it mattered how you broke the news to the deceased's loved ones. You could still make a difference, even after the patient had died.

I was scheduled to work at the hospital later today, so I went out for a walk. The June weather was perfect. Not too hot or cold, at least in the morning. But I was still incredibly bored.

Days like this, I wished I had made more of an effort to make friends at school. Not that I missed my roommates. They were nice girls, I guess. Just a bit silly for my tastes.

Frivolous, I thought with a smile. Brady loved to tease me about taking things too seriously, and I knew he was right sometimes.

Still, it was hard to make time for a social life when school was in full swing. My senior year would be no different. Harder, really. So it was probably best to just deal with summer boredom and then buckle down again in September. Deep down, I knew it wasn't healthy to have my entire life revolve around school and Brady, but that was just the way things were right now. And Brady wasn't even really my boyfriend. It wasn't good for my mental health, not to mention my heart, to have regular sex with a man who wasn't technically mine. But it felt so good being near him, it was hard to care about future consequences.

I sat down on a bench to rest for a moment and to ponder my immediate future. Namely, what did I want for lunch? I picked up my phone to search for food places nearby.

That's when I saw the sports alert that the MLB All-Stars had been chosen. I clicked on the article, waiting impatiently for the news story to load. When it finally did, sure enough, Brady Keaton was listed.

I wished I was at home in the apartment so I could scream out loud with joy. Instead, I did something I never did. I called Brady while he was out of town.

He answered right away. "Hey? Everything okay?"

"I would say so, Mr. All-Star."

Chuckling, he said, "So you've heard."

"Just now. I'm so excited for you!"

"Thanks. I'm super excited too. It'll be such a fun trip. Will be so great to finally bring you along on a trip instead of having to leave you behind."

I closed my eyes and drew in a deep breath. It really made me think about our relationship when he said stuff like that, especially when he was speaking quickly and talking off the top of his head. And hopefully, from his heart. Sure, we always said we missed each other when he was away, but this felt more significant somehow.

"Yeah. That will be so much fun. I can't wait," I told him, hearing the smile in my voice.

We fell into an awkward silence, despite the fact that there were so many things I wanted to say to him. I wanted to tell him I missed him and wished I was there with him. I wanted to tell him how things were going at the hospital and that I was feeling a little lonely. Weird thing was, if he was at home and we were just hanging out in the kitchen, I probably would have told him those things. Because then, it was like we were allowed to talk. Since we were both home and were sex buddies, we expected to talk to each other. But talking on the phone while he was away? That felt more relationship-like. Uncharted territory.

"Well, I guess I'll talk to you later," I said reluctantly. I didn't really want to hang up. "Good luck at your game tonight. I'll be watching."

"Cool. Thanks for calling."

I tried not to read into the fact that he didn't call me Doc or sweet Lyric. I was going crazy trying to figure out exactly what was going on with us. Brady was always so sweet with me, especially when it came to sex. Though technically we were just friends with benefits, the way he touched me felt like it was so much more. But what if all the tenderness he showed me was just because he was a genuinely nice guy and he didn't want me to get hurt? Maybe he never used to initiate sex before because he was being careful that I wouldn't get the wrong idea about him. About *us*.

The only thing I knew for sure was that our friendship was deep and real, and it would last after our arrangement was over. But then what? Would he go back to sleeping with a bunch of different women again?

That thought made me want to cry. Suddenly I wasn't so hungry anymore. Instead of getting food, I trudged back toward the empty apartment.

THE NEXT FEW weeks went on as usual. Working at the hospital, going to baseball games, and sex with Brady. Those were all good things in theory, but they were complicated by being shrouded in uncertainty. I still wasn't sure if becoming a doctor was the right path for me, and I didn't know if Brady could ever love me the way I loved him. I did my best to go with the flow, but as a serial planner, it went against my nature. Where Brady was impulsive, I was *compulsive*.

The All-Star trip was something to look forward to. At last, the day finally arrived when we would go to Washington, D.C. by way of Baltimore. We took his Maserati, which was a great way to travel. The plan was to spend the day exploring Baltimore, then meet up with his friends for dinner. After that, we'd head to D.C. We toyed with the idea of staying at the house Brady owned in Baltimore overnight, but ultimately decided against it. He said he would feel more comfortable if he was already in Washington on the day of the game. For all we knew, we could hit bad traffic trying to get there from Baltimore and wind up missing the game.

Traveling in the car with Brady was a blast. We opened the windows so we could enjoy the fresh air, and we had more time than usual to just talk. He told me all about his recent trip to New York with the team.

"Going to different cities can be fun, but at this point, there's nowhere I haven't already been a bunch of times. Only so many times you can do the touristy stuff, you know?"

"Yeah, I get that," I said.

"And it's hard to know what to do with myself now that I don't go out drinking after the games anymore."

"You don't go out at all anymore?"

"Not really," Brady said, flipping the car's sun visor down to block out the bright sunlight. "I don't want to sound cocky, but women approach me all the time in bars. Though most people seem to love the idea that we're together, there's plenty more who would love nothing more than to snap a picture of me with another woman."

"They've already managed to do that," I said, slightly embarrassed at how jealous I sounded.

"I know," he said, shaking his head. "Sorry about that. I always tell them straight away that I've got a girlfriend. I figure it's not worth the risk going to bars any more. That, and I don't like going out like that since …"

I held my breath while I waited for him to finish that sentence. Since he'd decided he only wanted to be with me?

"Since you told me about that girl's accident. Not only will I never drink and drive ever again, I guess I kinda realized I needed to tone down the partying altogether. I don't really want to be the kind of jerk who gets drunk and smashes stuff, you know?"

"That's great, Brady," I said. I meant it, of course, but it wasn't exactly what I'd been hoping to hear.

"You've made me a better person, Lyric." That made me smile for sure.

My phone dinged with a notification. I glanced at it and gasped. "Oh my God."

"What's wrong?"

"My MCAT results are in. Oh my God." My hands trembled as I clicked on the email.

"How'd you do?" he asked.

"I don't know yet. You have to go to the website and punch in your info to get your score."

Nearly hyperventilating, I frantically navigated to the website. Every cell in my body felt like it was on edge with fear. There was nothing like knowing the next few seconds might very well determine the course of the rest of my life.

"Dammit. Dammit! The goddamn website is taking forever to load," I said, watching that phone cursor spin maddeningly.

Wordlessly, Brady took his right hand off the steering wheel and placed it reassuringly on my back. His touch comforted me.

"Okay, okay, it's loading …"

"What did you say a good score is?" Brady asked.

"Highest score is 528," I said shakily. "I gotta at least score 500."

We both kept silent while I checked, knowing the next words spoken would be when I said the number out loud. *Please, please, please, please be a good score.*

"512!" I yelled.

Brady squeezed me hard with his right arm, then let go so he could bang on the steering wheel.

"I knew it. I knew it! What did I tell you?" he yelled back.

Clutching my phone to my chest, I said, "Thank God!" Then I checked my screen again to make sure I actually saw what I thought I'd seen. 512. 512. 512. It was real.

"I knew you were gonna make that test your *bitch*, Lyric."

Laughing happily, I said. "I wasn't so sure. I can't believe it. I just can't believe it."

"This is so awesome. It's so cool that we both have such great things going on at the same time. You're an All-Star too now."

"Thanks. I appreciate all your help and support through all of this. I know I've been unbearable sometimes."

"No way. You've never been unbearable. I just hate seeing you so upset and stressed out." Brady glanced over at me. "But I love seeing you like this."

Letting out a deep breath, I said, "Well, I love feeling like this."

"Can I ask you something?"

"Of course."

"I'm not trying to push you into making any decision or anything."

"Okay," I said, my mind and heart filled with the possibilities of what he was getting at.

"Does getting this awesome test score change anything for you? As far as the whole doctor thing?"

"Oh," I said, doing my best to hide my disappointment. "I

don't know. Helps my confidence, so that's something. You're right about how I always stress out about all my tests but I usually wind up doing okay. And this was the mother of all tests so far. My chances of getting into a good medical school just got better, that's for sure."

"But do you still want to go to medical school?"

"That's the question, isn't it? I'm not sure. I still don't know if I can handle all the bad stuff about being a doctor."

"Yeah. The job would be great if it weren't for all those icky sick people."

I burst out laughing and he chuckled along.

"You don't have to decide anything now. For today, enjoy this victory. You've earned it."

"Thanks, Crush."

CHAPTER 25

rady

I WAS LOVING every second of this road trip with Lyric. She was way more fun to travel with than the team. I felt like I could talk to her about anything and everything, and she looked so beautiful with the wind whipping her dark hair around her face.

I decided to take a short detour on the way to downtown Baltimore. Lyric looked out her window curiously as we drove down a quiet, unassuming side street packed with a bunch of rowhouses. Double parking in the middle of the street, my Maserati got some curious glances from the neighborhood kids.

"See that house?" I said, pointing to one of the homes near the end of the row. "That's where I grew up."

"Oh wow, really?" Lyric said, staring at the tiny house.

"Yeah. At least, my brother and I lived here until my

parents split up. Then we were here half the time and then my dad's place the other half."

"It's so cute," she said with a smile. "Nice neighborhood."

Lyric watched the kids playing in the yard next door.

"Yeah, it is. Just a few streets over, it's a different story. That's how Baltimore is. Some pretty scary places, but it's not the horrible, crime-ridden place everybody thinks it is."

I couldn't help feeling defensive of my hometown, which admittedly had its problems. I was lucky to have been born into a good, loving family who took care of me, and while they weren't rich, they had been able to provide for me. My philosophy had always been that unless you were born in a poverty-stricken, sometimes violent neighborhood, you had no right judging people who had been.

A car drove down the street behind me, so we had to get going.

"I'm glad you showed this to me," Lyric said.

"There's a lot of stuff I wanna show you while we're here," I said with a laugh. "Hope you don't get too bored."

"Of course I won't," she said, gently touching my back, sending delicious shivers up and down my spine.

"Lucky for you we don't have that much time, so you'll just get the whirlwind tour."

We made our way downtown and I parked my car in one of the garages near the Inner Harbor. From there, we took a walk along the harbor, looking out at the Chesapeake Bay.

"Used to come here a lot as a kid." I said, looking out at the water. "My mom and dad would bring Eric and me out here. Then, in later years, it would be my mom and stepdad that took us. It was fun. In those two big buildings there," I said, gesturing at the large, green-shingled structures, "there was a food court where you could get some great seafood and there were lots of shops inside. Then you could come out here and see street performers and people with their kids and their dogs and stuff. Live music. It was great."

I fell silent for a moment, and Lyric waited for me to continue. "There's some of that still going on, but not as much. Money problems. The place has fallen a bit into disrepair. It's a shame, really. I don't know. I guess there's a part of me that thinks maybe I could help, you know? If I could play here for Baltimore."

"That would be so great, Brady," she said, gazing at me sweetly.

"Lucky for me, Baltimore has always been a sports town. We love our baseball and our football here." I hesitated for a moment, and then said, "I hate to ask, but do you mind if we take a few selfies here? For social media and stuff?"

I really did hate to ask, because I was starting to despise the whole pretending Lyric was my girlfriend thing when I wanted it to be real. And yet, I still had a plan to carry out. I wanted to play for Baltimore almost as much as I wanted Lyric to love me.

"Of course not. That's a great idea! Photos of us together all around Baltimore. Let's do it!"

Grinning, I gratefully pulled her in close and snapped a few pictures of us in front of the water and the Inner Harbor buildings. Lyric smiled at me as I posted them right away online, using as many hashtags as I could think of. When we started walking again, I pointed out the Maryland Science Center, the National Aquarium, and other touristy stuff. Glancing discreetly at her, I saw her face bloom into a beautiful smile as she looked ahead to see where we were going.

"I was hoping you would take me here," she said softly.

God help me, I had to fight back tears when she said that. My throat choked up as I caught sight of Old Bay Stadium coming into view, and now seeing and *feeling* how touched

Lyric was completely overwhelmed me. As usual with her, I didn't have to say how I was feeling. She already knew.

The gates to the stadium were locked up, of course, but there was still plenty to look at on the outside. We wandered around the front of the place, exploring the metal statues erected of Baltimore baseball legends.

"Oh wow, there he is," Lyric said when she discovered the statue of Ray Renner Jr. "Your guy."

"Yeah," I said. "My guy."

Lyric paused reverently in front of the statue, taking the time to read the plaque listing all his accomplishments.

"He's a Maryland native like me," I said. "And he still lives here."

"That's really nice," she said. "I'm sure he could afford to live anywhere in the world with all the money he must have made."

"Oh, no doubt. I love that he still lives in Maryland. He does baseball clinics for underserved populations, all that kinda stuff."

"No wonder he's your hero," Lyric said with a smile.

I nodded, not knowing what else to say and at the same time, knowing I didn't have to say anything.

"Come on, we gotta get some pictures here," she said, her pretty blue eyes glowing.

We took pictures in front of the Ray Renner Jr. statue, in front of the iconic brick warehouse that formed the backdrop of Old Bay Stadium, and we got a nice photo with the seats in the bowl of the stadium in the background. Thumbing through the photos on my phone, I almost didn't want to post them publicly. The way Lyric and I stood close together, smiling and holding each other, felt private. Like we were a couple on vacation and exploring the city together. For most people, when they put photos up on their social media, only their friends and family would see them. My photos would go viral the moment I posted them.

These photos were gold, and I knew it. Pictures of me and my doting, wholesome medical student girlfriend at Old Bay Stadium. How could the Baltimore owner resist me now? So I posted them.

I didn't ask Lyric to pose for any more pictures for the rest of the day. That way, I could pretend we really were a normal couple spending the day together in my hometown rather than being on some weird publicity tour.

Lyric and I had an absolute blast walking all around the city, and we were super hungry when it came time to meet up with Angel and his wife for dinner. I was excited to have Lyric meet my best buddy from Baltimore. I felt bad about not telling Angel the truth about my fake relationship with Lyric, but part of me hoped that it wouldn't be fake forever. Maybe the next time I saw him after tonight, Lyric and I would be official anyway.

"Angel, my man!" I said when Lyric and I stepped into The Crab Mallet restaurant.

"Brady!" he exclaimed, hugging me and clapping me on the back. "Mr. All-Star himself."

"Yeah," I said, shrugging. Turning to his wife, I said, "Jana, you look amazing."

Rolling her eyes, she said. "You're such a liar. But I love it."

Smiling, she hugged me as best she could, her generous baby bump smooshed between us.

"I'm serious. You look great," I told her. She had put on some weight of course, but honestly that made her look even prettier somehow. She looked so *happy,* and Angel was visibly bursting with pride. With his dark brown eyes wide with excitement and that tousled brown hair of his, he exuded boyish charm.

"Angel, Jana, this is Lyric," I said with enthusiasm. My buddy wasn't the only one bursting with pride.

"So great to finally meet you," Angel said, shaking her hand.

"You too," Lyric said with a lovely smile.

"I would have known your face anywhere," Jana said, offering her hand next. "I've seen you on all the sports shows."

"Ugh, I know," Lyric responded.

"How are you doing with all that?" Angel's wife asked. "I know how overwhelming it can be sometimes."

"Yeah, it sure can. It's scary. I mean, overall it's not too bad. But I can't help being afraid I'll say or do the wrong thing."

Jana nodded with empathy at Lyric's words, and my heart squeezed in my chest. I'd never heard Lyric talk about that before. Then again, I hadn't really asked.

"Like when I go to baseball games, I feel like the camera's always on me. And tomorrow, at the All-Star Game, it'll be broadcast nationally and ..." She stopped and looked at me. "But it'll be fine, I'm sure. I'm really excited to be there to support Brady. I'll be wearing my Keaton All-Star jersey and rooting for him all the way."

"That's great," Angel said, clearly pleased that my girl-friend was so supportive.

Our table was ready, and I could feel lots of eyes on our party of four as we made our way to our seats. For once, it wasn't just me people were staring at. We were having dinner just blocks away from Old Bay Stadium where Angel was a star pitcher.

"You have to order crabs," I told Lyric.

"Well yeah, I figured it was the law in Baltimore," she said. Picking up the shaker of Old Bay from the table, she said, "Is it true you Baltimoreans put this on everything?"

"Yes," said Angel, Jana, and I in unison.

Lyric laughed. "Yeah, that's what I thought."

The namesake of my beloved stadium, Old Bay was a local seafood seasoning that natives put on everything from crabs to popcorn to french fries and pretty much everything else.

The drinks we ordered arrived quickly.

"I miss beer," Jana moaned.

"I know, sweetie," Angel said. "I feel bad drinking around you."

"It's okay," she said, tenderly touching her husband's back.

"How are you feeling?" Lyric asked. Maybe it was my imagination, but she looked worried as she gazed at Jana.

"Oh, pretty good, all things considered. I get so tired these days, though. Easily winded, you know?"

Lyric nodded slowly. "Yeah, I bet. Have you had a lot of nausea?"

"Not in a few months, thank goodness. That's mostly gone away."

"That's great," Lyric said. "I've heard that morning sickness can be brutal. Have you had, uh, any other aches and pains?"

"Not really. Been getting headaches of late, though."

Lyric sucked in her breath and nodded.

"So Brady tells me you're studying to be a doctor," Jana said. "That's amazing. Must be a lot of work."

"Oh, it is. This is the perfect time to go away on a trip, though," Lyric said. "I don't have any classes for the summer, so I'm mainly just volunteering at the local hospital. The next step is to apply to medical schools."

"Tell them about your MCAT score," I said proudly.

Laughing, I said, "They probably don't even know what the MCAT is."

"Tell us," Angel said with a grin.

"It's the Medical College Admission Test," she explained. "Now that I finally got the results back, I can start applications."

"The MCAT is like this super hard test that you spend months studying for," I explained, since she was seriously undercutting how tough it was. "It's like the bar exam but for med students."

"Wow," Angel said. "That must be intense. Jana's a lawyer. When we first met, she studied for the bar eight hours a day. It was like a full-time job."

"Yeah, the MCAT is a lot like that. And Lyric *nailed it*. Got a great score," I boasted.

"That's great!" Jana said. "Good for you."

"Thanks. I need to apply to a bunch of different medical schools to make sure I get into at least one. Like with college, I'll apply to a lot—the easier ones and then the one dream school I'd love to attend. But it might be a long shot to get in."

"You'll get in," I said.

Lyric laughed. "I appreciate the vote of confidence, but I don't think you understand how tough it is to get accepted."

"But I do know how smart you are," I said.

"Ain't you two the cutest thing together," Angel said, batting his eyelashes at us. I was about to say something smart to him, but our food arrived.

"All right you guys, you'll have to help me because I have no idea what I'm doing," Lyric said, eying up the crabs. Naturally, they were heavily seasoned with Old Bay.

"No problem. I'll help you," I said, grabbing a wooden crab mallet and showing her how to expertly crack open the crab shell and eat a crab like a native.

"Hope you don't have any cuts on your hands," Angel said. "'Cause you'll find 'em when you eat these."

"Yep," Jana agreed. "Old Bay is full of salt, and you'll feel it if it gets in a cut."

"Good to know," Lyric said. "You know, I never cared much for seafood, but this is pretty good."

"Glad to hear you say that," I said, beaming with pride. "God, whatever you do, don't get caught on camera in Baltimore dissing crabs or Old Bay."

Giggling, she nodded.

Despite her light tone, I got the niggling feeling she was upset about something. I hoped she was okay. Maybe she was worried about being in the spotlight too much during All-Star week. I made a mental note to ask her later and make sure she was doing okay.

"I'm gonna hit the ladies' room," Jana said after we'd finished with the crabs. "Gotta wash up. Got Old Bay stuck under my rings."

Angel watched as his wife eased herself out of her chair. He glanced at her precious baby bump and smiled.

The moment Jana was out of earshot, Lyric spoke up.

"Angel, I'm worried about Jana."

"What?" he asked.

Lyric glanced at me and then back at my friend.

"Look, as you know, I'm not a doctor. There's so much I don't know yet ... but still. I'm worried about her. She's gained a lot of weight, hasn't she?"

"Well yeah," Angel said defensively. "But the doctor said that's pretty normal. And I think she looks great."

Lyric smiled gently. "Oh, she looks beautiful. But it's just that she has a lot of swelling in her face. Brady and I saw you guys on TV a few months back, at some fundraising gala, so I know what she looked like before."

"Don't lots of women swell up during pregnancy?" Angel asked, looking bewildered.

"Yes," Lyric said. "Swelling in your hands and in your feet

and ankles is normal. But Angel," Lyric paused, glancing toward the ladies' room where Jana had disappeared. "Swelling in the face is not normal. It can be a serious warning sign of preeclampsia."

Angel nodded slowly, looking deeply concerned.

"Like I said, I'm not a doctor yet. Far from it. But I am concerned. You might want to get her checked out by a doctor as soon as possible. I didn't want to upset her by saying—"

Jana was coming back, so Lyric stopped talking.

Angel and I exchanged worried looks, and I knew he would do as Lyric suggested.

I hoped Jana and the baby would be okay. Lyric was level-headed, not an alarmist. If she was concerned, I knew it was for a good reason.

We finished up our meal, doing our best to hide our concerns from the mother-to-be.

CHAPTER 26

L yric

"Okay, so don't get mad," Brady said as I was getting dressed in our hotel room in Washington, D.C.

"I hate when people start sentences like that," I said.

"I know. I'm sorry. But there's something I've been putting off telling you because I didn't want you to stress out about it."

I finished getting my clothes on, then sat down on my bed and looked at him expectantly. He had gotten us a hotel room with two double beds, which was thoughtful but also disappointing. It would have been nice to have had no choice but to sleep next to him all night.

"My blood pressure is rising with every second. What already?"

"It's not that bad, really. Not bad at all. It's a good thing."

"Brady. Out with it."

He walked over and sat on his bed across from me.

"My family will be at the All-Star Game tonight. Sitting with you."

"Oh," I said. "That makes sense I guess."

"Yeah, I mean it would have looked weird if I had you sitting somewhere else and all that."

"Right. I can't believe I never considered that your family would be there."

"They go to occasional Dominoes games and stuff, but so far never at the same time as you've been there."

"So, it'll be your mom and dad and your brother?"

"And my stepdad, too."

"Wow."

"Don't worry. Everybody gets along great."

"I love that they're all coming out to support you. But I feel bad about lying to them."

Brady sighed. "Yeah, I get that. But ... it's not all a lie, is it? I mean, we *are* close friends, right? At least I like to think so."

"Of course."

"Well, then think of it like you're there to support me as well." He smiled. "I love when you're sitting close enough to the field that I can hear you cheering me on. And I know you probably hate being featured on the jumbotron, but I get a kick out of seeing you up there."

I laughed. "Yeah. I don't think I'll ever get used to that."

"It'll be cool, really. Just sit with them and cheer me on like you always do."

"Okay. I will."

"Thanks, Lyric. I really appreciate it."

Then he grinned at me like a schoolboy.

"What?" I asked, laughing.

He hopped up from the bed and said, "I'm just really excited about tonight!"

"That's good," I said, enjoying his enthusiasm. It warmed my heart to see him so happy, and I was glad that someone as well-deserving as him was chosen to be an All-Star. Clearly, it meant a lot to him and I would be proud to cheer him on tonight.

Even if it meant meeting his family and more or less lying to their innocent faces.

* * *

WE GOT to the stadium early, when the seats were mostly empty and before his family arrived. It was rather exciting to be on the inside of such an important event. Crazy to think that baseball fans all over North America would be tuning in to watch the All-Star Game on television. Sure, lots of regular games were broadcast nationally on TV, but this was different. In the baseball world, it was literally the only game going on. While sports fans were usually watching their respective home teams, during the four-day All-Star break, there were no other games scheduled.

Slowly, the seats began to fill up.

"Hey, are you Lyric?"

I'd been staring at Brady on the field as he talked to other members of the American League team, and I whipped my head around at the sound of an unfamiliar male voice. It was a young man with sandy-blond hair and brown eyes that looked just like Brady's.

"Umm, yes. That's me," I said, smiling nervously.

"I'm Eric, Brady's brother."

"Of course. He's told me all about you. Nice to meet you."

"You too," Eric said, taking a seat next to me.

I immediately relaxed once he sat down. I had been a little apprehensive about who would wind up sitting next to me. My biggest fear was that it would be Brady's mother, and that she might ask all kinds of questions, like when was I gonna give her grandchildren? Lying to somebody's mother was the worst.

Eric gazed out onto the field, and I saw him smile once he caught sight of his big brother. His eyes were filled with unmistakable pride, which made me like him immediately. That, and he just had an overall easygoing vibe.

Glancing over at me, Eric grinned. "Nice jersey."

"Thanks," I said, quite proud of my Keaton All-Star jersey. "I wanted to wear one with Huntington on the back, but he wouldn't let me." Darren Huntington was another guy on Brady's team who was selected to be an All-Star.

Eric laughed heartily. "That would have been funny."

We chatted pleasantly for a few minutes as he asked me nice, safe questions about how Brady and I had spent the day in Baltimore yesterday. I was grateful that Eric was there to introduce me when the rest of his family showed up. Their mother had the same sandy-blond hair as Eric, while their father had those familiar brown eyes. He was heavier and balding; their stepfather was shorter and wore glasses.

Brady's mother eyed me with interest when we were introduced, like she was sizing me up. It was a little nerve-wracking, but not too bad. Everyone was pleasant and cordial, and Brady's dad sweetly refused to let me pay for any of my food. I marveled at how he and Brady's stepdad drank beer and talked sports together. Such a lovely, blended family.

A family that would be wonderful to become a part of someday.

I knew it was dangerous to get too wrapped up in thoughts like that, so I turned my attention to the festivities around me. There were a bunch of ceremonial first pitches and some brief speeches before the game began. I had never felt prouder of Brady than when I watched him take the field wearing his official All-Star uniform. I knew how much this moment meant to him, and I was proud to be a part of it.

Thankfully, Brady's family was more focused on him and on the game than on me. He had made the right call by not telling me about them until the last minute. I would have done nothing but obsess from the moment he told me, and I was sure he knew it.

I'd hoped that everybody else in the stadium would focus on the game and ignore me, but that wasn't the case. Lots of fans stared at me the whole time. I was kind of a quasi-celebrity. Not famous in my own right, but people knew who I was. I saw myself up on the jumbotron during the first inning. Well, me and the rest of Brady's family. I knew from watching games at home that the media loved to point out the player's families. Honestly, I understood why they did. I found it particularly endearing when they showed the family of a player making his major league debut. That made me tear up a little every time I saw it.

Everything was going great for a while. Then, in the sixth inning, Brady got drilled by a pitch to his shin. I gasped, as did all his family members around me.

Wincing, Brady hobbled around in pain. A trainer jogged out onto the field.

I held my breath while they checked him out, dimly aware that I was back up on the damn jumbotron interspersed with images of Brady dealing with his injury. Though I understood the human-interest angle and that it made for exciting drama to show the worried girlfriend, I wished they would leave me alone.

Focusing on Brady, I hoped with all my heart that he would be okay. The errant pitch was most certainly an accident, given the good-natured spirit of the All-Star Game and the fact the bases were already loaded when he'd gotten hit.

Much to my relief, Brady walked to first base after a few

minutes of recovery. The crowd applauded, and we all breathed a sigh of relief.

In the end, the American League lost 6-2, but it was still a good game. Getting hit by the pitch resulted in one of those two runs, so that was something.

Brady never lost that giddy, childlike excitement throughout the game, and it was a joy to watch him play.

CHAPTER 27

rady

THE ALL-STAR GAME WAS GLORIOUS, and I'd loved having my family and Lyric there to cheer me on. I got back to the hotel late, and it took me quite a while to fall asleep since I was all keyed up. We each slept in our own bed, though I would have much preferred to sleep next to Lyric. But at home she had her own room, and I wanted to be respectful of her personal space.

When I woke up late the next morning, Lyric was already in the shower. I checked my phone and saw I had a text from Angel.

Call me ASAP.

I sat up in my bed and called my friend immediately, hoping to God everything was okay.

"Hey man, is everything all right?" I asked when Angel answered the phone. Just then, Lyric wandered into the room, toweling off her wet hair, another towel wrapped around her body.

Lyric eyed me with concern when she saw the serious expression on my face. She went about getting dressed quietly as she listened to my side of the conversation, which wasn't much.

"Yeah," I said into my phone. "Right now? Yeah, yeah sure. Lemme grab my laptop. Okay, yeah."

I pressed the end call button and looked over at Lyric.

"Is everything all right?" she asked.

"I don't know. That was Angel. He wants to do a video call with us both."

"Now?" Lyric asked, eyes wide. "Oh, okay."

She'd already managed to throw on shorts and a T-shirt, and she quickly dragged a brush through her wet hair. My laptop dinged with the notification and I quickly answered the video call. Lyric sat close to me on the bed so she could see.

Lyric and I both gasped when we saw who was on the screen. There were three people. Angel, Jana, and their newborn baby. The look on my buddy's face told me everything I needed to know as he cradled the child in his arms.

Everything was okay.

"I'd like you both to meet Enrique," he said, glowing with joy.

"Oh my goodness," Lyric said softly as she gazed at the tiny little bundle wrapped up all snug in a blanket. "Is he okay?"

"He's perfect," Angel said, his dark brown eyes filled with happiness. "He's a little on the small side. Only six pounds, two ounces. But he's a strong little guy. Jana's doing great, too."

Jana waved from where she lay on the hospital bed. She smiled, looking weak but happy. She had a fair number of wires and hoses hooked up to her, and I couldn't help wondering if that was normal.

"Lyric," Angel said, looking directly at her as he spoke. "I did what you told me and took Jana to her doctor. Turns out her blood pressure was up pretty high, and he was concerned. He was also worried about the swelling in her face."

I watched Lyric's face as she nodded, intently listening to Angel.

"The doctor said we should take her to the hospital and hook her up to a monitor to check things out and see what was going on. While we were there ..." He paused, his voice choking up with emotion. "Jana started to have seizures. It was the scariest thing I'd ever seen in my life."

"Eclampsia," Lyric said softly.

"Yes," he said. "That's what they said it was. Her eyes rolled back in her head and ... God, it was awful. They took her into the emergency room."

Trembling, Angel wiped his eyes with his one free hand while clutching his newborn son with the other.

"Pretty much the only cure is to get the baby out. So they did an emergency C-section. Thank God almighty Jana was nearly to term, 'cause they'd have had to take him out no matter what."

"Oh wow," I said, my head spinning with all the ways this whole thing could have gone down.

"Yeah. The doctor said ... He—he—told me ... if Jana had seized up like that when she was home alone, I might have lost them both." Tears dripped down Angel's face, and my mind grappled with how close a call this really had been.

Lyric pressed her hand to her mouth for a moment and then slowly dropped it. "My God."

Baby Enrique opened his little eyes and started fussing.

"It's okay, little man," Angel soothed. "It's been five

minutes, so I guess he's hungry again. Better give him over to mama to feed. I just had to let you see for yourself what you did for us, Lyric. I ... I don't have the words to thank you for everything."

"Oh, I'm just so glad everything worked out the way it did," she said, her gorgeous blue eyes sparkling with joy.

The baby cried louder, and Angel laughed. "Talk to you guys later."

Angel ended the call, and Lyric and I sat in silence for a few seconds. Then I turned to her and said, "Good job, Doc."

Lyric's face blossomed into the most beautiful smile I'd ever seen, and I was suddenly overwhelmed with the feeling that she was gonna be all right. Moments like this were undoubtedly why she'd always dreamed of being a doctor. I knew this was her home run in the World Series moment.

I pulled her into my arms and held her close, wishing I had the words to tell her how proud I was of her.

* * *

I TOOK her out to breakfast before we headed back home to Richmond. As usual, there were lots of people staring at us as we sat at a table near the back of the diner. I tried to ignore them as I wanted my attention where it belonged: on my breakfast date.

Lyric smiled warmly at me as I sniffed my coffee before drinking it. She sipped hers and let out a soft sigh.

"Sooo good. Never would have made it this far in life without coffee."

"I hear that," I said.

Lyric seemed happy and content, and it made me hope that she felt more confident about her ability to be a doctor. Between her MCAT scores and performing the incredible feat of saving my best friend's life, hopefully she realized how amazing she was.

As we waited for our breakfast, I thought about all the things I wanted to say to Lyric. My mind kept replaying nightmare scenarios of what might have happened to Angel's family if not for her. That guy was like a brother to me, and I couldn't bear the thought of his indescribable grief if Jana had died in childbirth. Or worse, if both she and the baby had died. My throat tightened just thinking about it. I wasn't sure what to say, but I knew I had to say something to her.

As soon as I opened my mouth to speak, I saw somebody approaching our table. And it wasn't the server. It was a young lady wearing a baseball cap with the Washington D.C. All-Star logo on it. I pasted on a smile, ready to force myself to be polite.

"I'm soooo sorry to bother you," the girl with the cap said, her green eyes lit up. "But you're Lyric Rivers, right?"

Lyric blinked in surprise. "Uh, yeah?"

She looked at me with uncertainty, and I shrugged.

"That was so amazing what you did for Angel Jimenez. I'm a huge Bay Birds fan and, you know how it is, you get attached to all the players when you watch them on TV every day. He and his wife are so cute together, and I just knew he was gonna be this great dad and, well, just wow. To think what almost happened if it wasn't for you. I just wanted to say great job. You're gonna be an amazing doctor."

"Uh, well. Thank you," Lyric said. "Thank you very much."

"Anyway, sorry to bother you." Then shyly, almost as an afterthought, she said, "Hi, Mr. Keaton."

After she walked away, Lyric asked, "Did you tell people what I did?"

"No, I haven't even had a chance. I've been with you all morning. Believe me, I'd put it in skywriting if you'd let me, but I know how private you are."

I took out my phone and quickly scanned the sports headlines. "Oh, I see what happened."

"What?"

"Looks like Angel released a statement though his publicist all about Brady Keaton's med school girlfriend and how she diagnosed his wife correctly and potentially saved her life and the baby's."

"Oh, wow," Lyric said. As usual, her reaction was different than a lot of people's would have been. Even when it came to medical stuff, she still didn't crave the limelight. She drew in a deep breath and looked a bit shaken.

"You okay?"

"Oh, I'm fine."

I wasn't too sure. I could see being recognized in public had rattled her a bit. Sure, people knew her as my girlfriend when we were out together, but this was the first time a stranger had actually approached her.

"Sorry about, you know, this," I said, halfheartedly waving my phone in the air. "I'm sure Angel didn't mean any harm."

"Of course he didn't. He's just excited about his baby and relieved that Jana is okay. It's totally fine."

The server brought our breakfast and set it down in front of us. Steak and eggs for me, french toast for the lady. Might have been my imagination, but it seemed like our waitress glanced at Lyric with recognition. I hoped, for Lyric's sake, that the attention would die down soon.

After eating a few bites to take the edge off my hunger, I asked, "So, does this change things for you? Saving two lives?"

She smiled. "Oh, I don't know that I definitely saved them. I just—"

"You heard what Angel said about what might have happened," I said sternly, determined not to let her downplay the importance of what she'd done.

She ate a forkful of her french toast and then said, "Yeah. It does change things. Made me realize I was being selfish by dwelling on how upset I was when that patient died."

"It wasn't selfish. How can you say that?"

"I don't know. Maybe you're right. Maybe selfish isn't the right word. I guess I just mean I was so busy feeling sorry for myself about how traumatic it was that a young girl died, I forgot what was important. But now it's like … it really is possible that there are two people who are still alive because of me."

Lyric shook her head in wonder.

"Not just any two people," I said, swallowing hard to keep my emotions in check. "Angel is my best friend, Lyric. I don't even know how to begin to thank you for …"

Words failing me, I reached over and grabbed her hand and squeezed it firmly. She nodded and smiled, gazing into my eyes. I knew I didn't have to figure out how to tell her what I was feeling. She simply understood, the way she always did. I let go of her hand so she could finish her breakfast.

"So yeah. This changes things. I want to be a doctor again. More than I've ever wanted it before," she told me, her blue eyes shining with determination. "Dr. Bennett told me that even though I won't be able to save everyone, it still matters how you treat your patients. The sick people themselves and their loved ones. Compassionate treatment makes a huge difference, even when the patient dies. Kindness. Dignity. Respect. That's what she taught me. So I figure if I bust my ass to become the best doctor I can be, I can save some people and I can still make a difference to the ones I can't save in the way I treat them and their loved ones."

Lyric spoke with such deep passion about her dreams. I had never been more tempted to tell her that I loved her than right then and there.

"Anything else I can get for you?" the server asked, arriving at either the best or the worst time possible. I genuinely wasn't sure.

"No," I said. "I've got everything I need."

I just hope I get to keep her.

CHAPTER 28

yric

THE NEXT MONTH and a half were busy, even though I wasn't
back in school for the first semester of my senior year yet.
The media attention continued, and it was bizarre to say the
least. I still wasn't crazy about being in the spotlight, but it
was kind of nice to be known for something other than just
being the girlfriend of Brady "The Crusher" Keaton. And if I
had to be famous for something, I was thrilled that it was for
my medical diagnostic abilities.

I still couldn't believe I'd correctly recognized the signs of
preeclampsia in Jana Jimenez. I had been quite nervous about
saying anything, since I'd known there was every chance I
was just being paranoid. My gut told me that the puffiness in
her face wasn't right and thank God I'd spoken up when
I did.

I'd noticed Brady had stopped calling me Doc after that
terrible night when the teenager died. He must have been

worried that using the nickname might upset me while I was questioning my future. Right after we found out about Angel's wife and baby, he'd called me Doc again. Like he knew I was back on the medical path. And he was right.

Brady and I were already a popular, high-profile couple, but the whole Angel Jimenez thing launched us into the stratosphere. It was like the media couldn't get enough of us. Though it was unnerving to be the focus of so much attention—I had actual paparazzi following me now—I tried to look on the bright side. Not only did it make Brady's image more squeaky clean than ever, I figured my notoriety could only help with my school applications. Medical institutions were always on the prowl for big donors, and admitting the girlfriend of a fabulously wealthy MLB star might benefit any school that would have me. I felt slightly guilty about having an unfair advantage like that, but I couldn't help grasping for any leg up I could get. After all, once I got *into* school, getting good grades and just surviving medical school was all on me.

During the summer, I worked with one of the biology professors at my university to help with his research. The work was interesting, and that kind of project looked great on my medical school applications. I also continued working at the hospital as much as possible, soaking up as much experience and knowledge as I could. I had renewed vigor for becoming a doctor, and I actually felt up to the challenge. Several patients died while I was working, and I handled each loss better than the last. Both Brady's and Dr. Bennett's advice was invaluable, and I learned that not only was it okay for me to try to forget those losses as quickly as possible, it was necessary for my survival as a healer. I simply could not help the next patient if I allowed my emotions to bottom out every time they threatened to spiral.

The Richmond Dominoes were still playing well and

were very much in playoff contention as we headed into September. Time was flying by too fast. On the one hand, I was eager for the semester to start. The sooner I finished up college, the sooner I could get to medical school and be well on my way toward my dreams. On the other hand, I felt like crying every time I thought about what might happen when baseball season was over. Playoffs were in late September, and hopefully the Dominoes would make it that far, and then would come the World Series. And after that would be the moment of reckoning. Either Brady would make it to Baltimore, or he wouldn't. As much as I hoped with all my heart that Baltimore would choose him, I also hoped he would choose *me*. We'd been together—or kind of together if not officially—for months. Our lives were as entwined as if we were a married couple. I knew his schedule and he knew mine, and we coordinated meals and everything else depending on what was going on and how busy we were. I'd reached the point where it was nearly impossible to imagine my life without him. But as difficult as it was to keep going despite all the uncertainty, I knew all I could do was continue to hold up my end of the bargain and see what happened when the deal was over. The ball was in his court. Or his dugout. Whatever the baseball version of that metaphor might be.

One morning in mid-September, I awoke to hear banging, like somebody was pounding on the front door of the apartment. Glancing at my phone, I saw it was 10am. I hoped Brady was still home to deal with whatever was going on.

Frightened, I cracked my bedroom door open. I cautiously wandered into the kitchen.

"Sorry. Sorry! I didn't mean to wake you," Brady said. He was standing at the kitchen counter.

"Oh, that was you?"

"Yeah," he said with a grin. "I was kinda sorta banging my fist on the counter."

"I see. May I ask why?"

"My agent just called. Looks like Baltimore might be interested in me after all," he said, eyes shining.

"Crush! Are you serious?"

Brady nodded, and I knew that giddy look. I *loved* that look. The happy, excited expression he had every time something cool and baseball related happened to him. His eyes were all lit up and he couldn't stop smiling if he tried. It was the way he'd looked when he stood on the field as an All-Star.

"Yeah. Oh, I can't believe they're actually giving me another shot. And I owe it all to you, Lyric."

"I don't know about that."

"I mean it. All this time we've been together did just what I'd hoped it would do. Made me seem like I've finally calmed down and stopped being so immature."

"I guess."

"And now that you're this amazing, life-saving doctor-to-be, that just makes me look like I've got the best girlfriend in the world. And you are. You really are!"

"I'm what?" I asked breathlessly.

"The best, Lyric. You are truly the best," he said, rushing over and giving me a hard squeeze.

Everything was working according to plan. Just like he wanted. And I was happy for him. I really, truly was. I was thrilled and elated for Brady and his promising future. I just couldn't help wondering if I would be a part of that future.

Though no official contracts could be signed until after the World Series, because apparently that was how free agency worked, that didn't mean they couldn't at least negotiate a bit in the meantime. For a stressful few days, we waited for any more word from the Baltimore Bay Birds.

Brady's agent seemed pretty optimistic, though, and did his best to stay in touch, apprising Brady of any new developments, no matter how small. I appreciated that so much, because seeing Brady on edge with the excruciating wait was awful. I wished there was something I could do to hurry this up for him.

Then one morning I woke up to find him sitting out on the patio staring into space. My heart seized in my chest. The only other time I'd ever seen him sit out there like that with no coffee and not looking at his phone was after that patient died and he was upset about his past as a drunk driver.

"Brady?" I said as I stepped outside. "Are you all right?"

He gazed up at me with dark, hollow eyes.

"They know," he said quietly. "Everybody knows. It's all over the news. They know the truth about us."

CHAPTER 29

rady

I'D BEEN SITTING out on the patio in a daze for over an hour, going over and over in my mind, trying to figure out how in the hell this could possibly have happened. The only thing I knew for sure was that news headlines from all over were screaming about what a fraud we were as a couple.

"Wh— what do you mean they know?" Lyric asked, looking every bit as shaken up as I was.

"The sports pages, the gossip pages, they're all saying that our relationship is totally bogus. And they know it's because I was trying to trick the Baltimore team into thinking I had changed just so I can play for them."

"How did they find out?" she said, slowly lowering herself into the patio chair next to me.

"I have no idea! I don't have a clue how anybody could have found out about this. Lyric, be honest. Who did you tell about this? Your parents? Your roommates?" I asked.

"Nobody, I swear," Lyric said, her eyes wide. "Not a soul. Believe me, all this time, I've been wishing I could. The lying is the worst part. I hate having my parents thinking I'm in a serious relationship, and I can't stand lying right to my mentor's face at the hospital. But I promise you, Brady, I never told a single soul the truth about this."

I shook my head.

"You don't believe me?" she asked angrily.

"No, no. Of course I believe you, Lyric. I just don't know how the hell this happened. It makes no sense," I said, dragging my hand through my hair.

"Do you think it could be your agent? I know you told him you would take less money to go to Baltimore. He would make more money if you kept playing for Richmond, right?"

I considered that for a moment. "That's true. Hard to imagine he would screw me over like that. I mean, I guess it's possible, but I never breathed a word to him about the plan."

"You must have told *somebody*, Brady. I mean, not only do they know our relationship is fake, they know why we did it. So you can get into Baltimore."

Lyric froze for a second, and then added, "Do they know about my part in the deal? About getting into medical school."

I nodded slowly. She gasped and covered her mouth.

"Brady! *Who did you tell?*" she wailed.

God, it hurt to look at her. All morning I'd been feeling sorry for myself and dwelling on what this meant for my future. I couldn't believe it hadn't occurred to me what this might do to Lyric and all her dreams. That horrified, panicked look on her face wrenched me out of my self-pity at last.

"One person. I told one person," I confessed to her.

Lyric's breath came in gasps, like she was on the verge of a panic attack.

"But he wouldn't rat me out. Not in a million years."

"Brady, you can't possibly know that. Who did you tell?" she demanded, eyes blazing. It was kind of a relief to see her go from panic to fury.

"My brother," I said. "But I'm telling you, Lyric. He wouldn't do that."

I wasn't sure about many things in life, but that one was a certainty.

Lyric shook her head. "You never know. People can surprise you sometimes."

"Doc," I said, grabbing her hand and staring into her eyes. "I promise you. I swear on my life, my little brother *would never sell me out.*"

She drew in a deep, steady breath and slowly let it out. Then she nodded. "Okay."

She trusted me. Thank God. I let go of her hand.

"Then there has to be somebody else you told, Crush. Because I swear to God it wasn't me!"

I groaned out loud. "I believe you when you say you didn't say anything, but neither did I. Gah, this makes no sense! I've been trying to think if maybe somebody overheard us talking about our deal. But I don't think we ever did that. We were always careful about what we said in public. Maybe somebody bugged my apartment or something."

"Oh God," Lyric moaned, looking like she might be physically sick.

"That's pretty unlikely," I amended quickly. "Security's tight in this building."

"What exactly did the news articles say? I don't want to look," Lyric said, physically trembling.

I had to tread carefully with what I told her. Some of the news reports had been nasty.

"They're saying that an anonymous source said that I hired you to be my fake girlfriend to help clean up my reputation so the Baltimore Bay Birds would consider offering me a contract," I said, shaking my head.

"And they know what I get in return for my part of the deal," Lyric said, lips quivering as she spoke.

"Yeah," I said quietly. "I'd pay for college and for medical school for you."

"No medical school will accept a student who's a proven liar, whose reputation has been completely trashed in front of the whole world."

Then my precious Lyric covered her face with her hands and began to weep. My heart felt like it was being torn out of my chest as I helplessly watched her cry.

I got up and sank down to my knees in front of her. Wordlessly, I pulled her into my arms and held her as she sobbed.

Rubbing her back, I told her, "It's okay. It's all gonna be okay. We're gonna figure this out. I promise."

For the first time, I wished I'd picked someone—*anyone*—else for this ridiculous scheme. Some money-grubbing, fame-hungry woman who could have easily been bought off and would have gotten away scot-free once this was all over. I never would have dragged Lyric into this if I had thought for a second she could have gotten hurt.

Then and there I vowed to figure out who the fuck had screwed me over and exact revenge in any way I could.

I ARRIVED AT THE DOMINOES' clubhouse to find the whole team was pissed as shit at me. Not that I could blame them. Nobody needed a scandal right now with us being this close to clinching a playoff berth. Now one of their most popular players was being branded a fake and a liar in the media, and it didn't make them look good to have me apparently eager to get the hell off the Richmond Dominoes team.

Dave Green, our left fielder, was the first one to greet me when I got there. If you could call what he said a greeting.

"Dude, whatever the fuck is going on with you, you better not let it screw up your game. Few more wins and we can take the AL East Division."

"Yeah. I know," was all I said.

"Is it true?" Dave asked. "Everything you got going with that girl was all fake?"

"It's not fake," I said truthfully. It might have started out that way, but I felt differently now.

Dave shook his head with disgust, and I hardly blamed him. I hadn't sounded exactly convincing with my weak-ass denial just now.

"I just can't figure out who would say something like that to the media," I said.

"Oh, I can tell you who did it," Dave said.

"Really?" I asked.

Dave turned his head and shot a pointed look in Tyler Maxwell's direction.

"No way," I said. "Tyler?"

He was my best buddy on the team. We'd been through so much together, and nobody on the Dominoes knew how much I wanted to play for Baltimore more than he did. Besides, as close as we were, I never told him about the deal between Lyric and me.

"Yeah, Tyler," he said. "He spoke on condition of anonymity, but I heard him give the interview. I'm tellin' you. It was him. And I don't know which one of you assholes I should be madder at. You for doing something so dumb, or him for rattin' you out."

I charged over to Tyler.

"Don't do anything stupid, man," Dave called after me.

Tyler's green eyes opened wide with alarm when he saw me coming at him. He'd seen that raging look in my eye before, but it had never been directed at him.

"What did you tell the media?" I asked slowly and deliberately, my fury evident with every syllable.

"H—how did you know th—that I—"

"Cuz you got a big fucking mouth and somebody overheard you going off about me," I said, seeing no reason to drag Dave's name into this mess. He'd done me a solid by telling me who was to blame.

Backing away slightly, Tyler said, "It was only a matter of time 'til people figured it out anyway. Sure, you and your girl are the toast of baseball right now, but you're the same drunk partier you always were. I don't know who the hell you think you're fooling with this act."

Everybody, I wanted to yell. I'd had everybody fooled until this jackass interfered.

Lowering my voice, I asked, "How did you even know about the deal? Nobody knew but my brother, and I know he wouldn't stab me in the back like this."

"You told me yourself, you dumb fuck."

"The hell I did," I said through clenched teeth.

Tyler laughed and shook his head. "Just because you don't remember telling me doesn't mean you didn't. It was early in the season. Back in Boston."

I thought back to that trip so many months ago. I remembered that night at the bar; it was the first time I hadn't taken some random girl back to my hotel, because of Lyric. At least, I remembered *some* of that trip. Somehow, I'd made it back to my room, but I didn't know how. Yes. It was entirely possible that I'd drunkenly spilled my guts about my plan to Tyler.

"Oh God," I said.

"Yeah," he said with a laugh that made me want to choke

him. "Was the dumbest thing I'd ever heard. Never thought it would work."

"But it did work. It was working. Then you decided to fuck it all up. Why?" I demanded. "Why the hell would you do something like that?"

"I told you. You're a big-time drinker and partier, and that wasn't gonna change. You were just hiding it for a while 'til you got what you wanted."

"So what? Why the fuck would you care that—" Then suddenly it all made sense why Tyler would screw me over like this. "Because I help get you laid, that's why. Women recognize me because I'm more famous than you. With you sitting right next to me at the bar, it was easy to get a lady in every city we visited. So that's why you destroyed my life? So you could get *pussy*?"

By now, everyone in the locker room was staring at me and Tyler. Nobody made a move.

"You're a goddamn phony," Tyler said. "Pretending to be such a good guy ballplayer with a saintly little girlfriend."

Up until that moment, I'd been yelling at Tyler for potentially destroying my career. But his mention of my "saintly little girlfriend" conjured up images of Lyric's tear-stained face. Fuck *my* career. This bastard may have ruined her chances at getting into medical school.

I saw white.

Rage overtook me, and I simply could not control it. Clenching my fist, I pulled back and punched him square in the jaw with all my might. Tyler fell back hard against the metal locker. My only regret was that I hadn't punched him in the nose. I could have easily broken it.

Tyler managed to stagger to his feet. He started to charge toward me, and I gratefully accepted the challenge to continue the fight. However, several of my teammates grabbed me while others grabbed Tyler.

"What the hell is going on here?" Our manager stormed into the clubhouse.

"Brady goddamn punched me, that's what happened," Tyler said, holding his jaw. "And I'm pressing charges for assault. Whaddya think Baltimore's gonna think of that?"

Tyler's sneer made me want to punch him again. What did it matter at this point?

I was totally fucked, and that's all there was to it.

CHAPTER 30

$\mathcal{L}$yric

I REALLY DIDN'T WANT to read any of the news stories about us, but they kept popping up on my phone because I'd set up news alerts to tell me whenever the Richmond Dominoes were mentioned. The alerts had helped me keep up with the team's baseball scores when the games ran too late for me to stay up and watch. That, and up until now, all the mentions of Brady and me had been good news. For months, there had been photographs of us out together and talk of my helping Angel and his family. Now, all the articles were terrible.

Worst of all, the news had broken that Brady had gotten into a fistfight with Tyler Maxwell in the clubhouse tonight. Apparently, some member of the Dominoes cleaning staff had witnessed the fight and given an interview to the media about it. I sat on the couch, unable to stop reading the news and feeling like I was going to throw up. How had everything crashed and burned so quickly?

Having lost track of time, I was still sitting on the couch and obsessing over everything when Brady got home. I was surprised the Dominoes manager let him play in the game tonight, but I guess maybe he was hoping to make it look like whatever had happened was no big deal. Tyler had played, too, but only as a pinch hitter late in the game.

"Hey," Brady said when he walked in the door. He looked like hell. He was often tired after a long game, but this was an entirely different kind of exhaustion. The same kind I was experiencing, no doubt.

"Hey," I said in return.

After he set down his gym bag by the door, he came over and sat down next to me on the couch.

"How are you doing?" he asked.

"I don't know," I said wearily, and he nodded. "What the hell happened tonight? You got in a fight?"

Brady nodded. "Yeah. I did. I punched Tyler."

"So I see," I said, holding up my phone.

He winced. "Was a dumb thing to do, but he had it coming. Believe me. He's the one who sold us out."

"You told him about us? You swore you didn't tell anybody but your brother!"

"I know, Lyric. And I swear I wasn't trying to lie to you. Turns out I did tell Tyler about it, but I was totally hammered and I don't remember doing it."

I groaned and buried my head in my hands. "I should've known. Dammit! I thought you stopped drinking so much."

"I did! Apparently, I told him a long time ago. During that road trip when you were still making up your mind about whether or not you were even gonna go through with it."

"Oh," I said. I was still angry with him for making such a reckless mistake, but I felt slightly better that it hadn't happened more recently. Hugging my arms around my chest, I said quietly, "This is just so awful."

"I know. Even good media coverage makes you uncomfortable. Can't imagine how you're feeling right now. Doc, I'm so sorry."

"I know you are," I said with a heavy sigh.

"Do you think you can still get into medical school with everything that's going on?" he asked, sounding really worried.

"I have no idea. All my applications have been submitted. To my safety school, my dream school, all of them. It's totally out of my hands now. I'm pretty sure they will know what happened. These days, you can't even go on a simple job interview without them looking you up on the Internet to see what they can find about you. It will all depend on how much my reputation bothers them."

"I am so, so sorry, Lyric. I never meant for any of this to happen," Brady said, his brown eyes so filled with sadness and regret that it was nearly impossible to stay mad at him.

"I know you didn't, Crush. But what's done is done. You can't change the past."

He nodded, wearily rubbing his temples.

"But," I said sternly, "you listen to me."

Brady dropped his hands from his head and focused on me.

"You need to get your shit together. I mean it. Lashing out at Tyler or anybody else is only gonna make this worse. The last thing you want to do is start drinking again and lose control. The Dominoes are headed to the playoffs. A couple more wins and you'll clinch your division. You could make it to the World Series. Don't lose focus now."

"It's hard to care about that now, knowing I might have destroyed your life."

"It'll be okay," I said, though I wasn't sure of anything right now. All I knew was there was no sense in Brady throwing away his dream of playing in the World Series. Not when he was this close. "When you feel yourself losing control, try to slow yourself down. Take a deep breath and think about something you find calming."

"I don't want you worrying about me," Brady said. "You need to focus on your schoolwork, on the hospital. On everything you've got going on."

"I will. Crush, let's do our best to get through this together, okay? No matter what, we're still friends, right?"

Looking pained, Brady nodded.

"Then let's help each other through this. I want to lay low for a bit. Not come to games right now, is that okay?"

"Of course. I can't stand the idea of people giving you shit in public."

"You focus on baseball, and I'll focus on school. We're going to survive the storm together, okay?"

Brady nodded. "Lyric, I ... "

"What?"

I could see there was something he wanted to say to me, but he was struggling for some reason.

"I just want to thank you for being so amazing through all of this."

Smiling at him, I pulled him to my chest and hugged him. "It's gonna be okay. You'll see."

Brady held me for a long time, neither of us wanting to let go.

* * *

MY MOTHER CALLED me the next morning, just after I'd finished getting dressed.

"Are you all right?" she asked, concern in her voice.

"Yeah. Why?"

"Lyric, what in the world is going on with you?"

"What do you mean?" I asked, though of course I knew

exactly what she was talking about. Sinking down onto my bed, I mentally prepared myself for a difficult conversation.

"Is it true? Did you just move in with this guy to pay for your medical school?"

I sighed deeply, which was all the answer my mom needed.

"Oh, Lyric," she said with dismay. It broke my heart to think that my parents were probably incredibly disappointed in me. "Are you in any kind of danger?"

"No, of course not."

"This man apparently has a violent temper. He beat up one of his teammates!"

"Yes, well ..." I wanted to say that Tyler kind of had it coming, but I didn't want to get into all of that. "Brady's not a violent person. Really."

"The man gets drunk and trashes hotel rooms. I've read all about him, honey," she said.

"I know that all looks really bad, Mom. But it's not. Really. Brady's a real sweetheart once you get to know him. You have to understand. He grew up in Baltimore, and ever since he was a little boy he's dreamed of playing for them. He used to be pretty wild. Unfortunately, those stories about him getting drunk and all are true. *Were* true. And the Baltimore Bay Birds didn't want to take a risk on him because he used to be unstable. So when I met Brady and we became friends, we made this agreement to pretend to be boyfriend and girlfriend so the Baltimore owner would see that he'd settled down and could be trusted. And in return, Brady would pay for my school, because he literally has millions of dollars to spare."

What I had told my mom was mostly true. The only white lie was that we'd really been relative strangers when we'd first made the deal. But what did that matter now?

"I'm so sorry, Lyric."

"Sorry for what?"

"I'm sorry that your father and I couldn't help you with your school tuition. Maybe if we'd been able to contribute more, you wouldn't have felt you had to …"

My mother was struggling to find a nice way to say I wouldn't have had to whore myself out to some wealthy stranger if they'd had more money.

"Mom, it's okay."

"I always felt bad, you know," she said quietly. "Maybe if your dad and I had more traditional, steady jobs, we could have provided more for you."

My eyes welled up with tears at hearing the sorrow in my mother's voice. This was exactly what I had been afraid of, and why I hadn't wanted to tell her the truth about our arrangement. I knew my sweet mother would wind up blaming herself.

"Mom, please don't say that. I'm so proud of you and Dad for following your dreams. You've been an inspiration to me, and I'm really sorry I never told you that. You two have been the most wonderful, supportive parents anybody could ever ask for. My science and medical path has been so different from your artistic one, but you guys had my back all the way. You always told me I could succeed at whatever I wanted to do. That's worth way more than any amount of money you could have given me."

"I'm just so worried about you," she said, sniffling a little.

My heart broke, knowing I'd made my mother cry. How did I manage to make such a mess of things?

"I know you're worried, but I promise you I'm all right. Brady is very sweet to me. And he's always been a perfect gentleman to me. Nothing more than friendship has ever been expected of me in this deal."

Sure, we had sex, but that had been all my idea. And I saw

no reason to discuss that part with my mother. I just had to reassure her that I wasn't being abused.

"Sometime after the season ends, you can meet him, and you'll see what a nice guy he is. We're still gonna be friends after this is all over." I closed my eyes as I said those words out loud. God, how I dreaded the end of the season and what might be the end of my time living with Brady.

"You're sure you're okay?"

"Yes," I said, opening my eyes and nodding as if she could see me. "I promise, I'm just fine. Please don't worry."

"You know you can call me and Dad if you ever need anything. We will drop everything and come get you at a moment's notice."

"Thanks, Mom. I appreciate that. I love you."

"I love you too, sweetie."

I reflected on how fortunate I was to have my incredible parents to lean on. I was actually grateful that my mother knew the truth. It was nice to have somebody to talk to about all this insanity.

That, and I might need to move back in with them when the baseball season was over.

CHAPTER 31

rady

I WAS worried sick about Lyric. I would give up playing for Baltimore—hell, I would give up just about anything— if it could fix the mess I'd made of her life. She had worked so hard and for so long to get into medical school, and all I could do was hope and pray I hadn't completely screwed that up for her.

Lyric kept reminding me that I needed to keep a level head, but it wasn't easy. The Richmond Dominoes did manage to finish first in our division, which meant we were headed to the playoffs. Lyric was such a sweetheart, cheering me on all the way even with her own future in doubt. Though she steered clear of the stadium and avoided the paparazzi as best she could, she still had to go to school and to the hospital. I was concerned both for her emotional well-being and for her physical safety. She told me to quit worrying about her, as if that were possible, and to concentrate on playing ball. Her advice really did help. Whenever I was tempted to give into some stupid impulse, whether it be swinging recklessly at the first pitch or swinging recklessly at Tyler's face again, I took a deep breath to try to slow things down. She'd told me to think of something that calmed me in those moments, so I did. I thought of her.

As terrible as things were, they could have been worse. At least the team's manager had talked Tyler out of pressing charges against me for decking him. That would only have made things worse for the team, and we didn't need any distractions right now.

I came clean with my agent about what was really going on, and we released a carefully worded statement saying I didn't have to defend my relationship with Lyric to anybody, and that I was protecting her by keeping her out of the public eye. After that, I "no commented" my way through any and all media queries, making it clear I would talk baseball and nothing else with them.

As much as I hated the way I'd dragged Lyric into this mess, I couldn't help being grateful to have her by my side as we endured the firestorm together. I don't think I could have gotten through this had I chosen anybody else for my partner in crime.

THE DOMINOES MADE it through a truly harrowing round of playoffs where we were on the brink of losing it all. We made a comeback after being down two games in a best-of-five series. Lyric was with me through it all, even when she couldn't physically be present. When we played at home, she watched every game on TV and waited up for me to get home, no matter how late it was. For the road games, she kept in touch via phone call or text message to cheer me on.

It always lifted me up and made me stronger to know she had my back. Emotions ran high during playoff season, and each and every loss hit hard. This was the first time I'd ever gotten this far with a team. I'd never played in a Divisional Series, and it was incredible. The World Series was so close I could almost taste it. And there was nobody I wanted to share it with more than Lyric Rivers.

If we did make it to the World Series, I desperately wanted Lyric to be there, wherever we were playing. Like at the All-Star Game, she'd be surrounded by my family. Eric would make sure nobody in the stands harassed her during the games. Hell, I'd hire a bodyguard if need be. Of course, I wouldn't pressure her to come to any of the games if she didn't want to, but the experience wouldn't feel real without her. Nothing felt real without her.

Dear God, how I loved her. I had no idea how the hell I would be able to live without her once the season ended.

We started off stronger in the next round of playoffs— the American League Championship Series. We won the first three games in the best of seven against New York. All we needed was one more win—just *one*—and the Richmond Dominoes were headed to the World Series. As much as I still wanted to play for Baltimore, playing in the baseball world championship was *the* dream. Most players would never make it that far, and I couldn't believe how close I was. Just being a part of the World Series was incredible, but the idea of actually winning a ring was utterly mind-blowing.

The Dominoes lost the next game against New York. It sucked, but it wasn't the end of the world. Then we lost the next game, and I tried not to panic too much. Those two games were played in Richmond, and I came home both nights to find Lyric waiting to give me a consoling hug. She reminded me to take a deep breath and to take one thing at a time. We had two games left to play, and we only had to win one of them. That was doable.

Game six and the potential game seven were to be played in New York. If we won game six, we headed to the World Series. If we lost, we headed to game seven, the tiebreaker.

We lost game six.

Now was the time to panic.

"I wish you were here," I said to Lyric when she called me while I was alone in my hotel room.

"I wish I was too, Crush. I know you're scared, but you got this. You really do. When it comes down to it, it's just one game. You just have to win one game and you're golden," she said in that voice that never failed to soothe me. "These last few games were so close, and they easily could have gone your way. There's no reason why tomorrow's game won't be yours to win. *You got this.*"

I smiled, remembering saying those same words to her when she took the MCAT. She had been scared, too. But she nailed it. Maybe I would, too.

GAME SEVEN TURNED out to be one hell of a nail-biter. It was a slugfest, back and forth the entire game, with each team scoring runs in nearly every inning. My emotions were all over the place. I would be on top of the world, thinking we might actually win, only to have my hopes dashed again when the New York Kings had another big inning. At one point we were up by three runs, but all too soon we were losing again. It was, without question, the most nerve-wracking game of my career.

Then, to my utter horror, somehow the entire game came down to me.

It was the ninth inning; the score was 13-12 with New

York in the lead. The Dominoes had runners on second and third. Two outs. And I was up to bat.

All we needed was one run to tie the game to stay alive. Somehow, some way, I had to get that runner on third base home.

As usual, the New York fans were rowdy jerks, and they were yelling some truly vicious things about me. Worse, they yelled some sick stuff about Lyric. As much as that could have gotten me riled up, it didn't, and it was all because of her. She wouldn't want me to lose my focus, no matter what the fans were screaming.

Taking my place in the batter's box, I thought about her advice.

Take a deep breath and think about something you find calming.

Drawing in a deep breath and then slowly, deliberately letting it out, I pictured Lyric's beautiful face. Her bright blue eyes. In my mind, I heard the sound of her soothing voice saying *You got this.*

It was all too tempting to hack away at that first juicy pitch that looked like it was straight down the middle. But I didn't swing, and it was slightly outside the strike zone. Ball one.

Breathe.

I held still during the second pitch as well.

A walk would be okay. No need to be a three-run home-run hero, as incredible as that would be. My job was to get that runner on third home, or at the very least, I needed to get on base. A walk would load the bases.

The next pitch was too good to pass up, so I swung at it. And missed. Strike one.

Breathe.

I was still doing okay. It *had* been a good pitch. I was in the zone, being cautious. Careful. For once in my life I wasn't letting my impulsive nature get the best of me.

I swung at the next pitch and fouled it off.

Strike two.

My heart began to race. One more strike and it was all over. New York would be headed to the World Series and my team would be headed home for the season.

I fouled off the next three pitches, one of which I sent sailing way into the right-field seats. Just *barely* foul. Had it been a few feet to the left, we'd be up 15-13.

I drew in a deep breath. Thought of Lyric. Calmed myself. Remained in the zone.

The next pitch was tempting to swing at, but it was too high and up out of the strike zone.

Or so I thought.

"Strike three!" called the umpire from just behind me.

And just like that, it was all over.

CHAPTER 32

$\mathcal{L}$yric

I SAT ALONE in an empty patient's room in the hospital, staring at the television in utter disbelief. My volunteer shift had ended an hour ago, but I didn't dare head back to the apartment for fear of missing the end of this critical game. I'd ducked into the unoccupied room so I could watch the game by myself.

Trembling, I knew I had just witnessed Brady's worst nightmare. He'd made the last out, and his team was going home instead of to the World Series. He'd done everything right as far as I could tell. Took his time and had been patient at the plate. But sometimes even doing everything perfectly wasn't enough. No matter how hard you tried, sometimes your dreams ended in heartbreak.

I wept openly as I sat on the hospital bed. My sweet Crush was all the way in New York City, far away from my arms. I couldn't hold him and comfort him. I felt so helpless knowing there was nothing I could do to take this pain away. My mind suddenly flashed back to the memory of watching *Field of Dreams* with him, and I recalled that look on his face when we talked about his baseball dreams. Naturally, that only made me cry harder.

I composed myself as best I could before leaving the room. Mr. Watkins, one of the heart patients on this floor, was standing just outside in the hallway. Though I hadn't worked in the cardiology department in a while, I still visited the patients there frequently because I loved watching Dr. Bennett work.

"Your boyfriend's team lost, huh?" he said, his gray eyes filled with sweet concern at seeing how upset I was. He was one of several hard-core baseball fans here at the hospital. It was common knowledge that Brady was my boyfriend. If any of the patients knew about the controversy about our relationship, they'd been too nice to say anything.

"Yeah," I said, wiping fresh tears from my eyes.

"I'm sorry, sweetheart," the old man said. "You must love him a lot to be so upset."

"Yes, I love him very much." It felt good to say those words out loud to another human being. I'd kept those feelings bottled up for so damned long.

"Well, he'll be home from New York soon enough and you can take good care of him. There's always next year," Mr. Watkins said.

"Yeah," I said, my stomach filling with fresh dread as I wondered what would happen to Brady and me next year. Hell, I wondered what would happen when he got home tomorrow. The season was over. Now what?

Mr. Watkins looked at me like he wanted to say something else.

"Are you all right? Do you need anything?" I asked,

glancing at the oxygen tank he had to wheel around with him.

"No, I'm fine. I'm sorry. Don't mean to stare at ya like that. You just remind me of my wife. She used to fuss over me all the time. She died five years ago. We were married almost forty years."

"I'm so sorry for your loss, Mr. Watkins."

"Thank you," he said. After a pause, he asked, "Do you mind if I take a picture of you?"

"A picture?"

"Yes," he said, fishing his cell phone out of his robe pocket.

It wasn't the first time a baseball fan had asked for my photo. It felt weird every time, since Brady was the one who'd earned all that fame and not me. But I never said no. And I certainly couldn't say no to sweet Mr. Watkins.

"Sure."

Hands shaking, he held up his phone. "This okay?" he asked, holding out his other arm as if to put it around me.

"Oh, sure," I said, realizing he wanted to take a selfie. "Here, I can do it."

I took the cell phone and took a few selfies with him. Though I smiled for the photos, I knew my face was still a mess from crying.

"Thank you, dear," he said, happily looking at the photos. "My grandkids taught me how to take pictures with this thing."

"That's nice," I said.

"You go on home and get some rest now."

"I sure will. Take it easy, Mr. Watkins. I'll come see you again soon."

"You be sure and do that!" he said with a smile.

* * *

IT TURNED out I never should have trusted that allegedly sweet old man.

No. That wasn't true. He *was* a sweet old man. And I knew in my heart he was only trying to help me when he sent those pictures to the local Richmond news.

Mr. Watkins had apparently been aware of the ugly rumors about my relationship with Brady being fake, and he'd wanted to set the record straight. The old guy had been standing in that hospital hallway for a lot longer than I'd thought. He'd been watching me as I watched the playoff game on the television. And that selfie wasn't the only picture he took of me.

I'd already been dreading the inevitable news coverage of the team's loss, and I knew my phone would blow up with news alerts all about it. Figuring it was best to get it over with, I grabbed my phone as soon as I woke up the next morning to see how bad it was. I hoped to God they wouldn't mention Brady too much. It really wasn't his fault. Somebody had to make the last out, and it was just his bad luck that it was him.

The last thing I'd expected was to see my face splashed all over the news.

I had to hand it to Mr. Watkins. He'd gotten several pictures of me looking tense and afraid as I stared at the TV, and he'd managed to capture one hell of a photograph of me as I sat on the bed watching that terrible final moment of the game. I had tears streaming down my face, my hand over my mouth, and my eyes filled with horror and sadness.

Or, as the headlines put it "The Agony of Defeat," "A Devoted Girlfriend's Nightmare," and "The Face of True Love."

Those harrowing photographs of me, combined with the fact that Mr. Watkins had *quoted what I'd said about loving Brady*, had convinced the world overnight that we really were the fairytale couple people had thought we were in the beginning.

But that still didn't make it true.

God love Mr. Watkins, his heart had been in the right place. No doubt he was thinking of his precious wife and their decades of life together. He thought—no, he *knew*—that I loved Brady genuinely. Anyone who'd seen me last night, or had now seen the pictures, knew that. He thought he was helping me by providing solid proof that my love for Brady was real.

"I love him very much." I read my own words in black and white over and over again.

There was no doubt in my mind that Brady had seen them by now, too.

Shockwaves of horror and humiliation raced through my body, and I honestly might have passed out had I not been lying in bed. Putting my hand over my face, I seriously considered leaving. Just packing my stuff and getting the hell out of there before I had to face Brady when he got home.

I dismissed that thought rather quickly. The idea of never seeing him again was torture, so I knew I had to face the music. I'd always known that the end of the baseball season might mean the end of us as a couple. For the first time, I feared that it might also be the end of us as friends. Even the strongest friendship bond couldn't survive the awkwardness of unrequited love.

* * *

I GOT DRESSED and put some makeup on so I would look at least halfway decent when Brady got home from New York. He texted me his travel itinerary so I would know when to expect him, but he said nothing more. Right after the game last night and before everything went to hell in the media, I'd texted him that I was so sorry about the game and that I hoped he was okay. He wrote back *Thanks, Doc* and added a heart emoji. I hadn't called him because I wasn't sure he wanted to talk. Sometimes he didn't want to talk after a tough loss, and I knew this was the worst one he'd ever endured.

I'd been nauseous all day and couldn't even think about eating anything. I didn't even have any coffee since I was jittery enough. There was nothing left to do but to get this over with. All of it. If nothing else, when Brady came home, we would figure out what came next. Should I move out? Wait until the World Series was over since that had always been the deal? Would we still be friends? Would we be *anything* anymore?

As desperate as I was to get this over with, I nearly jumped up off the couch to run away when I heard his key card the lock. But I knew that was stupid. There was no running away from this.

I sat stiffly on the couch, not looking up when Brady came in. I heard him set his bags down near the door.

"Hey," he said.

"Hey." A fresh wave of nausea coursed through me, and I knew it was a good thing I hadn't had anything to eat.

He walked over to the couch and stood near me.

"Please look at me," Brady said. His worried tone told me what I already knew. He had seen the news articles and knew exactly how I felt about him.

"I can't," I said, my voice quivering.

"This was just supposed to be pretend," he said.

My eyes welled up with tears of pure mortification. In that horrible moment, I honestly wished I would just die on the spot.

"I know that, Brady. I know!"

I did jump up from the couch then, ready to run off.

"Lyric!" he said so sternly it stopped me cold. I turned my face to see him.

"Let me finish," he said. "This was just supposed to be pretend. But I'm not sure it ever was just a fake relationship. At least not for me."

My entire body tensed. My mind and heart were at their breaking point. I struggled to comprehend what he was saying.

Brady sat down on the couch. He took my hand and pulled me down next to him.

"That first day when you tried to kill me with hot coffee, I wanted to ask you out. But you hightailed it out of there so fast when we were done eating that I figured you weren't interested. I tried to let it go, but I kept thinking about you."

He tenderly ran his fingers through my hair as he gazed at me.

"Then I came up with the insane idea of marrying you to help get me into Baltimore." Laughing, he said, "But you managed to talk me down from that ledge. The live-in girl-friend compromise worked pretty well. For a while. But after living with you and being with you physically, something happened."

The knots in my stomach slowly began to untwist. Brady dropped his hand from my face and began to gently massage my tight shoulder muscles. My body relaxed at his tender touch.

"Was like every day I was falling harder and harder for you. It got to the point that I felt sick to my stomach every time I thought about what might happen when the season was over. I was afraid you'd want to move out. That I might lose you. Doc, you know how crazy and impulsive I can get. So you can imagine how hard it's been to keep from telling you how I feel about you all this time. But I didn't want to risk making things awkward between us."

I drew in a shaky, nervous breath and let it out. Brady's sweet brown eyes were filled with compassion. He could see what a complete wreck I was.

"My plan was to wait until after the season to tell you how I really felt about you. But looks like you beat me to it."

Staring into his eyes, I willed him to say the words I longed to hear. And then he did.

"I'm in love with you, Lyric."

I closed my eyes and let his beautiful words wash over me. Then his strong arms wrapped around me and held me close.

"I love you too, Crush," I said. Squeezing him tight, I started to cry. I held him for a moment, then leaned back so I could see him.

"Oh, Brady. I'm so sorry about the game," I said, wiping my eyes.

He smiled softly. "I think you're taking it harder than I am."

"Maybe so. It's hard to see the person you love suffer," I said, relieved that I could finally be open about my feelings for him.

"I'm okay. Really."

"You did great, Crush. You really did. I saw how careful you were. Kept your eye on the ball. Never just swung wildly."

"Yeah," he said wearily. "I've been obsessing over and over about those last few moments of the game, and I'm not sure what I could have done differently."

"Nothing. You did great. It just didn't work out," I said. "Believe me, I've read every news article I can get my hands on, and *nobody* blames you for the team's loss."

Gently caressing my face, he said, "Are *you* okay? I can't believe how everything just blew up like this."

"I know," I said grimly. "But yeah. I'm okay. If it weren't

for Mr. Watkins, I'm not sure I'd ever have had the guts to tell you how I felt about you."

Brady laughed. "He's a cute li'l man. Love the photo of you two."

I laughed, too. "Yeah. He meant well, the old dude."

"So, does this mean you'll stay here? With me? Like, for real?" he asked.

"I would love to," I told him.

He leaned over and kissed me. And in that perfect moment I knew everything would be all right, no matter what happened. Our love, and our friendship, was strong enough to withstand anything that life could throw at us.

"It's okay if you want to keep everything on the down low," he told me. "I want to be with you because I love you. You know that, right? Not to get to Baltimore, not to prove anything to anybody. You're gonna be in the public eye no matter what because of me, but that doesn't mean you have to be front and center all the time. I know how hard that is for you. So I don't want you to feel like you have to come to games or—"

"No," I said firmly. "I'm tired of hiding. And Brady," I said, tenderly tracing his lips with my finger. "I'm sorry I wasn't at the game. I should have been with you. There by your side."

"That's sweet, Doc. But your schooling is important. I wouldn't have wanted you to miss that."

I nodded. "Yeah. But I want to be there for you. Support you. In public and in private."

"Cool. And there is something I'd like to do with you in private right now," he said, leaning over to press his lips to mine.

rady

I TOOK Lyric to my bedroom where we made love for what felt like hours. I'd thought nothing could make me forget my agonizing playoff loss, but being with the woman I loved made the pain simply drift away for a while. Being with Lyric had always been awesome, but this was some next-level sex. Both of us *knowing* we were in love made all the difference. Now, in addition to hearing her scream my name in moments of intense passion, I had the honor of hearing her softly saying words of love to me when we held each other afterward. The best part was she no longer left my bedroom after sex. This time, she stayed in my arms where she belonged.

Due to the strain of all the media attention and the stress of the playoffs, it had been quite some time since we'd had sex. At first, we were desperate to get our hands on each other and finally release all that emotion, tension, and sexual frustration. The second time, we went slowly and it felt more intimate. After we'd worn ourselves out, we lay cuddled up together in my bed.

Staring at the ceiling, I said, "Wow. What a wild few months this whole crazy experiment turned out to be."

"Yeah," Lyric said, nuzzling my neck. "I was afraid to hope we'd end up together. I really had no idea how you felt about me."

"Believe me, I know what you mean. I'm thrilled that we're together. I'm just sorry for the hell I put you through along the way."

"Not your fault. And I'm sorry you didn't make it to Baltimore." I could hear the sorrow in her voice, and it was such a comfort to know how much she cared.

"Don't be sorry. For a long time I never thought there could be anything better than playing for Baltimore, but there is. You. You're everything I never knew I needed."

Lyric smiled and kissed me.

"You know what I need besides you?" she asked.

"Name it."

"Food. I've been such a wreck all day that I haven't eaten a thing."

"Awww. And here you used up a bunch of energy on me too," I said.

"Sure did."

"Do you want to just order in?" I asked, getting up to get dressed.

Lyric considered it for a few seconds, and then said," No. I want to go out."

"Really? You sure?"

"Yeah, I am. I meant it when I said I didn't want to hide anymore." She laughed. "It's funny. It'll be like our first non-fake date."

"You're right," I said with a grin, warming to the idea. I still couldn't quite believe I could actually call Lyric *mine.*

* * *

WE GOT DRESSED and I took her out to a not too fancy place for dinner, per her request. She said she didn't have any clothes that were nice enough to wear to an expensive restaurant, and I promised her I would take her shopping to remedy that. Lyric shrugged but then agreed to that future trip. That was my girl, all right. Always so low maintenance.

Once we were seated and had started on our drinks and dinner rolls to take the edge off our hunger, I said, "So, there's something I've been wanting to give you."

"Oh? And what's that?" she asked, nibbling on her buttered roll.

Reaching into my pocket, I said, "Don't worry. It's not a ring. You know, *yet.*"

The sweet smile that played on her lips gave me hope that she just might say yes someday if—well, *when*— I asked.

"I know you're not big on bling and all that, but I can't help wanting to spoil you. I had this specially designed for you. Was just waiting for the right moment to give it to you."

Lyric gasped when I opened the jewelry box and held up the gold necklace with a diamond in the shape of a Caduceus, which is the Greek symbol for medicine on doctor's pins and paperwork and stuff.

"Oh my gosh, it's beautiful!"

"Can I put it on you, Doc?"

"Yes! Please!" Lyric said, those gorgeous blue eyes lighting up. I walked over behind her chair and she lifted her hair so I could clasp it around her neck. I could feel lots of eyes on me as I did so, and I was already imagining the pictures in tomorrow's news articles. Being a celebrity must have been so much easier before everybody had damned cell phones.

Oh well. People could write whatever they wanted about us. I loved Lyric, and she loved me. For *real*. And that was all that mattered.

After we dug into our entrees, Lyric asked, "So what happens now?"

"What do you mean?" I asked, eagerly stabbing a forkful of steak.

"Are you going to re-sign with Richmond?" Her question was tinged with sadness. She wanted me to play for Baltimore almost as much as I did.

"Yeah, I think so. I mean, you've got another year of college to finish here, so no sense in going anywhere else."

"Brady, don't feel like you have to stay for me." Lyric frowned as she twirled pasta around her fork.

"No, it's cool. Makes sense. The team's been good to me. Well, except for Tyler maybe. The Dominoes are a terrific team, and they might make it back to the playoffs next year. It doesn't really matter where I play, as long as I'm with you."

Lyric smiled, fingering the dainty pendant around her neck. "I couldn't agree more."

* * *

A COUPLE OF DAYS LATER, my agent called me. I figured he wanted to discuss the terms of my new contract for the Richmond Dominoes, but it turned out he had a surprise for me.

The owner of the Baltimore Bay Birds had requested a meeting. The strangest part was that Gary Devilbuss wanted to meet with *me* and not my agent. That was all we knew because the man wouldn't elaborate.

"You sure you don't want me to go with you?" Lyric asked as I was getting ready to leave for the meeting.

"No. I don't want you to miss any school. And it will be mostly driving all day."

"I like riding in the car with you," she said.

I smiled. That was one of the coolest things about my girl. We didn't have to go to fancy restaurants or on exotic vacations to have fun. I had a good time wherever I was when I was with her. We'd had so much fun talking on the long drive to Baltimore in July.

"So do I," I said. "But school's more important. The meeting shouldn't take long, and I'll be back this afternoon, depending on traffic."

"Good luck, Crush," Lyric said, and then stood on her tiptoes to kiss me. Three simple words, but they were loaded with emotion. I loved that she knew how important this was for me.

It was a long drive to Baltimore, and traffic was a bitch. It sucked because I had nothing but my obsessive thoughts to occupy me without Lyric there by my side. Still, I knew I'd done the right thing by not letting her come with me. Senior year for a pre-health student was tough enough as it was without having to miss classes.

Fortunately, Mr. Devilbuss was ready to see me right away when I got there, saving me the stress of having to sweat in his reception area for too long.

"Thanks for coming today." Mr. Devilbuss shook my hand across his desk.

"Always a pleasure to visit my hometown," I said, happy to butter him up in any way I could.

The portly man with glasses and white hair smirked a bit at that. We both knew why we were here, and I hoped he would get right down to it.

"Well, let's get right down to it!" the man said.

Okay then.

Mr. Devilbuss was a retired attorney, and I could feel him

scrutinizing me as if I was on the stand in court.

"Your play for the Richmond Dominoes has been quite impressive, and you seem to have matured quite a bit. Fielding remains stellar as it's always been, but I note you're much more patient at the plate. Two-time All-Star."

I nodded, waiting for the *however* part …

"*But,*" Mr. Devilbuss said sternly. "There's a huge *but* here. Do you see the big *but* here?"

I might have matured more over the last year, but I wasn't made of stone. I had to bite the inside of my cheek to keep from laughing about this stern old man going on and on about a "huge but."

"Uh yes, sir. I think I do understand the … well, your concerns," I managed to say without cracking up.

"The huge *but* here," he began again.

Oh God, please make him stop.

"Is your off-field behavior. You've gone from drunken frivolity and property destruction to dominating the headlines with your bizarre love life. Frankly, I'm not sure which one is worse. All I know is that it's all a huge distraction from baseball."

"You're right, sir," I said, feeling much more serious now. My career in Baltimore hinged on this critical conversation. "I can totally understand your concerns and your hesitation in bringing me in to play for the Bay Birds."

My heart pounded hearing myself say the words "play for the Bay Birds." Being on the team had been my dream for as long as I could remember. And now I was *so close.*

"But I can assure you that I really have changed very much over the last year. I'm just not sure what I can do to convince you."

Mr. Devilbuss sighed heavily. "As recently as a few weeks ago you punched a teammate. Does that indicate a significant change in maturity to you?"

My heart sank. Yeah. That one was a little hard to explain.

"Uh, well. Yes. I can understand your concerns about that. But I assure you that—"

"*Brady*," he said, slamming his fist down on his huge mahogany desk and startling me. "The thing I need most from you right now is the truth. Level with me here and tell me exactly what in hell is going on with you. And what in blazes is your deal with that woman?"

Inwardly, I bristled at the way he referred to Lyric as "that woman" and the dismissive way he waved his hand in the air when he said it.

"The truth," I said, stalling for time while I tried to figure out how much I should tell this guy.

Then I did what I always did nowadays when faced with a stressful situation. I drew in a deep breath, let it out, and pictured Lyric. I also recalled what she'd said about being tired of hiding, and I realized how much I agreed with her. Enough was enough. If I was gonna play for Baltimore, I guess old Gary here deserved to know what he was getting into.

"The truth is that I made a deal with Lyric Rivers at the start of the season. Though I barely knew her, I struck a deal with her that I would pay for her schooling to become a doctor if she pretended to be my girlfriend. I wanted to make you think, sir, that I'd settled down and fallen in love with a nice, sweet, good girl. And Lyric was perfect. A hardworking, intelligent woman working her way through school. No scandals. No skeletons in her closet."

Mr. Devilbuss pursed his lips grimly. He was clearly not pleased at my deception.

"It was totally fake when it all started, and it was supposed to be a temporary arrangement." I smiled as I said the next part. "But then we fell in love for real."

The old man audibly scoffed at that, and I shrugged my shoulders.

"It's okay if you don't believe me. Lyric and I know the truth, and that's really all that matters."

Mr. Devilbuss shook his head, clearly not buying it. I let out a deep sigh. It was tough to have gotten my hopes up, but talking about my love for Lyric reminded me about what was really important. No matter what happened at this meeting, I would go home to her. She would kiss me and console me. She *loved* me. And that was more than enough for me.

"You're saying you're actually in love with this girl," he said dryly.

"Yup. That's why I punched Tyler Maxwell square in his stupid face. He knew about my scheme, and he ratted me out because he missed having me as his drunken partier friend." Clenching my jaw, I said, "He might have fucked up Lyric's chances at getting into medical school. If I had it to do over again, I'd still punch him. And *that's* the truth."

I was surprised at how good it felt to be honest for once. No more having to worry or care about what the media thought about the two of us. It simply didn't matter anymore.

"I want to make you an offer to play for Baltimore," he said, shocking the hell out of me.

"Wait, what?"

"You're devoted to Baltimore, *that* I believe," Mr. Devilbuss said gruffly. "I want to make you an offer, but there's a huge *but* here ..."

Not this again.

"Okay. I'm listening," I said, my heart in my throat.

"But you can't ever see that woman again."

Staring at him, I said, "You can't be serious."

"Serious as a heart attack, and I've had two, so I know whereof I speak," he said, his stern eyes boring into me.

"Enough of this insane media circus. I appreciate the lengths you've gone to in order to catch my attention with this clever scheme of yours, but enough of this nonsense. So you go ahead and honor your promise to that woman and send her on her way, and you'll be a Baltimore Bay Bird."

You'll be a Baltimore Bay Bird.

That phrase got my heart to racing again, but not half as much as the other stuff he'd said had raised my blood pressure.

"First of all, her name is Lyric Rivers. Not 'that woman,'" I snapped angrily. "And no, I'm not about to 'send her on her way.' My home is her home. Home is wherever she is."

The crusty old man actually rolled his eyes at that.

"Look. You don't have to decide right this minute. I'll give you forty-eight hours to think it over."

Jumping to my feet, I said, "I don't need forty-eight *seconds.* There's nothing for me to think about. I love her. I love her more than *baseball.*"

How about that? It was true. I *did* love her more than baseball. Wow. Cool.

"We coulda just hashed this out over the phone instead of you dragging me down here," I said, shaking my head. I was rather enjoying the fact that I no longer had to kiss his old, wrinkled ass. Seriously, fuck this guy. "Now, if you'll excuse me, *I'm going home to my girlfriend.*"

As much fun as it was to storm out of his office, a bit of melancholy set in as I drove away from the building. I made an unscheduled stop at Old Bay Stadium. I parked at a garage down the street and strolled the grounds outside the park. Though I had zero doubt that I'd made the right decision, I still needed to take a little time to mourn the loss of my dream.

In all honesty, I wanted to indulge in some self-pity.

My throat tightened when I peered past the gates and

into the stadium. Staring at the green grass, I knew I'd still play on that field soon enough. But I'd always be on the opposing team. On the outside looking in.

Gross. Okay, even I was sick of myself. Yes, I had every right to be sad, but I was luckier than most people. I still had my dream job and my dream girl. Thinking back to my years in the minor leagues, I thought of all those guys who never made it to the big leagues.

Yeah. Enough whining. I had it pretty good.

Pausing by the Ray Renner Jr. statue, I smiled. I had a feeling my hero would approve of my decision.

Feeling lighter, I hurried back to my car so I could be in Lyric's arms as soon as possible.

CHAPTER 34

*ℒ*yric

"Hey! How did it go?" I asked, rushing toward Brady the moment he walked in the door.

He just looked at me and shook his head sadly.

"Oh, Crush," I said sorrowfully. Crushed was exactly how I felt, and I couldn't imagine how he was feeling. We'd both been so hopeful that it was actually going to work out for him.

"It's okay. Really," he said.

I wrapped my arms around him and held him close. No. It wasn't okay. And suddenly, I was really pissed off about it. Pulling back, I said, "So, what? The guy drags you all the way to Baltimore to turn you down in person? What the hell?"

"Yeah, pretty much. Look, I don't want you to get too upset about this," he said, gazing at me fondly and stroking my hair.

"Too late for that!"

He chuckled and nodded. I think it made him feel better to see me so angry on his behalf.

"It was the same old crap. Mr. Devilbuss wasn't sure I'd calmed down enough for him to be able to trust me. And me decking Tyler recently didn't help my case."

"Oh," I said. Even I had to admit I could understand the Baltimore owner's concerns there.

"He was just kinda on the fence about me, and he told me what he wanted most from me was total honesty. So that's what I gave him."

"You did? As in, you told him *everything*?"

"Yeah."

"Wow," I said. Though I wasn't a fan of lying, I would have been okay with it if it meant Brady could have finally achieved his dream. Besides, we'd come this far with our scheme, there was no reason not to see it through.

"I told him that I'd hatched a plan with you that we would pretend to be in love, but then we fell in love for real," he said, still stroking my hair with affection.

"You told him that?" I asked softly, touched at his honesty.

"Yeah. I did. And he told me to dump you."

"He *what?*"

Brady laughed. "Yup. Told me to dump 'that woman,'" he said, using air quotes, "and I could play for Baltimore. Said he didn't want all that media attention to detract from the team."

"Oh, Brady," I said, my heart feeling heavy in my chest. "I'm so sorry."

It was my fault he wouldn't get to live his dream. I couldn't believe it.

"Don't be sorry. Told me I had forty-eight hours to think about it."

"Oh. Well, then ..."

Brady laughed harder. "Doc. There's nothing to think

about. I told him I loved you more than baseball and then I stormed out of his office."

His brown eyes sparkled with excitement and not a hint of regret.

"You really said that?"

"Yes," he said, dipping his head down to kiss me. "And I meant every word."

"Brady, I would have understood if—"

He shut me up with another kiss. After he lifted his lips, I gazed up at him sorrowfully.

"Please don't feel bad. If it weren't for you, he never would have even considered me in the first place. Besides, it was a dick move making me choose. Screw that guy."

I sighed heavily, and he wrapped his arms around me. "It's okay, Doc. Really."

"I should be the one consoling *you*," I said.

"Let's console each other. Shall we drown our sorrows?"

"Please."

Brady grinned and grabbed some beers from the fridge. We had pizza delivered and ate it while watching TV and drinking beer in the living room. We laughed a lot together, and it felt good to know we really would be okay, no matter what happened. In the end, it didn't matter where we lived and worked, as long as we were together.

His phone rang later that evening. Covering the mouthpiece, he said, "My agent."

I nodded. No doubt, Doug Ryerson had heard about Brady storming out of Gary Devilbuss's office. I hoped he wasn't in trouble.

"Yeah, I know," Brady said to his agent on the phone. "Can't believe the asshole did that. Felt like charging him gas money for dragging me all the way to his office."

He put his feet up on the coffee table as he spoke. "Yeah. He what?"

Brady put his feet down and sat up straight on the couch. My heart seized in my chest. What if he really was in trouble? That Devilbuss man was a powerful guy. Could he mess up Brady's deal with Richmond?

"Okay. Okay, yeah. I understand."

Brady ended the call and looked at me.

"What?" I asked, my chest tight.

"So turns out my meeting with Gary today was some kind of test. Looks like I passed."

He sat there, looking dumbfounded.

"What do you mean?"

"Devilbuss was testing me to see if I was telling the truth. When I said I loved you and chose you, I guess that convinced him. He believes I've changed. Baltimore wants me for sure. All that's left now is for my agent to hash out the details of my contract."

Gasping, I covered my mouth. Brady and I stared at each other in utter disbelief. Then we burst out laughing at exactly the same moment.

I grabbed him and pulled him to my chest. "Crush! Crush! I can't believe it."

Holding him by the shoulders, I said, "Brady Keaton, you're gonna wear the orange and black. You're gonna be a Baltimore Bay Bird!"

His sweet brown eyes welled up with tears. I would never forget the sheer beauty and perfection of this moment, and how honored I was to be able to witness it.

I pulled him close again and we held each other tight, not wanting to let go. And the great thing was, we didn't have to.

Eventually, he let go and leaned back on the couch. I reveled in the look of sheer exuberance on his face. That made everything we'd been through worth it and then some.

"So much to think about," he said. "My head is spinning."

Brady sat up and grabbed my hands. "You'll come with me to Baltimore, right?"

"Well, yes. Eventually. I still have to finish school in Richmond this year."

"Right, right," he said, nodding. "Okay, we'll keep this apartment as long as you need it. I can live here with you during the off-season. Then I go to spring training in March in Florida, and then I've still got the house in Baltimore for when I start playing."

I heard the catch of emotion in his voice when he spoke about playing for Baltimore. The reality that he was really going to be a Bay Bird was still sinking in, and it was lovely to see him so excited.

"Sounds perfect," I said.

"But wait? What about medical school?" Brady asked.

"Well, you know that dream school I applied to?"

Eyes wide, he asked, "Did you get in?"

"I don't know yet," I said. "But the school? Brady, it's Johns Hopkins Medical School."

"In Baltimore!" he yelled,

"Yes," I said with a laugh. "That's my dream medical school. I mean, it's everybody's dream school. But Crush, it's really tough to get into."

"You got this, Doc," he said with enthusiasm.

"I hope so," I said softly, gently stroking his face. "But you know more than anybody. Sometimes you can do everything right and things still don't work out."

His face fell a bit, and he nodded. "I see your point."

"But wherever I end up going to med school, we'll find a way to be together."

"Yes," Brady said firmly. "No doubt about that."

"You know what we should do now to celebrate?"

"Go into our bedroom and have crazy, celebratory sex?"

Smiling, I said, "Well, yeah. We can do that. But it's not what I was gonna say."

"Okay, Doc," he said, eyes shining. "Tell me what you were gonna say."

"I think we should grab some more beers, get super drunk, watch *Field of Dreams*, and cry our eyes out."

"Oh my God. I love that so much," he said, gazing at me with tenderness. "Yes. Let's do that."

My eyes filled with tears. "God, I'm a mess already. Brady, I'm so proud of you!"

Brady pulled me into his arms and held me close. "I love that we're like the only ones who know about Baltimore right now. The news will break soon enough, but tonight? Tonight's just for us to celebrate."

"Yes," I whispered. "Just for us."

EPILOGUE

rady

THE DAY LYRIC found out she got into medical school was
one of the happiest days of my life. I found her crying in the
kitchen, which struck terror in my heart at first. When she
lifted her eyes from her laptop screen, I immediately recognized these were happy tears.

"Was this ... Did you hear from Johns Hopkins?" I asked
hopefully.

"Yes!" she squealed, jumping up from her seat.

I held her in my arms as she cried with relief. That night,
we stayed up late drinking beer and watching a double
feature of *Patch Adams* and *Awakenings* in our living room.

We both cried a little, just as we had when watching *Field
of Dreams* to celebrate my becoming a Baltimore Bay Bird.

God, what an incredible feeling it was to be able to share
my life with Lyric. Everything felt heightened, more fun,
more exciting because I had her to experience it with.

After much careful deliberation and discussion, Lyric had decided to come clean to the media about everything. We told our story to *People* magazine for a cover article just in time for opening day at Old Bay Stadium.

And what a cover it was. *People* got a magnificent photograph of the two of us, now framed in our living room in our house in Baltimore. The picture was of Lyric and me smiling with our arms around each other, me wearing a Johns Hopkins University T-shirt, and her wearing my Baltimore Bay Birds baseball jersey.

Telling our story really endeared us to the fans in Baltimore, which meant the world to me. They knew how much I really wanted to play for the team, and people seemed charmed by our unusual love story.

And what a love story it was. We had lots of challenges ahead, to be sure. Come September, Lyric would begin the grueling pace of medical school. And as much as I adored the Baltimore Bay Birds, they'd finished last in their division last year. There would be a lot of rebuilding for the team, and reaching the playoffs again seemed a far-off dream. But Lyric and I had weathered lots of challenges already and had supported each other every step of the way. And I knew we would continue to stand by and support each other.

For the rest of our lives.

I wasn't exactly sure yet when or how I would propose to her, but it wouldn't be a public spectacle with me dropping to one knee on the baseball field in front of a bunch of reporters. Lyric had graciously endured far too much media attention already. Even though we continued to be in the public eye, when it came down to it, our love was between the two of us. It was like a best man speech I once heard at a wedding. He'd said the couple was like a pair of scissors: always together, and punishing anything that got between them.

Yeah. That was us.

Opening Day surpassed all my dreams, which was really saying something. They introduced me as "Baltimore native, Brady Keaton," and I jogged out onto the field to a standing ovation. I glanced up at the jumbotron, and sure enough, there was my lovely Lyric wiping tears away. My brother Eric laughed and wrapped his arm around her, pride shining in his eyes. Her mom and dad were there, too. They were incredibly sweet people and they had become fast friends with my brother and all three of my parents.

I was a Baltimore Bay Bird. I had my entire family there in the stands cheering me on. I was in the city of my dreams with the girl of my dreams.

I was *home*.

* * *

THANK you so much for reading the first book in The Boys of Baltimore Series! If you want more steamy baseball romance, you can join my email list and get Starting From Zero, a prequel to the series that is available EXCLUSIVELY to my email list subscribers!

STAY TUNED for the next book in the series, Second Base, Second Chance!

WAIT! BEFORE YOU GO!

Don't forget to join the email list if you want the <u>FREE</u>, <u>exclusive</u> prequel novella, Starting From Zero.
Join the email list so you will always know when I've got a new book out.
I promise not to cram your inbox with too many emails – pinky swear!

You can also keep in touch by:

Following me on Amazon
Following me on Bookbub
Following me on Instagram
Joining my Author Reader's Group on Facebook.

Why Leave a Book Review? I'll give you 3 good reasons.

You can do it in <u>less than a minute</u>! Just choose a star rating from 1 to 5 stars and add a sentence or two on how you felt about the book.

1. Most readers choose the books they read based on the reviews, but <u>only a few readers </u>are kind enough to leave a review.
2. Most readers are not aware of this, but authors live and die by reviews. We really do.
3. It only takes a minute to leave a review, but the impact lasts for the lifetime of the book.

Thank you so very much.

ATTENTION ROMANCE NOVEL FANS!

I hope you'll join my romance novel fan club, Romance Novel Addicts Anonymous, on Facebook, Instagram, Twitter, and Pinterest. Join the email list, and you'll receive WHAT'S YOUR PLEASURE? RNAA'S OFFICIAL GUIDE TO FINDING YOUR NEXT GREAT ROMANCE READ.

Made in the USA
Columbia, SC
30 March 2022

58321691R00172